BOOK #3

PHOENIX

RECLAIMED

THE PROBED

SAGA FINALE

Skye Falcon™© 2015

For you, my readers. Thank you for the support!

A long while back, I held a character naming contest in my Fierce Falconettes Facebook group. These were the two winners, and their names, which are both vital parts of this novel! Thanks, ladies! I appreciate your support!

Character Name Recognition
Pierce Talon- Kathy B.
Lizzie St. James- Sunni B.

Phoenix Rising, book 1
Phoenix on Fire, book 2
Oh, Forks! A Little Bit of Everything and All That's Gluten Free
OH, Forks! Collections e-cookbooks

1

"You're all *mine*..." I groaned, pulling out of her as I rolled over. I was again sated.

I couldn't help but look at her lying there, so beautiful. Her long blonde hair had fallen off her back, and sprawled across her shoulders. Her skin was glowing in the sunlight, which only accentuated her curves. I needed more... Rolling back over, my body pressed into her side. Deliberately, she began to roll over into me. Her eyes slowly met mine, and I was lost in them.

"Gabe!" she said in a hurried, sexy whisper. Her hand came around to me, and she slowly stroked the side of my thigh. Giggling, she wrapped her hand around my hard cock. Her eyes blazed into mine, and her grip tightened as she pulled at my flesh. "I guess the answer is yes..." Her eyebrows rose, and her lips sealed around my cock before I could stop her. I glanced over at the time, and it was already 8:30am. I needed to be out of the house soon to get to the site on time.

Her warm wet lips were such a distraction. *And her tongue, oh my God...* I lost my breath. The suction was so intense, and I was still sensitive from her riding me moments before. I could feel my heart speeding up, and my eyes were rolling back into my head. *Bliss.* Ah! I have to get ready. Refocusing my thoughts, and breaking her seal, I pulled her up to me.

"Janie," her gaze was warm, and so incredibly inviting. "I've got to get ready for work." She smiled, and nodded, burying her head into my chest. I wrapped my arms around her, and listened to her inhale.

"That's okay, Gabe. You'd better get ready, and I suppose I need to get up, too." She swung the sheet off of her leg, and rolled back to the side of the bed to stand. For those moments, I was completely mesmerized by her. After all these years, she was still stunning. I watched the curve of her hips change as she stretched from side to side. I imagined my tongue rolling up her rib cage, and back down again... *Ah! Damnit!* I shook my head to attempt to refocus, and opened my eyes to see her smiling back at me. "Having trouble focusing?" She smiled wider, and stood before me, slowly wrapping herself in her robe.

"You know it." I nodded and winked at her. She continued to dress, and pull her hair back while I headed into the bathroom to get ready to get to work.

"I'm going to be packing Lilah and Galen for summer camp today." She paused, and in the mirror, I watched her touch their picture on her desk. She loved our kids beyond measure, and this made me love her even more. "Hard to believe they'll be gone for so long..." Her voice was heavy, and started to shake.

"They're going to have so much fun at camp though, and then with your parents at the lake!" I paused, and pulled on my grey pants. Checking the mirror briefly, I added my black polo. "I would have killed for a summer like they're going to have!" I turned to see Janie standing there, nodding in agreement, with tears streaming down her face. "Aww, baby! No! Don't cry! It's okay!" I quickly gathered her into my arms.

"I know," she cried. "I'm just really going to miss them!" She turned her face away from me, and I patted her hair.

"Have I ever told you how beautiful you are when you cry? Especially when our creations are the reason?" Putting my thumb under her chin, I raised her mouth to mine. She trembled at first, but was quick to relax while my probing tongue dancing around her lips. Her tongue was eager to wrestle with my own, and I had to break the kiss. "Easy, love." I wiped the tear off of her cheek. "You'll get to visit them at the lake, you know. So, you just need to get through these first few weeks of camp!" I smiled at her with my best silly smile, and she sort of cracked a teeny, tiny smile back. She shook her head, patted my biceps, and headed out to the kitchen to start breakfast for the kids.

I headed back into the bathroom to quickly put on deodorant, and touch up the hair. Catching myself in the mirror, I noticed my tan was already quite dark. Spending time in James' gym was helping, too. My muscle definition had really formed nicely over the past year. *What?! Gawking at yourself again?* I suddenly had a quick flash of a naked Janie on my lap, stroking my now ripped chest with her own bare skin... Ah! A spray of cologne, and I headed to rush out of the door.

"Daddy!" I heard him yell as he ran through the house towards me. I turned to him quickly, and picked him up to hug him.

"Good morning, Galen." I put him down, and ruffled his hair. "Daddy's in a hurry this morning, but I'll be home early.

Maybe we could go for a swim tonight before camp starts?" He nodded vivaciously.

"Yes Dad! That's perfect!" He high fived me, and headed over to help Janie at the counter. I caught Janie smiling at me out of the corner of her eye, obviously proud of my parenting move. I smiled back widely, and walked towards her. My hand instinctively enclosed around her perfect ass, and I pressed myself into her completely. She tipped her ear to my mouth, and I heard her breath hitch.

"I've got to run. I'll be done early today, so plan for a swim later with us, okay?" She nodded into my neck, and kissed my cheek.

"Have a good day, Gabe. Be safe, and I love you." She reached up on her tip toes for one last kiss, and I headed for the door. As I passed by Lilah's room, I couldn't help but poke my grumpy little bear. "Good-bye Lilah! I'll see you later when you're not hiding in your room!" I winked at Janie as I closed the door.

Jumping into my Nissan 370z, I was quick to step on the gas to get to Donovan's. This was by far the best early Father's day present I had ever gotten. Turning around the corner, I keyed in my code, and pulled around to the back storage house. I hated feeling this rushed with these projects, but there was no way I'd give up those extra minutes with Janie. I found today's delivery quickly on the roster, and proceeded to have it loaded into my car. All the while, my mind was thinking about her. I don't know why I am feeling so nostalgic, but I am so lost in memories today.

As I climbed back into the car, and hit location number one on my GPS system, I thought of those first days, soo many years ago, when I first laid eyes on Janie. I rolled the windows down, and turned off the radio. Losing myself to random thoughts wasn't normally my style, but today is just different. As I merged on to the highway, the comforting GPS voice told me I had roughly 30 minutes until I arrived at the location. I felt a smile creep across my lips, and there she was walking through my mind again.

I remember when she started at the Phoenix. She was awkward, and a bit clumsy. She had a quiet, mysterious confidence about her, and seemed to be somewhat untouchable. She smiled at everyone, all while keeping the same people at an arms distance. *But what I saw...* It was the way she held your gaze whenever you spoke to her. How I knew when she took the time to talk with me, she was so invested in that moment. How smart she was, and somewhat smart mouthed. Suddenly my mouth went dry. I realized then that there was really no way to remember the past with Janie, without the baggage that came with her. The crazy, psychotic assholes that she brought, but didn't deserve or ask for.

Before I knew her personally at the Phoenix, I knew him. He was everywhere she was, lurking in places no sane person would waste their time for hours a day. I knew what the relationship was to him, and I felt a huge pull to save her. Michael, the person I blame for Janie's entire view of the world, and people. I could see what he was doing to her, and couldn't help inserting myself into her life in any way I could. *Who knew you'd fall in love?* I smiled to myself in the rear view mirror. I knew, after about ten minutes of talking to her. I never saw the other two coming. That may haunt me the rest of my life. That and the things she did with my business partner...and friends. *Not like you're a saint in life, Gabe.*

Past all of that, and even my own indiscretions, she still wanted me. Wants me, still, so much. The love she pours out to me, and to the kids, I'll never understand. She's beautiful. So, so beautiful. *Ah, Jesus.* Looking down quickly, I noticed I had started to get myself hard. Pulling at the crotch in my pants, I tried to adjust for comfort. GPS informed me that I was only minutes away from my destination, so I focused on the last few turns carefully.

Pulling in to their drive, I stopped next to the security hut and smiled at the officer. This building was harder to get into than the Pentagon, and its officers were scarier than any secret service agent I'd ever seen.

"Good Morning, Mr. Lazarus. Normal monthly shipment?" He raised his sunglasses to check my ID, and scan the barcode on the paperwork. Strapped to both hips were his guns, and behind those, some handcuffs, mace, and a Taser.

"Hey Manuel, how've you been? Yes, normal monthly delivery. Will it go in the normal bay area?" He handed me his paperwork to sign, and I briefly read it over, and signed.

"Yes, bay #1 is ready for you. Andre is waiting for you to help unload." I smiled, and handed him back the clipboard. "Good to see you, sir. Take care." He nodded, and opened the gate. I drove through the gates, and headed to the back storage building, pulling into bay number one. I was greeted by a smiling, friendly guy I didn't recognize. *He must be new.*

He directed me to back in, and when to stop. At many of our locations, we did not leave our vehicles. I was thankful for that here, as it looked like a prison yard. The "yard" was littered with old exercise equipment, junked out cars, and old delivery vehicles. Everyone around was staring at the white guy in the truck, and some of their tattoos were most likely done by their prison bunk-mate. Slightly intimidating, but they were normally very nice guys.

"Hey, want me to help you unload?" *What? You're offering?* I smiled at him, and motioned to the trunk. While breaking protocol wasn't something I did regularly, this guy looked harmless.

"Sure. You must be Gabriel?" I nodded, and picked up a box. "You work for Mr. James?" I could tell he had some interest more in my cause, but no bother. *Yet.*

"Yes, I work for James Industries. I am the Vice President, actually." As I finished putting the box down, I caught a glimpse of his "holy shit" face. "Is there something I can help you with?" He hurriedly finished unloading the boxes, and signed off on the paperwork. I placed the lock on the bay, and snapped it closed.

"Oh, I just think it's a great company. I would love to have a job there." I smiled at him, as many people wish to be as lucky as myself.

"Well, you're welcome to come to our main office, and put in an application. We do hire on crews often, as our building projects and orders just keep coming in. Business is indeed booming!" His smiled widened. "I'll check over your resume myself. It's been a real pleasure to meet you." I smiled, and extended my hand for him to shake. He quickly took it, as if I had promised him the world. I didn't have the heart to tell him that Donovan has a stringent hiring process, and higher quality assurance levels than most humans can function with.

I climbed back into the truck, this time needing some tunes to drive to. I blared 'Life After You' by Daughtry, and kept the windows down. My phone rang into the car speakers suddenly. I was still getting use to this new technology.

"Ah, hello?" I asked, trying not to shout my hello, and remembering there were speakers everywhere.

"Gabe! It's Don. Just checking on you, as that was a huge, huge order!" I smiled, and felt my eyebrow raise in the air.

"Oh yeah, I'm great! So great, that I'd like to do another delivery today, if I could." I could hear his happiness with me, yet again. "I saw that location seven called in an extra order. I thought I could run that out, since it would take a few hours."

"See, my friend, this is why we work so well together. Yes, I'll have more packaged for you, and ready by the time you get here. Give me your ETA, Sir?" I chuckled. *He must be drinking.*

"Ah, give me about 30 or so."

"See you soon. Just pull in and honk. Talk later." I cranked the radio, and sped down the highway. Laying my head against the head rest, I couldn't help but be thankful for the place we were in right now. Money was no longer an issue for us, and we had the most security we could ever need. Our kids are happy, thriving, and our family is intact. I parked and smiled at Pierce as I pushed the trunk button. I noticed there were only three small boxes going out. This was not the normal order for this location, so I stuck my head out the window to verify.

"Hey Talon, can we double check this order? Normally location seven gets bales, not boxes." He quickly checked his clipboard, and verified the box numbers.

"Nope, looks like they're getting some Oxy this time. Lots, and lots of Oxy." I nodded, and smiled. He closed the trunk, and gave the signal knock to head out.

I pulled back out on to the same highway, and headed towards location seven. This was a longer run, so I found a good CD to play for the drive. Pink Floyd carried me the whole way through another flawless delivery. As I pulled into the driveway, I was greeted by the kids at the pool, and my wonderful wife, toting a beverage for me in hand.

"Hello Gabe. How was your day?" I smiled, as she handed me the cold bourbon. A taste I had acquired after hanging around Donovan for too long. Words escaped me suddenly, and all I could do was pull her in, and kiss her. She tasted of strawberries, and lip gloss.

"My day was great. Managed two deliveries today." I smiled her, as my phone vibrated. I pulled it out, and noticed the text update from Donovan.

$86k for today. You are my favorite man ever! Wait. Is that gay? Oh well. ;) D.

I said nothing, but instead turned my phone to Janie, so she could read the message herself. As I did, she steadied my hand with her own, and her eyes almost came out of her skull.

"Gabe, is this for real? This is the biggest one yet!" I was sure she was going to explode, or strip everything off and do me right there. Even after two years of this job, she still had her reservations, and worries. *What mother wouldn't? No, what sane person wouldn't??* If only being a runner was legal. If only the things I was running were even slightly legal. I smacked her ass, and kissed her again.

"You bet it's for real. I am damn good at this job." I turned around and checked on the kids, who were playing away in the pool. I noticed Mom was out there with them, too. "Now, I'm going to change so we can go for a swim! Let's order in tonight, All right?" She nodded at me, and I headed inside. I heard her head towards the pool, and announce that I would be out in minutes. The squeals that followed were priceless. I called in our dinner, and headed outside the only way I knew how... with a soaking cannonball.

2

The kids finally calmed down after s'mores and swimming about 10:30. Janie and I finally had some down time. Janie was finishing up her work on email, and smiled as I walked by her.

"Hey, you want to sit outside with a fire for a bit? It's nice out." I grabbed my bottle of bourbon from the counter, and a glass, and stood waiting for her answer. She rifled around some papers on her desk, and turned to me again.

"Absolutely, that sounds perfect. I'll be out in fifteen or so, okay?" I nodded, and headed out on to the deck. Last summer we renovated our back patio, keeping the hot tub, but adding on a covered roof, and permanent bar area out here.

This made it so much easier to enjoy regardless of what was falling from the sky. I looked around at the seating choices, and decided on our old favorite patio lounger. Even though Janie had it recovered last summer, it was still tattered showing signs of wear. *Truth be told, it is your most used piece of furniture out here.* Pulling it closer to the fire pit made me think of all the parties we've had here, and all of the good times.

Some of the people I missed from the Phoenix, but for the most part it was a good break. After the whole Simon scandal, I just really began to see everything for what it was. And that people had motives that you could never dream of. Donovan stepped in with the job offer, and the rest seems like history. I lit the wood I had just stacked, and poked at it until a good flame began bellowing from the pile. I headed over to the bar where my drink, and glass waited. Mesmerized by the flame, I managed to pour myself a drink, and recap the bottle. My ass had just hit the cushion when she emerged from the house.

"Sorry about that, Mylah called." She shook her head, as if confused. "That girl, I swear. Are you sure Don can really handle that much extra bullshit?" She was fiddling around with her jacket, and putting her wine down on the table.

"Yeah, she's a trip, I've noticed as well. He seems to like her though, and she apparently gives great head." I couldn't help hold in the laugh as I took a drink, and swallowed to see an angry faced Janie directly in front of me. I chuckled loudly again. "What?! I didn't say I knew she gave good head. Only know what Don *tells* me. And anyway…." I nudged her with my nose, conning her lips into locking on to mine, while my hands gently massaged around her scalp. "Yours is the only head I ever want!!" She locked on again, and broke the embrace with laughter.

"You ass!" She was still laughing, and lighting the smoke. She took a long draw, and I watched as she inspected

14

the joint. Since we started getting company product, her standards had risen quite high. *Ha, funny man...* She inhaled again, handing it back to me.

We passed it back and forth for nearly a half an hour, and finally I could snuff it out. The fire was still burning nicely, and the moon was floating in a cloudless sky. There was silence around us except for the sounds of nature... and the low hums our bodies were beginning to make towards each other. Her hand slowly wandered on to my thigh, and without uttering a word, she was on me.

"Please, Gabe?" She moaned into my mouth, and she dove into me with her tongue. My tongue was more than ready to greet hers, and make everything that I had thought about during the day come true. Her fingers dug into my shoulders, and she fisted my hair. I could tell she was full of heavy desire, and extremely needy. I could barely break our kiss for air.

As she came up for a breath our eyes met, and her giant smile told me this was exactly what she wanted. I pulled the rope on her robe, and it opened to reveal a small nightgown. *My favorite.* As she bent over me to lick and bite my neck, her breasts and belly were exposed. I couldn't help but reach out and squeeze on to them. Her nipples immediately hardened as I continued to brush my hands over, and back over their pertness. She shuddered. Chills ran down her spine with each tug to her chest. She melted more, and further into me.

With a sudden jerk, she sat up, and threw the robe to the floor. She whipped the nightgown over her head, revealing her completely naked self. The throbs began immediately and I wanted inside of her badly. I thrust my hips upward towards her core. Feeling her rub against my hard flesh was almost too much. *Focus.*

Placing my left hand on her thigh, I stuck my fingers in my mouth and sucked. Her eyes stilled on me and her pupils dilated. I slipped my fingers into her tight, hot center and I was met with slick, warm, readiness. I pushed around with my fingers inside and out, feeling for that rough patch of tissue. If I was lucky enough to find the spot, she would surely cream all over my hands.

She rose a bit, and did a half turn so her ass was now in my face. She leaned forward reaching for her toes, exposing her entire self to me. Palming my own length, it pulsed with desire in my hand. With her splayed out in front of me using my cock as a whip, I smacked her with it. The jolts sent such pleasure through my body, and she loved the intense cock torture on her clit. The more into it she got, the farther her legs opened. This was one of Janie's secret weapons. *One of her secrets that made it impossible to take her immediately. The longer you waited, the more beneficial and amazing it got!*

Lifting my knees helped raise her ass high enough to slip the tip of my hard cock into her tight pussy. She gasped, but I was faster than she was, and I slid completely in to her, making her take every solid inch. She rose slowly so she was sitting upright on my length, and began to move up and down at her own pace. Her fingers came to her clit, and began circling around and around. Her left hand grasped on to her breast, and my teeth clenched automatically at the sight.

I quickly pulled out of her, spinning her to face me. No way was she getting off without letting me see every fucking detail! She turned quickly, and spread herself open for me to sink back into. I pulled her back down on to me, and began to rock under her. She held on to my shoulders, and our mouths crashed together passionately. I could feel her clenching around my cock, but I wasn't ready to finish yet. Grabbing her shoulders, and holding her all the way on to me, I felt her body squeeze me, and hold on for dear life. Her eyes rolled back in her head, and she stopped breathing. *Classic Janie...*

After the orgasm rolled over her, I let go of her shoulders, and rammed into her tight space as hard as I could.

16

Her hot liquid oozed all over my cock, and that made me even harder. The closer I came, the tighter she clamped around me. Just before I was going to go, I felt her hand close around my balls, and pull. *Fuck yes!!* My body tightened, and released into her. Over, and over, and over again. With each pulse, she matched with a tight squeeze. She collapsed on to my shoulder, and her heavy breath ended in my ear.

"Thank you," she mustered out breathlessly, husky as ever. I couldn't force out any words, so instead I kissed her cheek. She eased off of me carefully, and fell to the cushion below. She looked exhausted, so I scooped her up sans pants, and carried her to our bed. I set her down gently, and kissed her forehead.

"I'm just going to clean up outside, and lock up. I'll join you in a few." I pulled the covers up around her, and headed out to clean up. Putting the cover over the fire, the flames ceased quickly. I grabbed our glasses and booze, and headed back in to the house. Arming the system, I turned to check on the kids one last time for the night. Both so peaceful, happily dreaming away. I closed our bedroom door behind me, and fell into bed with my entire life, who was already snoring next to me.

Janie.

~

When I woke up this morning, I felt refreshed. I was still in shock about how much money Gabe was earning working with Don, and I knew things were still looking up. Almost two years with no hang ups, accidents, stalkers, or court appearances. *Oh, come on Janie… you know you shouldn't even speak of it. You're going to jinx it!* I chuckled, knowing my thoughts were probably right. I quietly slunk around the kitchen, finishing up the last bit of packing I had to do to take the kids to camp later on today, after I met with my employees for our monthly meeting.

I piled up some paperwork, and sat down at my lap top to shoot off some emails. My newest employee, Bradley, was fabulous. The clients he was servicing were more than satisfied with his tricks, and methods. *Well, of course they love him! Everyone loves a little bit of voyeurism...even boys like Bradley Butch!* Hiring Bradley on was one of the best things I'd ever done. At first, I was hesitant to expand the business to more of the unspoken, naked, and adult side of cleaning. Even with Donovan's reassurances and Gabriel's support, I just needed to experience and know it on my own. A new email pinged in.

"To: Janie Lazarus, At Your Service, LLC, Owner
From: Donovan James
06/06/2010 7:34:06 am

Hey Beautiful, I'm going to need a June party planned. We've got another boat launch coming up, and I'd like to have a party here at the estate. A pool party, perhaps. Something fun, and welcoming. Let's go with the 24th or so. Also, when are you coming over with Gabriel? I owe you two dinner. Please give my best to the Princess and Prince for me.

All my love, D."

I smiled at his sentiment, and opened my calendar to next month. Lucky for him the 24th was open. I immediately emailed the caterer, DJ, and decorators to save the date, and week before, to assist in set-up. Next came emailing Don back.

"To: Donovan James
From: Janie Lazarus, AYS, LLC., Owner
06/06/2010 7:56:12 am

Good Morning, Boss. The 24th has been reserved, and dates blocked out by all party helpers. We can chat more about it tomorrow when Gabriel and I come over. We have to take the Royalty to camp this afternoon, so Gabe's playing entertainer this morning for my meeting with the employees. Dinner then, maybe? Let me know later.   J ☺ "

I heard some commotion coming from the bedrooms, as if on cue all three doors opened at once, and my sleepy people appeared. Both kids were already bouncing off the walls, so I handed them some fruit, and pushed them into the fresh morning air. Gabe was moving a bit slower, and headed for the coffee pot.

"Good morning, baby." He rubbed his eyes, and hair. He wrapped his arms around me, and pulled me into a hug. "Thanks for last night," he whispered.

"You're welcome. It was much needed. I slept so well! I feel like I have a grasp on my emotions today, and am ready for a bit of work, and a drive to camp later." I nudged him out of my way, as I had to go prepare before my meeting.

"What do you need me to do?" *Ah, what a man he is….that's the best question ever.* I smiled, and poured his coffee for him.

"If you could just keep ahold of the kids for the morning, we can head up to Camp Potawotami to drop them off then after." He nodded in agreement. "I figure we'll be back late, so no plans for tonight, but tomorrow Don wants us to stay for dinner."

"That sounds fine. I can do some of my paperwork then, too. And maybe schedule some of the pick-ups, since we'd be there a bit." He shuffled with his coffee, and grabbed a donut. *Who is making these plans?!* "I'll head out with the kids. What time is the meeting?" I glanced at the clock. It was 8:26am.

"Meeting starts at 9am. Thanks, honey." I smiled, and disappeared into the bedroom to dress. While I threw on my cut offs and tank top, I played out the meeting in my head from start to finish. Nothing too complicated to cover today, really. Just some new clients, and check-ins. *Don't forget the new security documents!* Oh, my poor busy brain.

Over the years I'd been given the best opportunities to ensure our safety procedures were up to par. *Unfortunately for you, you were often the guinea pig...* On top of having all new clients screened, our new security also verifies their tax ID numbers, previous taxes filed at the address location, and runs a background check on any potential clients *before* my employees ever step into the place. After the strip mall incident, I'd vowed to never put myself or an employee in danger again.

I made some fresh lemonade and set it on the back patio table for our meeting. I turned on some tunes softly, and sat down to wait. It didn't take long before I heard the chimes in the house signal the gate was open, and visitors had arrived. I saw Bradley and Caty pull in, and Kiara's car soon after. My phone vibrated suddenly, and I checked to find a text from Mylah. *Who now, after hooking up with Donovan, was always late!*

Janie, on my way! Will be just a few bits late!

"Janie!" I heard Bradley shout from the driveway. He was so full of life, and energy. He was flamboyantly gay, and so proud of it. He loved being able to use his skills with men to max out his tips after he cleaned for them. His confidence in himself and his abilities made him so popular with some of our male clientele, that some had grown to be weekly regulars. He was strictly watching only, and hands off. I knew we all had our limits, and his were never questioned.

"Hey Bradley! How are you doing?" I stood to hug him, and Caty. They sat at the table, and quickly poured some lemonade.

"Oh girl, so glad you made this! Yours is neither too tart, nor too sweet! Right in the middle!" He took a drink. "MMMmmm, so good!" He pulled out his planner, and Caty giggled at his antics.

"Well, no sense in wasting time! Let me give you your new client information, and you can update me on things." I handed Caty and Bradley their new client info, and welcomed Kiara to sit with us. "No new ones for you this week, as you requested Kiara. Did you have any troubles, or updates?" She handed me her paperwork for the month, and smiled widely.

"No mam, everything is going very well. Tips are still up super high, and all of the clients seem very happy! I can't believe that I've had some of them for two years!!" I smiled with her.

"Yes, I was thinking about doing something for our long term clients...a party, or something. Just as a thanks, you know?" Kiara nodded. "Anyone else have any issues? Good things?" Just then, I heard the gate code chime again. All heads turned to check. "It's just Mylah, no worries."

"I'm soo happy with this company, and you Janie. Thank you for hiring me!" Bradley put his paperwork away. "These two new clients will give me the boost of income we discussed, too. I really appreciate it, Jane." I smiled at him, and noted all his thanks.

"Hey everyone!" Mylah said as she approached cautiously waving, covering her chest.

"OOoohh!!!" Kiara shouted. "Late agaaain?" she laughed.

"You know damn well it's all Donovan's fault. Sometimes he finds the damn dirtiest things for me to clean…. Again…" she laughed loudly, and sat to finish our meeting.

Roughly an hour later, we wrapped up, and I cleaned up my meeting area. Gabe suddenly appeared in the kitchen with me, and helped prepare lunch for the kids.

"I can't believe this is our last lunch with them for a while, except for at the lake!" I felt my stomach heave.

"You've got this, baby. You'll have me all to yourself, in a quiet empty house." *Oh, very valid point…* He put their lunch on the table, and called them in from outside. "Lilah, Galen! Come in for lunch!" Suddenly my mind was taken with thoughts of Gabe and I… all over the house. The kids came in, and sat for lunch. I was still smiling a bit from Gabe's comments, and Lilah was quick to notice.

"Mom! What's so funny?!" she demanded. "Are you that happy we're leaving?!" Her face was kind of disgusted. I frowned at her comment.

"Of course I'm not happy you're leaving! I will miss you though." I wrapped my arms around her, as I piled more chips on her plate. She smiled at my hug, but I figured it was probably more for the chips. Turning to Galen, he was oblivious to everything else but the spicy chips on his plate. "Those good, Mister?" He smiled, and nodded huge.

"Now Mom," he said, though there were more chips falling out, than staying in. "First is camp, right? Them Gramma Sam will take us to the lake?" I nodded.

"Yes, bud. Camp for three weeks, and then to the lake. I'll be up to visit at the lake once you're there, too. You guys are going to have so much fun!" Even though I sort of had to push the words out, once they were out, I knew they were true. "Hey

Gabe, could you pack up the Jeep for me?" I smiled at him, and could feel my cheeks flush when I saw the look on his face.

"Of course, baby. I'm on it." He was off packing the car up, and the kids were done with lunch before we knew it. They were eager to get to camp, and away from us for the month. We sang loudly together on the ride up, and I was thankful that Gabe was able to go with us. We checked them in to camp, and saw that their bags got to each of their bunks, respectively. They changed into their suits with us, and we walked them down to the "welcome" beach party. Seeing them smiling with friends they made last year, and hearing those squeals…. *You hearing them Janie? Those giggles? That happiness?* That's what let me walk away from camp, and leave them there today. I climbed back into the Jeep, and Gabe took my hand. Raising it to his own mouth, he kissed the back gently, and winked.

"Kid free for the first time in a year… Wow love, where should we begin?" I couldn't hide the yawn that had just escaped my lips, and Gabe laughed out loud. "Well, then. Home it is!" I reclined in my seat, and rolled the window down. The air hit my face perfectly to nap the whole way home.

3

Driving back down the highway with the windows open and music blaring was perfect. Until the phone rang straight into the speakers, which were obviously now set on the loudest setting known to man.

"Ah, fucking technology!" I couldn't help react to the piercing ring, pushing every button that was on the steering wheel. "Hello?!" I answered exasperated. There was a bit of static on the line, but could definitely hear chatter and commotion in the background.

"Gabe! Sorry about the static! It's Don. I need two hours of your afternoon for an extra delivery. Can you swing it?" Pushing my lips together, it was hard to turn down the money.

"Which location is it? I looked over at Janie, who was now staring out the window while the wind blew her hair into a mess behind her.

"It's Location 5. Should be quick." I checked the clock quickly before committing, and noticed it was already 2:46pm. I knew if I did it, I'd be home early enough to still enjoy our evening. Money is money.

"Sure Don, I'll be over after I drop Janie at home."

"Perfect! Thanks, man. See you soon." The line disconnected, and although she showed no visible signs of disappointment, I could've sworn I heard her sigh. I glanced in her direction and as if on cue, she turned and smiled.

"I won't be late, I promise. It's just a quick one, and…" I paused. Should I ease her mind and tell her what Location 5 orders? Donovan's words were heavy on my mind whenever these situations happened. I know Janie, and she's a mess of worry and wonder on every run. *"Gabriel, the less she knows, the safer she is"* was always running through my head.

"What Gabe?" she spoke softly, and broke my thought.

"Oh, I just don't want you to worry. You know, Don says he's going to invite *all* of our clients to this pool party…so maybe you'll get to meet some of them there." Checking again, her eyebrows were up as if she was entertaining the idea.

"I'll be fine. I'm really tired, and sort of bummed the kids are gone. I'm just going to watch a movie or something on the couch tonight, I think. I'll wait for you." She patted my thigh, and leaned on to my shoulder. I pulled my arm behind her, and hugged her best I could while turning on to our street. Over the years our road had become even more grown over with trees, and it created a nice privacy for all of the houses down our long block.

Turning into the drive, I pulled up to the security box, stopping when my antennae lined up with the wooden pole marker. Donovan's new technology knows what cars belong, and which cars are unknown. This perk was a job-seller for me-security. After everything, knowing that someone else is watching out for her when I'm out on runs helps to rest my mind. As I pulled down the driveway, I couldn't help scan the tree lines all around, just in case. She started to sit up, and collect her things.

"I'll be as fast as I can, baby, promise." She smiled. "I'll text you on my way back, and I'll grab us some dinner."

"That sounds good. Don't forget to text me, please." She walked around to my side of the car, and leaned in through my open window. Her kiss was soft, sweet, and apprehensive. *The typical time-for-a-run kiss. Maybe it's because you always forget to text her??* "I love you, Gabe." She blew me one more kiss as she went into the house. I couldn't wait to get back here to quietly lay with her, and just watch her sleep. *MMmm, Janie.*

~

I pulled into the James Estate and was directed away from my norm loading area. Perplexed, I parked where directed, and met Pierce with my paperwork for this run. I heard Don's boisterous voice coming from somewhere, so I waited to touch base with him.

"Hey Gabriel! Thanks for coming so quickly." I smiled and tossed him a wave. "Why don't you take the company van they've got packed. You just need to park it, and exit the vehicle for a few at Location 5. They'll take care of the rest." I nodded, seemed east enough.

"All right, I'll be back in a bit then. Hey," Donovan turned to me. "What time tomorrow?"

"OH! Let's say four-ish? Sun is still on the pool then, we could grill out." I smiled, and nodded. "That work for you guys?"

"Sure does. If I don't see you when I'm back, we'll both see you tomorrow." He tossed a wave back, and put his phone to his ear. His loud laughter told me what was on the other line was either a female, or a huge business deal just sealed. I climbed into the company van, adjusting the seats. Turning around, I checked out the contents of the van, which looked like boxes of boating accessories. *Works for me...* I quickly changed the radio station, and headed through downtown to the north side of the city.

Traffic seemed to move in slow motion, as it always did on days when I wanted to be home with my lady. Driving through downtown, there were women on some of the corners selling pieces of ass for pretty cheap. I shuddered as I went around the corner, as it brought me close enough to touch to one of the torn-purple "lingerie" clad women whose teeth were missing, and decaying more with each lip retracting smile. I finally came to the address, which seemed to be only one block out of the bad area of town.

I pulled into the lot, and up to the front garage door, as I was directed. A shorter man approached the van cautiously, walking all the way around. He nodded to me as he walked around front of the van, holding mirrors to the underneath checking for what I can only imagine were bombs. He then motioned to someone in the distance, smiled at me, and pointed for me to drive into the now open garage door. Slowly creeping, I parked, and hopped out of the van.

"Hello. We've been expecting you." A voice spoke over the speakers. "Please find your way into our lounge, and we will let you know when your vehicle is ready to go." I nodded, and head towards the door marked, 'Lounge.' "Thank you, Mr. Lazarus." I smiled, and kept going. Entering the lounge, there were a few chairs, and a couch. *Who knows how long this will take?* I sat down on to the couch, and pulled my phone out to text Janie.

Hey Love, at site, shouldn't be too much longer

I scanned the room, and there wasn't much for excitement. A dirty, barely used coffee pot on the small table, with a few packs of crackers, and what looks to be the leftover packets of ketchup from fast food lunch runs. The magazines were over a year old, and riddled with dust. Thank God my phone vibrated when it did. *Janie.* An instant smile came to my face.

Okay, please be careful. Sort of lonely here without your warm body.

My mind was wandering again, right back home to Janie. I knew this payout would be big, and that's why I agreed...but honestly, I'm glad I'll have a few new guys to train on all of this soon. Just then, I heard shuffling coming from a different area in the building. There were voices, and they seemed to be getting louder. I could hear a few men, and maybe a woman. Suddenly the doorknob turned, and in walked my worst nightmare. *In heels.* Her shriek was just as I had remembered.

"Oh hell no." I shook my head and crossed my arms. I remembered our last interaction all those years ago at the Phoenix. I remember the trouble she caused after ending things, because she didn't agree. *How in the hell had the world shrunk so much?* She looked the same, maybe a little more filled out... but bitchy as ever.

"Gabriel Lazarus." She shook her head, and wrinkled her nose. She slunk closer to me, watching my every expression. "It sure has been awhile since I've thought of you, but now that you're here." I shook my head, and put my hands up to ward off her advances. She laughed loudly.

"God, Lizzie. Save me the dramatics, I'm here on business." She nodded as if in disbelief. I really didn't have time for this, and I could see that obnoxious-as-shit twinkle in her eye. "So, how much longer until my van is ready?" She walked closer to me, and took a seat at the end of the couch.

"It's actually ready now, but I needed a few minutes," she said, adjusting herself on the cushion. "You know, we ended things so abruptly before. We were so hot together..." She began to reach out for my thigh, and I moved it quickly.

"Lizzie, you're still delirious after all these years? Come on now. No chance in hell." I sat up to pull myself off of the couch and before I could react, her salty, dry lips were covering mine. Her hands dug into my collar, and she feverishly tried to push her tongue through my sealed lips. Finally getting a good enough grasp, I pushed her away and threw myself off of the couch. "What the *fuck* is wrong with you!? I don't want you! Business, Lizzie. Hands the fuck off!" I stood up, and dusted off my shirt. I couldn't hide the look of disgust, and confusion that was surely slathered all over my face. "Business, please. The van is done. Please give me the keys." I held out my hand and waited patiently.

She held her stare, directly in my eyes, for nearly ten minutes. We stood in silence, and I could only imagine the things that were going through her head. In years past, I'd awoken to her sitting on the end of my bed, staring at me while I slept. The trouble was, she wasn't in my locked house before I went to bed... *So, she's a whack job?* Finally, her hand dove into her pocket, and fished around for a minute. She pulled it back out, and forcefully put the keys in my hand.

"Well, if not now, maybe later. You know, it's been years... I'm a different person now. One who gets what she wants." I shook my head, and scowled more. *She's insane.* "Sounds like we're going to be seeing each other a whole lot more then, huh, Gabe?" I hated the way she was twisting her voice to be cute. No way was I falling for it again. "We're due for regular deliveries twice a week beginning very soon." She

29

smiled wider than ever, as if anticipating our next unscheduled run-in. "Well, I must get back to the office, so my boss doesn't worry." She winked, and reached out for a hand shake. Not knowing who was watching, I kept my business cool.

"Miss St. James, until next time." I nodded and as I tried to pull away she squeezed my hand hard enough to get me to turn around, where her open mouth was waiting. *Gabe?! What the hell?!* Her tongue was hot and soft, but too persistent. She tasted bad, and it repulsed me. I pushed her away again, walked away, and spat her out of my mouth.

"You held on longer that time, didn't you baby?" She taunted as I walked away. "Just like old times, huh? Remember the things you use to do to me? We could have that again!" *Oh my God.* I just wanted to get out of ear shot of her pain inducing voice. I still didn't truthfully know what I was thinking all those years ago... but back then my hormones did most of the talking. I got back to the van, all but jumping inside. I was back on the road in the silence, for nearly twenty minutes. Then I was angry. I dialed quickly, and barely waited for the hello.

"Donovan. I can't do Location 5. I'll get Talon taught, introduced and ready." I swallowed hard.

"Easy buddy, what the hell happened?" Donovan cleared his throat.

"I didn't know that someone from my past works at this location. A person who could cause us more trouble, and I cannot do that to Janie." I could hear him shuffling paperwork.

"Well, I don't see the problem training Talon. I'm assuming this problem is a woman?" He laughed aloud.

"No Sir, not a woman. A walking, manipulative cunt. One who stuffs her tongue down your throat, while you're biting it off just to make her point." I sighed, and sped back through town. Reaching the higher speed limits reminded me I was almost home.

"I understand. Noted. We'll work on this as soon as possible. I've got your back. Let me know if you need anything, okay? And just swap the van and your 370z tomorrow." I agreed. "Oh, and tomorrow is still on, right?"

"Oh yeah, Janie's excited to party with you and Mylah. Me too, after today. Jesus Christ." We both laughed loudly. "All right man, thanks. I'll see you tomorrow."

"Great! Tell Janes I said hey! Talk soon!" Donovan hung up just as I pulled into the driveway. *Shit.* Now I've got to face Janie, after that nasty piece of shit was all over me. I shook my head, and gripped the wheel. So many years I've been able to skirt away from my own past, and just leave it there. And now, all these years later, I'm going to be emptying my pockets on the table for her. *Well, let's look at the bright side here, at least the kids are gone!*

4

I walked in to find the lights dimmed, and the glow from the television shining on the walls all around the place. It was only 8pm, surely she wasn't asleep. I crept up behind the couch, and peered over. She was wrapped up in a blanket, one leg out, clutching it for dear life watching the old *Tales from the Crypt* stories. I reached out and gently touched her exposed leg, and she screamed like I was trying to kill her. I instantly stood up, hands in the air.

"Jesus Gabe!" She sat up, and smacked the air in my general direction. "You scared the shit out of me! You didn't text me!" Her eyes rolled into her head, and she flopped back down to the couch. I headed around the couch quickly, and almost sat on her.

"I know. I'm wondering if we can talk a bit. Something happened at the location today, and I've got this feeling in my gut- you know, the one you say never to ignore. Well, I think we should listen." She wrinkled her forehead, and I smiled at her. "I'm going to get some drinks. You might need a few. What would you like? We're just going to have a talk night." I wasn't sure how she was going to take this, but suddenly she was grinning ear to ear. "Okay then, I'll be right back."

When I returned to the couch, I brought her a large cosmopolitan, and had poured myself a large glass of Jack on the rocks. I grabbed a joint on the way through, some of the new strain from Donovan's lot. I chose some mellow music, left the lights off, and we would use the glow from the TV as our light.

"Gabe, you're being crazy." She willingly took the cosmo from my hands. "After all these years, you're that worried about what you have to tell me?" I shook my head. It really wasn't that I was worried she was going to freak out, and leave me. I was more worried that the crazy bitch from Location 5 would appear out of nowhere, and cause my poor wife undue stress. I took a huge swig of my drink, and the warmth instantly started in my legs. She adjusted, and fired up the joint.

"I'll try to explain this so it's not complicated. And I think I can take you back in time so you'll remember, too. Today at Location 5, someone from my past showed up, out of nowhere." She frowned a bit, and took a drink of her cosmo. Then she nodded, and passed me the joint. I inhaled, but that didn't make it any easier. "So, years and years ago when you worked at the Phoenix, there was a day where you saw a woman yelling at me, and attempting to kiss me on her way out. You were upset by the situation, and we talked about her a little." I looked at her, and that face had appeared. *Do you know the one?* The lip is cocked, the eye brow is up, and her eyes became laser points boring into anything they stopped to focus on. "Ah, I see you remember."

"Yes, Gabe. I remember seeing her. I don't know anything else about her, because you never told me." I could tell she was getting a little hot under the collar, and I had full plans to work with that, too. "Can you please just tell me? I

33

can't handle the pauses." She was being frank, which was how she got before she blew up.

"Her name is Lizzie, and she's the friend I was screwing around with when we hooked up all those years ago. She's crazy and delusional. I haven't seen her since that specific day at the Phoenix, and all of the sudden, out of nowhere today, she appears. She kissed me twice." Her mouth fell open, and her eye brow went even higher. *I'm not sure I'd ever seen it get that high before*. She quietly took the joint back, and had a very long swig of her cosmo, which was now almost gone.

"Well, I guess if you couldn't help it…" her voice shook. *Oh no*. This is what we needed to avoid! I watched her shaky hands re-light the joint to inhale, and her body tremble as she exhaled. I could tell this news crushed her.

"Baby, I pushed her away as fast as I could each time." I climbed closer to her. "I refused her advances, and I told her there was no way in hell. See," I held her hand. "I'm not telling you this so you get worried, but just so you are aware. I don't know what in God's name this woman has up her sleeve. And now that she knows I'm working with Donovan, well, who the hell knows." She sighed.

"And Donovan knows what's going on?" I nodded.

"Yes, I called him first, on my way home. Which is why I didn't text you. I'm sorry about that." She smiled a little. Then her nose wrinkled, and I braced myself.

"I'm sort of grossed out that she kissed you." She pulled her head back a bit, and I couldn't control it. My hands grabbed the sides of her head, and pulled her into my mouth. She fought only for seconds, and my tongue pushing into her hot mouth was never denied. I pulled back only long enough to take the remaining bits of the joint, and set it in the ashtray. My mouth covered hers again, this time she was completely into it.

"Are you still grossed out?" She shook her head, and her fingers dug into my neck, pulling me back to her. Her loose nightshirt hung around her neck, and have me ample room to get to her beautiful breasts. While I suckled each of her perfect, alert nipples, she downed the last of her cosmo and seductively wiped her lips off with her forearm. "You know you're the most beautiful thing I've ever seen, right?" She nodded, and writhed for more.

Her back arched on the couch cushions, pushing her stomach to the ceiling, exposing her tight white panties underneath. I felt my heart speed up getting a full view of the warmest, best place in town. *My Janie.* My cock was ragingly hard, and I needed to free the beast. I sat back from Janie's breasts, and began to take off my pants. Suddenly she was on her knees, pushing me back into the couch. She finished removing my pants, and gently cupped my balls, and shaft in her hands.

I love watching her squeeze my shaft. Gritting my teeth together with each tight pull, she was making my blood boil. Her eyes were locked on mine, and her tongue licked her lips over and over again. My dick was throbbing for her, and she knew it. I could tell by the small smirking smile creeping across her face.

"You want me to suck it, baby?" Her grip tightened, and I lost my words for a moment. My gaze met hers, and just like always, I was lost. I nodded as my eyes rolled back in my head, and I felt her hot breath end on my shaft, then down to my balls. *Oh, Shit!* I felt her taking deep, long, hot breaths, and they were all ending squarely on my balls. My dick is so hard for her, it's hard to focus on anything else. *What about that pussy, G?!*

I let my arm fall to her back, and gently caress her while she focused on my giant pole. Finally, as if the anticipation was killing me, her lips finally rested on my sack, and the warmth almost set me over the edge. Her hand tightened around my shaft while her mouth did the most amazing things to my balls. It was euphoric. *Heaven is for real... Jesus.* Releasing the suction, she rose and licked my tip with her tongue all the while smiling, and looking me right in the eye. Her deep green eyes were so vivid, and full of many colors. It was hard to focus on just one feature.

Just then, her mouth sank down over my shaft, taking me in as far as she could. My eyes rolled back again, and the thoughts of her tight pussy over took me. Her mouth felt so good, more than I had anticipated, again. But God, how I wanted to be deep inside of her. She sank on my cock again, and this time I pulled her off.

"Had enough, huh?" I smiled at her, and turned my body to face hers. "Ah, I see what you want." She lifted her night shirt over her head, revealing those sexy white panties.

"Baby, I want to rip those off." I crawled towards her, and linked my fingertips around the bands of her undies.

"No! Please don't rip them. I really like these!" She sort of pleaded, and giggled. *Oh my God, there's the giggle. We're done for.* Instead, I gently pulled them down, and when I did, the prize was all mine. As always, she was clean shaven, just waiting for my touch. I could see every quiver, and I could feel every single squeeze. Her slit was perfect, and I couldn't help finger her a bit. She was wet, so I spread it all around her hole. Pushing into her, she was ready to take me deep. I could feel her squeezing my fingers, wanting more.

I sat back, and looked at her nakedness. Her perfect human self, all mine. I stroked my cock a few times, hardening it even more. Her eyes followed my hands, wanting what I had so badly.

"Please, Gabe..." she was desperate. Her want for me was so heavy, and it turned me on even more. I bent over and lined myself up with her deep, wet hole. Pushing into her, I only gave her my tip. She moaned, and dug her heel into me, trying to push me in deeper. I smiled, and met her gaze. Even with just the tip in, I could barely control myself. *Perfection.* I still had three-quarters of a foot to shove inside, and now looked to be the time. I could feel her clamping on my head, and it was time to drive it home.

The warmth overtook me, and the throbbing was out of control. The wet pulses engulfing my cock were almost too much. I steadied myself, and took a few slow breaths. No way was I going to end this too soon. I slowly sank into her, and her body opened to me ever more. Her moans calmed for a moment, and she gyrated her hips in circles, begging for it. Pulling back from the warmth, and ramming back into it, her narrow hole was giving my cock a run for its money. I pushed into her again as deep as I could, and rested my hand over her abdomen. I could feel myself harder than ever, pushing into her, and it was more than hot. Just then, her hands came around me in a flurry, and grabbed on to my balls.

There wasn't much more I could do, and I felt my heart speed up again. I could feel my sack tighten, and the muscles tense, I knew I was close to coming. I opened my eyes again, and her beautiful face was mid-orgasm, clenching down around me, and completely yearning for my entire being. I pushed into her again, and felt the hot liquid ooze shoot deep into her belly. With each pulsation, I shot more into her. With every pulse, her tight pussy squeezed me even harder. I hadn't noticed that I had been pulling on her nipples, which was only prolonging her endless orgasm more.

"Oh, shit, baby. I'm sorry." She was breathless. Wanton and sleepy. She smiled, quickly sliding off of me, and rolled over on the couch.

"It's okay, but I'm exhausted. Let's watch a movie and sleep out here." She giggled, and reached for her panties. I couldn't help but watch her dress. It was like she was beaming with energy now after a few orgasms. Her smile was so contagious. It was these times that I was reminded how truly beautiful she is. And how lucky I am that she's all mine. "Oh," she turned, and I found her pointer-finger close to my face, lying next to me on the couch. "We're not done talking about this *other* woman." *Damnit.*

~

Morning came faster than I would have liked, but I was happy to be awake, and with Janie. She had gotten up before me, and was busily concocting something for breakfast. I knew what she'd want to talk about over breakfast, and I couldn't help sigh a few times to prepare myself. I heard my cell go off while I was in the bathroom, but figured it was probably Don, and we'd see him this afternoon. When I walked back into the kitchen, I was greeted with her peppy morning grin.

"Hey sleepy, here's some breakfast." She all but crammed me into the bar stool chair, and pushed the food into my face. I smiled, and poked around. Looked like a normal breakfast sandwich, so couldn't be too crazy. "So..." she said, opened ended as ever.

I took a big bite to give myself a few more seconds to think. She smirked, and knew exactly what I was up to. If there's one thing I've learned about my wife over the years is that she really does care what others do, think, and say. The wrong word choice could crush her, or anger her...and I really don't want to do any of that. Swallowing hard, I bravely stepped into the firing ring.

"Well, what else do you want to know exactly?" She paused, and looked at me perplexingly. "Seriously. Look Janie," I set down my sandwich, and took her hand. "I didn't bring this up with you to dive into my past, or bring up details that could hurt you. I just need you to know about Lizzie, and that she's a fucking psychopath." I guffawed aloud, shaking my head. "No, that's mean. She's just not all there, you know? Thinks that she owns anything she touches, and if you "defy" her, you're toast."

Janie wrinkled her nose. I took the moment of silence to slam another bite. *This sandwich is pretty damn good.*

"Will you see her more now with deliveries?" I shook my head quickly.

"Hell no. I already talked to Don, and I'm going to put Talon on it. We shouldn't have any other issues with her." She was searching my face for truth, or any bits I may have left out of the explanation. "Baby, I'm not lying. She's nothing, and honestly, wasn't really anything to me but a lay back in the day." She giggled, as she often does when I rhyme.

"You're a poet…" She drank from her orange juice cup. I couldn't help but watch how her perfect lips curled around the glass rim, and how her throat so gracefully swallows each gulp. FOCUS! "Okay Gabe. I'll watch out for her, or anyone else out of place." She smiled, and patted my hand. "Now, what do we need to take to Don's tonight?" *Oh, shit.* When she said that, I remembered my phone had gone off.

"Oh, not much. Mylah will be there, too, of course. He did say we'd hit the pool, and grill." I picked up my trash to throw away. "Can I take yours, too, beautiful?" She smiled, and handed me her plate.

"All right, I'll go pack our pool bag, and get my notes together for his June advertising party thing. He still hasn't told me if what I've done so far is okay or not." She shook her head in disgust as she walked into the bedroom.

It was so strange not having the kids around all the time, and so much quieter. That part was hard to adjust to. I missed their hugs, kisses, and constantly ramblings about God only knows what. Janie had gotten sent a few pictures of their camp activities, but we were yet to get any letters or calls. *If it's making me this crazy, I can only imagine how Janie's feeling on the inside.* I picked up my phone to check my text, and lost my breath.

Gabriel. You should think wisely about this decision. I'm not sure I trust this Talon.

I knew who it was from immediately. An unrecognizable number. *Lizzie.* I sat in my chair, and rested my head against the back. Surely Lizzie was only out for the best business deal for her boss, whoever that was. *Surely she couldn't be after me after all of these years*? No. It's just business.

I tried to brush off the latest text until I could talk to Donovan at his place later. Just then, Janie came blasting back through with a bag packed, and ready to go.

"We've got a few hours, love." She nodded.

"I know, I wanted to watch a movie before we left. Care to join me?" I smiled, and tipped my head.

"Depends. What are you watching?" She smiled, quickly opening our movie cabinet, and diving in like she knew exactly which she wanted. She pulled out the case and *'The Blue Lagoon'* shown across the title. I had to hold in a small burst of laughter. Whenever Janie is nervous, she always watches this movie! I remember years ago putting that movie in for her to relax to. "Yeah baby," I began, still shaking my head. "I'll watch that with you." She put in the movie, and jumped on to the couch.

I loved this spirit that she has, and that's been growing since all of the chaos has left our lives. Even the jail mail that still shows up occasionally doesn't tip her scales as much as they use to. I'd really like to believe we're out of all the drama in our lives. But in the pits of my stomach, I couldn't help feel like the tides of life were turning again. I just couldn't say in which direction quite yet. Cracking my neck, I turned back to the television to find her intently watching as the shelter is made on the beach for the children to live in...

5
Janie.

I walked into the James Estate like I owned the place. After all these years, and all of the crazy shit we'd all been through! I chuckled to myself. Don and I had a very hard to explain relationship. Thankfully it was one that Gabe seemed to understand, or at least pretend to and roll with. We did have a lot of fun together... *Janie! Focus!* I shook my head, and headed into the kitchen, where I put my cold appetizer, and drink. I could hear Don and Myl at the pool house out back. Grabbing Gabe's hand, I headed straight out back.

"Hey Donny!" I said flirtatiously as I could. His eyes lit up as they met mine, and he instantly came around to greet us both. His hand first outstretched to Gabe.

"Sir, it's a pleasure to see you on this fine afternoon." They finished their secret man handshake, and he turned to me. His smile was still one of the best I'd ever seen, and in certain cases, I'd still get the butterflies in my stomach if I wasn't prepared for his million dollar looks. "And Janie..." he took my hand, and raised it in the air. "Still fine as ever, MMmm!" He pulled me in to a hug that was rather low handed.

"Hello, Don." I smiled as he pulled away. "How're things going? It's been a few months since I've been over here! I sort of missed this place!" He laughed out loud. "On a business note," he winced. "I've got the June party set up...did you get my email?" He nodded. "Ohh, so you just didn't respond." I shook my head, and threw my hand into the air.

"It looked perfect, Janes. Like everything you do." I smiled. "I'll email you some extras specs and details next week. No rush. Let's just have fun tonight." Turning to head back to the bar, he stopped momentarily, and turned back towards me. "I'm glad you were okay with the extra guests. They should be here shortly." He smiled, tapped my cheek, and took his seat back at the bar. Extra guests? I think I was left out on something.

Looking around I saw Gabe finding us some bar chairs, and claiming them with his smoke, drink, and cell phone. I saw Mylah floating in the pool on her raft. I heard the music turn up a bit, and then it hit me. The mystery guests must be new employees. *But why the secrecy?* Probably someone I know… Some like Sean. I chuckled to myself a bit remembering those months a few years back. Slowly, I blew out my deepest breath through my mouth. *Let's not get too worked up about that again, huh Janes? Didn't seem to fair as well for you that last round.* That voice was right. I just need to focus on having a fun night with my love.

Taking my seat at the bar, I was handed a new drink. Mylah watched the interaction from the pool, and made sure to shout her thoughts over to me.

"Try that drink! It's so good!!" She smiled, and gave me the thumbs up.

"All right, I'll give it a go!" Gabe smiled even bigger, and as I took the cup from him he engulfed me with himself. He smelled so good. Clean and fresh, not overloaded with cologne like so many men are these days. While he hugged me, I tasted the drink. It wasn't too sweet, or too dry. It tasted of nectarines, strawberries and something…minty? "MMmm….this is good!"

Agreeing, Gabe released me back into my bar chair. He took the stool next to my own. I couldn't help but check my cell phone, as it had been a few days since we had dropped off the kids, and I hadn't heard anything from them yet. As if on cue,

Gabe's hand came crashing on to mine. I met his gaze, and his smile reassured me it would all be okay.

"I get it, love. I miss them, too." He stroked my hand, and I gulped my drink. "Let's just have fun. We don't get this chance very often, so let's live it up a little bit." He smirked, and reached for my glass. *He's right, you know. You need to let loose a little. You know you can feel it building up inside of you, getting ready to bust, Janes.* I handed him my glass without much second thought. I also grabbed the music controller, and turned it on to my own preferred station. *'Cats in the Cradle'* blared through the speakers.

"Well, let's just enjoy ourselves then!" I grabbed my newly made drink, and drank it in about four gulps. Gabe laughed heartily, and Donovan joined him at the bar. I handed my drink back to Gabe, and leaned over the counter to kiss him. As I did, I heard the speaker system announce the other guests, and Gabe turned slowly to see who had arrived.

"Well, I guess the rumors were true." He didn't even have to point out who he was talking about. I had already seen him standing on the deck, and knew I'd have to have that "special" moment with him at some point.

"Fabulous. I'm so..." I trailed off, trying to hide the worried and semi-disgusted look on my face. "Excited?" I shook my head idly. *Maybe the 'Cats in the Cradle' was playing for him*? I giggled.

"Great!" Donovan turned, and welcomed the new group of people. "I'm so glad you could come, Sean! It's been too long!" They briefly hugged, and I turned in time to see he wasn't alone, and was with two other men. "Hello, I'm Donovan James." I listened, as he extended his hands to the unknown men. Gabe nudged me, and he stood closely at my side.

"Be right back baby. Have to go meet the new prospects." He raised his eyebrows, as if not impressed, and headed towards the group of men. I watched them all intently, and drank a few more sips of my drink. I could hear Gabe enter the crowd. "Hello, everyone! Ready to party?!" The men all laughed, and agreed.

"This is Gabriel Lazarus, my right hand man." Donovan patted Gabe's back, and left the group heading back towards myself at the bar. He approached me slowly, seeing that I was eyeing the new crowd. "Hey Janie," he softly spoke. "Sorry if you didn't know Sean would be here. I can promise you-" I held my hand up.

"It's all fine. It's been years since those nights..." I trailed off quickly, and took another drink. He caught the gleam in my eye, and the sudden bent peak of my eyebrow. I smiled, and dropped my bathing suit cover up. As always, his eyes trailed up and down my body, hungrily.

"My God," he sighed. "Certain things only get better with time." I smirked again, grabbed my drink, the vodka bottle, and my towel.

"I'll be in the hot tub, if I'm needed." I winked at him as I walked away. "You never know what will happen at these parties, Mr. James." Leaving Donovan at the bar, I heard Gabe join him there. I took my seat in the massage section of the ginormous hot tub. *Donovan took party size to a new meaning, for sure.* I took another drink, and sank myself into the bubbling hot water that was now glowing with pink, blue and green lights. Closing my eyes, I rested my head back and listened to the chatter around the pool yard.

~

I watched Janie slink off to the hot tub, fully knowing what she was doing. I couldn't hold in my laughter as I approached Donovan, who was still standing there gawking at my wife. He held my drink out to me, freshly refilled and iced.

"You're gonna need this man," he said as he gulped a double shot of bourbon. "She only gets better, seriously." We both nodded and looked her over, now calmly relaxing in the steamy tub. Her breasts were perfect, and covered with one of her new bikinis. Glancing over, I'm pretty sure I saw Donovan wipe the drool from his mouth. I chuckled again.

"Easy camper, you know how she gets." He nodded, and drank again. As I refilled my own drink, I couldn't help but gaze at her. The water gently lapped on to her chest, and her boobs bounced freely behind the triangles barely holding her perfect nipples in place. She had just gotten her hair wet, and it was slicked back, and wildly placed around her shoulders. I finished mixing my drink, and dropped a few ice chunks into my glass.

As I walked back around the pool towards Janie, I could've sworn she was glowing. Looking down, my shorts began to get tight. *Oh, hold that monster in check!* I was suddenly stopped by Sean, who had already downed a few beers.

"Hey Gabe! How's it been?" His eyes met mine, and looked across the pool yard at what I was gazing at. His eyes stopped on Janie, and instinctively, he inhaled sharply at the memories. He slowly turned his head back to face me, and smiled awkwardly. I nodded, and took a drink.

"Sean, it's been too long." I extended my hand to him, and he quickly shook it. "I was sorry to hear about Delaney. I hope that now things have been calmed for the little guy." He nodded, and smiled.

"Thanks, and yeah, for the most part we've got it all worked out. We get pretty equal time, and it's nice because she's really flexible when I can see Dominic." He smiled, and took a sip of his beer. His eyes darted down into his cup, showing me he wasn't being the most truthful. "How about you and Janie and the kids? Everything going well?" I smiled wide.

"The kids are doing great! They're at summer camp, and then hitting the lake house with Jane's parents until we get there in August. We're taking care of some business, and spending some time together first." I winked, and motioned back to my beautiful wife. "And Janie, well, look at her buddy." He chuckled, and nodded with me. I tapped my glass to his, and said "cheers" as I walked away.

"Well, hey Gabe, wait up!" Sean jogged a few steps to catch up with me, and I knew Don wanted all the newbies handled with white gloves.

"Yeah?" I stopped, and turned to face him.

"I just wondered if you and Janie were still having parties. Are you? It's been so long since I've been! I'd love to come to one next time you're up for it." *Is this guy for real?* I smiled a disingenuous smile, and nodded.

"Sure man, I'll let you know. All our focus has been on the James Industries events, and stuff for Janie's business. Maybe later this summer." He tipped his chin upwards, and threw his hands in the air as he walked back to the bar with Donovan and the other new guys. *Shit, what were their names?* Armando and...? Uri, maybe? Pushing the thoughts out, I put myself back on track to my wife.

Finally reaching the hot tub, I walked over to Janie and smiled at her. I set my drink down on the table and chairs she had claimed, and I pulled my shirt off to join her.

"Oww-Oww!" She wolf whistled at me, and I almost blushed. I watched her tip her head back, and guzzle the last few sips of her drink. She was obviously tipsy, if not already drunk, and she was bouncing through the water towards me. She ended up in my lap, with her breasts surrounding my face. I couldn't help cup them, and pull her farther on to me, so I could bury myself in her chest even farther. Her nose pressed against mine, and her smile was beaming as she ground against my crotch.

47

"Ahh, what's that you want, my love?" Her lips circled my own, eventually taking over. Her tongue probed into my mouth, and she tasted of strawberry and liquor. Her hands clawed their way down to my shoulders, and down my back. She was more than eager. "You sure you want to do this here?" She looked around the pool, taking note of Sean, Mylah, Don, and the two newbies. She turned back to me, her eyes were dark and hungry.

"Yes, I want you here and now." I paused, and turned to her empty glass. "I'd also like a refill!" she shouted to Donovan who had already caught on to what was about to happen. Donovan smiled back at her, and held up his finger, motioning for her to have patience. She turned back to me, and quickly removed her top. *Oh, she's drunk...* I reached for my drink, and finished it off. The rush of alcohol helped this be okay....we haven't done this in public in over a year. *Fiends.*

She swung her bikini top around my head, and began grinding my crotch hard as she could. It was incredibly hard to resist her at times like this, and I wasn't about to start now. Her nipples were hard, and stabbing into my chest. I could feel the throb in my shaft, and my cock was heated up. I shimmied out of my swim shorts, and sat back on the upper seat of the hot tub. My legs were covered with water, and half of my shaft. She bounced around spinning, and splashing while everyone watched her.

I caught Donovan sneaking around behind us, bringing us both new drinks. He placed hers next to her in the tub, making sure to take extra time to focus on each nipple. He put one on the table for me, and a smaller glass with a few more shots into my hand. He winked, and disappeared into the crowd. I quickly drank the hot whiskey and again felt the warmth flow through me. I tossed the glass into the chair, and turned back to Janie.

48

"Hey, try this," I grabbed my cock and motioned it towards her. She licked her lips, and sank into the tub on her knees. She sucked me deep into her mouth, and I lost my breath. Her hands were swiftly cocking my shaft, and her lips were warm and wet all over my tip. I loved her tight squeezes, which meant she remembered our late night conversations about sexual favorites. *She is perfect.* My head fell back, and I relished this feeling of togetherness. She knew me so well, and I her. We were alone in a crowd of people, focusing only on each other.

Reaching down to her breasts, I pulled each into my hands, and pushed her back to an upright position. Slowly, I turned her around so I could take her from behind. Pulling each of the side strings on her bikini bottoms, the fell into the water. She bent over the side of the hot tub, and sipped on her drink. I gently pulled her cheeks apart, revealing her bright pink folds. Using my fingers, I pushed into her to spread her slick around for my entry.

My cock was rock hard, and ready to take her. She looked over her shoulder at me, and smirked. I knew she was ready, and wanted everything that was coming at her. Palming myself, I pushed into her tight hole. Her walls instantly clung to me in welcome, and I grit my teeth through the joyous pleasure she offered. Her head reared back with pleasure, and she screamed out in delight. The crowd appreciated the efforts, and clapped in awe. I pulled back and slammed deeper into her core. With each thrust, her walls tightened around me even more. I could feel her hot gooze coming out all over with each squeeze, and it made my balls quiver.

I wrapped her hair around my hand, and pulled it tight. My right hand rested on her shoulder, pulling her farther on to my shaft. I could feel her womb shaking, and dripping with wetness. I could feel my balls pull and constrict, and I tightened my grip on her hair and shoulder holding her firmly in place.

Taking all of me at once. I could feel myself shoot deeply inside of her, and I felt the aftershocks of orgasm flow through her for ten minutes after. Sometimes I was sure that those little quakes were the best part. I pulled back out of her, sinking us back into the warm water with the dark cover. Her lips covered mine in a deep kiss, and she hopped out of the hot tub to her towel in her chair. Curtseying to the crowd, she wrapped herself up, and sat down to smoke.

I found my trunks floating idly on the other side of the hot tub, and slid them back on effortlessly. Donovan joined me in the hot tub moments after, and Janie passed a joint down to me. He smiled at me, and sipped his drink.

"You are the best!" He laughed aloud. "Those two newbies signed the contract half-way through your show!" Janie coughed, and giggled.

"Aww, guess I haven't lost my touch, ehh… Don?" she adjusted herself, and crossed her legs as he looked up their length.

"Oh Janie, my God no. You could make movies…" he shook his head, and we all laughed aloud. "So, I owe you again, as those two new hires are going to make us all a lot more money!" He raised his glass to toast, and my love raised her smoke. "But seriously, where have you two been all my life? Man, seeing that shit, those guys were sure it'd be the same for them!" I couldn't help but chuckle. Sean appeared next to the group, and sat down in the open chair, dipping his feet in the hot tub. "And look, the years have even brought Sean back into our company." He patted Sean's back, and Sean still looked a little out of place.

"Yeah, Thanks Don! I'm excited to be back with everyone. I took the newbies back to their apartment for the time being. We'll see how fast they blow through their stash." Donovan and I exchanged disturbed glances.

6

"Hopefully they can get market value, or more, for that prime product, too." I couldn't help but add. I was still skeptical of Sean, being completely honest. I knew that deep down he was a good enough guy, but with everything that happened first with Janie, and then his own wife and child, I'm just leery of his commitment to anything, or anyone. Sean nodded at my comment, seeming to understand what wasn't said.

"You'll see Gabe, I'll make sure to keep these guys on track. I swear they seem truly legit, and know something about their area for sales." He shrugged. "It's worth a shot, I think." Donovan nodded, and patted his shoulder again. I didn't want to be the one causing tension between the ranks, so I quickly covered my own suspicions.

"Oh yeah, I'm sure they'll be great! We'll get them all properly trained on our fabulous lines of boats and boating accessories in no time!" I winked, and stood to pick up our things. Looking over, I could tell that Janie was spent, and that her head was no longer in the party. She was attached to her phone, most likely hoping for a message from our kids. I leaned over to her in her chair, and kissed her forehead. "You about ready, baby? You look tired." She yawned, and nodded.

"I'm all right here in the chair, if you want to stick around." I smiled, and nodded.

"Maybe just a bit longer then. I don't want to miss out on anything important." I picked up her cup, and headed to the bar to get her some water. Mylah met me at the bar, and was finishing cleaning up from the snacks, and prior evening adventures.

"Hey Gabe. How's Janie doing?" I checked over my shoulder to make sure that nothing had changed in the last few seconds, and she was still peacefully reclined, puffing away on her smoke.

"She's good, just recovering from our outburst a little while ago." I smiled at her, and resumed filling my drink. Donovan had some of his secret drink mix on the bar, so I filled up with that. "Hey, could you fill this up with ice and water for me real quick? I didn't want to knock you out of the way." She smiled, and took the cup. I headed back towards Janie, who was now sitting on the edge of her chair.

"I'm just going to take a stroll around the gardens." She smiled, and reached for her glass. "Thanks for the water. I'll be back in a few." I smiled at her, and knew she just needed a bit of space. I sat back down in my chair, listening to Don and Sean discuss their hopes for our company. I watched her drift into the dimly lit garden, smelling the flowers as she went along. No sooner did she leave my sight, and my cell phone vibrated. Digging it out of the bag, I flicked the screen on. *Shit, Mom.*

"Hey Mom," I answered quickly, hoping it was no news about the kids. I stepped into the house to talk to her away from the chaos and loud boisterous voices bellowing by the pool. As she talked, I listened as I walked around inside of the mansion. Stepping into the patio room, I was hoping I could catch a glimpse of Janie in the gardens. "Really? Well, that sounds like a plan." I tried to appease to get her off of the phone faster, but it wasn't working. I strolled into our product room, entering my code as I went through the barred, bullet proof, safe-like vault doors.

As my mom's voice rang clearly in my head, checking around our stock, I was floored by the massive quantities of everything. "Oh yeah, she really does like gymnastics! Maybe that would be a good thing, too. Did you mention it to Jane?" I idly flipped through the calendar on the schedule table, and noticed there were numerous notes on location five. I could feel my brow bend, as Lizzie was the last thing I wanted in my mind. Out of the corner of my eye, I caught a shadow walking near the garden.

Quickly heading for the door, I killed the lights and locked up. "Mom, I've got to go for now. I need to find Janie at this party we're at. Can I call you later?" Walking back through the kitchen and out through the patio doors, I noticed Sean was no longer at the table.

"Hey Gabe, bring back more drink-" Donovan stopped talking, and instead watched me lunge off the patio and towards the garden. The lighting down the path wasn't great, and the divots were making for one hell of a walk. There was a large bush I stumbled across, that was an appropriate size to hide my big body behind. I could hear voices. Quieting my breathing, and twisting myself so I could see through the bush, I could make out their images in the darkness.

~

Janie.

Sitting on the bench alone gave me a minute to collect my thoughts. My head just seemed so hellishly scattered. *Loved your show with G...* I smiled at the thought, and giggled a little while I dusted the grass and leaves off of the bench. I couldn't help but think of his warm hands caressing every square inch of my body. I leaned in towards the small garden pond. The dim lights showed the blooms in the pond, and maybe even a Koi fish. But suddenly, I knew I wasn't alone. Even in the dimly lit garden, I could see the shadow reflection appear in the pond next to me. I gasped, and jumped back.

"Sorry Janes," Sean laughed. "Didn't mean to scare you." I frowned at him. "I saw you come off back here, and I wanted to make sure you were okay." I dusted myself off, and reclaimed my seat on the bench.

"Hey Sean." I dully responded. "Yeah, I come out here all the time. Donovan doesn't tend the garden much, so he lets me do what I want with it." I nodded, and smiled. He closed the distance between us, and edged towards the open seat on the bench next to me. He motioned at the bench.

"Can I sit there?" he pointed in question. I nodded. I hadn't really been alone with him since all of the drama years ago, nor had I really discussed how he had left Delaney when she needed him most. But still, as he sat down next to me, I could feel the tension. He took the seat next to me, and his leg brushed mine. Instinctively I pulled away. "Oh man. Don't be like that Janes. I'd never hurt you."

"I know." I said flatly, not even believing my own words. "I just don't know what to feel around you after everything that's happened in the past couple years." I looked up to find him staring at me. "It's like I don't know you anymore." His head fell, and he closed his eyes tightly. He nodded, almost in agreement.

"I know, and I deserve whatever is coming at me. I was so horrible to all of you." I sighed out loud accidentally, because I couldn't believe his first worry wasn't his child. Or his wife, regardless of how "ex" she was. "I know. Delaney. Dom." He buried his head momentarily in his hands. He swallowed hard. Sitting up, he shifted on the bench to face me. "See, after we were together," he paused, and I was now on pins and needles. "Something in my head broke, and I couldn't stop thinking about you. Months later after things calmed down again, and..."

I could see the angry tears forming in his eyes. "She found out we had sex. She blamed me, over and over." He sighed, and then chuckled. "You know what she said?" He asked, meeting my eyes again.

"I have no idea Sean." I watched his face change through a myriad of expressions, finally ending on one I hadn't seen before.

"She told me she knew I was in love with you." He smirked, and sat staring at me. Obviously waiting for me to say something. But what in the hell was I supposed to say to that? Of all times for my inner voice to be hushed! "Specifically, she said it was "unrequited love,'" he made quotation fingers as he finished. I could feel my mouth hanging open, so I turned away from him, pretending to look out into the garden.

"Well surely that's not the case. You know, I've seen her numerous times," I turned back towards him. "She's never hinted at anything like that, but then again, I don't bring you up unless she does." I began to stand up, and he stood with me, taking my hand in his own.

"So, she's right then?" he asked, almost afraid.

"Right about what Sean?" I said, yanking my hand from his. Did I really need to say aloud what he was hinting at? Was he really this drunk? *This dense? This....asking for trouble?* I needed to head back towards the pool deck, and drown myself in Donovan's mystery drink mix. *For once we agree. This is leaning on being a completely psychotic event.* His hands were suddenly moving, and heading towards my face.

"I *know* you use to love me, Janie." I pulled away from his grasp, and forthcoming hand which fell upon my wrist. "We can't leave what we started unfinished. I know that Gabe would understand, after we talked."

"Oh, he would, would he??" I twisted my wrist from his grasp, and backed up a few feet. "Stop, Sean!" I held up my hand. "Just fucking quit." He still pushed on, stepping towards me as I backed up. "What the hell are you going to do? Rape me? You want to corner me, and have me as you will? You gonna be like *Michael*?" I asked, now sporting a disgusting smile. Stunned, he stopped coming at me, and backed up himself, hands in the air.

"Whoa, easy, Janie. I'd never..." I shook my head.

"No, you'll never! You're damn right about that!" I paused to collect my thoughts. I had no idea what he needed to hear. *Come one! Come all! If you're a crazy fucking nut job, come on over and chat with Janie!* "Sean, I *don't* love you. I *never* really have. You were a friend. And if we're being honest, one who left me to the wolves for years, right?" I stepped towards him slowly. "I just want to be able to be friends, so you can work with Gabe for Donovan. You and I both know the instant you overstep with me, or something else, you're out." I turned to head back towards the pool, not giving him any time to respond. "Please stop putting me in these situations, okay? My choice is always Gabe. You'll always just be a friend." I turned and headed back down the path, desperately hoping the arms of my husband were close by.

What was that?! I had no idea. *Where did THAT come from?!* I guess distance does make the heart grow fonder. I couldn't help but fall back to that day years ago at Donovan's house, when Sean had appeared at the top of the staircase. Our awkward relationship had gone on for the better part of fifteen years at this point, and at this moment, I wasn't sure where the hell it was supposed to end up with him. Turning the corner, I smiled at Mylah who was tending to the bar.

"Hey Boss Lady!" she yelled at me happily. "What can I get ya?" she smiled, and shook her chest at me.

"I'll have a shot of Donovan's Mystery punch, if there's any left." She nodded, and begin pouring it into the tiny glass. I turned around, searching the patio for Gabe, but he was nowhere in sight. "Have you seen Gabe?" She handed me the drink, and shook her head.

"I did see him heading into the house earlier, looked like he was on the phone." I nodded, took the shot, and headed back towards our chairs to check my phone.

~

I turned around, and leaned into the bush for support. I couldn't believe what I just heard, and after all these years? There was no way that Sean was going to get anywhere close to Janie, not ever again. I made the quick decision to end that bullshit before it even began. I stepped out from behind the bush, and Sean was more than surprised. He smiled, as if trying to block the knowledge he already knew. I had heard everything.

"Hello, Mr. Westing." I said formally.

"Hey buddy, how's it going?" he was jumpy, twitchy, and obviously drunk.

"Well, I just wanted to see if you fully understand your job here at James Industries." I looked into his face, and raised my eyebrow. "Missteps in this business are just not welcome. In fact, there is no room for errors that may jeopardize your own personal health." I turned towards him, face to face.

"Oh yeah, I know man! No worries, I'm ready!" He smiled, and pumped his fists together.

"Great," I paused and began to turn away. "However," I stopped suddenly, a few feet away. "You'll want to know that my wife, Janie, is off limits to you. Understand?" I smiled at him, wider than ever. As if finally understanding the unsaid words, his eyes grew larger, and his mouth fell open. He nodded, and looked at the ground. I turned and headed back to find my wife.

Thankfully, she was just taking her seat when I found her. I couldn't help but smile at her. She was so beautiful, and so strong. She didn't need me one bit in that garden, although, I'm glad I was there.

"Hey love," I called to her. Her heart stopping smile was the first thing I saw. "You about ready to head home for tonight?" She patted the chair next to hers, so I took a seat.

"I just have a few sips of water left, and then we can go. I'm probably going to need to sleep for a day or so." She swirled her fingers around her ear, symbolizing 'crazy', and wrinkled her nose. "This last round seemed a little stronger than Don usually makes. This must be 'Mylah's Mix.'" She nodded, and gulped the rest of her ice water. We gathered our things, and walked our glasses back to the bar.

"See you later, Mylah! We're outta here." I smiled and waved at her while Janie hugged her. I extended my hand to Don. "Mr. James," I shook hard. "It's been a pleasure, as always."

"Gabriel!" He stood, and pulled me into a hug. "My right hand!!" He patted my back.

"Absolutely. You let me know once their paperwork is done," I said, motioning to the newbies now hammered sitting across the table from him. "I'll get them all trained and ready." Don shook my hand, and nodded. Pushing me out of the way to get to Janie, I laughed aloud.

"Oh, sorry Gabe. I just need a moment with your wife." I laughed aloud again, as I couldn't help picture the garden scene all over again. *What is it with everyone and your wife?* She hugged him gently, and fell back into my hands thereafter. She climbed into the 370z, and instantly cranked the radio. I shook my head while she belted out the best drunken version of *'the Freshmen'* that there ever was.

7

By the time I woke up this morning, the sun was already at high noon. I felt around next to me, and she was already up and out of the room. I pulled myself out of bed, and checked my cell phone as I slid on my slippers. I headed into the bathroom to take a shower. For whatever reason I felt overly hung-over, and really hoped the shower would help. I put my head into the stream of scalding hot water, and supported it on the wall. The water felt so good rolling down my back that I was lost in the waterfall-like dream I was having in my head.

Suddenly, her hands wrapped around my cock and balls, and snugly held on tight. I could feel the creeping grin sneak across my face, and her body pressed into my back. It was amazing how her nipples drove into my skin, no matter where they touched. Her hands were gentle, but firm. *My favorite.* I pulled myself off of the wall, and leaned back into her even more. She took a few steps back, slowly readjusting me out of the direct shower spray.

I wiped the water from my eyes, and caught her ornery gaze. In moments, she was on her knees running her hands up and down my thighs. My flaccid self was no more after a few more minutes with my sexy wife. Watching her work, my dick twitched with need, rising even taller by the second. She smiled, and nibbled her lip before completely devouring me.

Watching her swallow me whole was one of my favorite sights in the entire world. There were no logical words in any language which would help describe how perfect her mouth truly is. I watched her lips slide up and down my shaft, and I fell in love with her more when she flashed those beautiful green eyes at me. *Holy. Cow. She's gorgeous.*

"Oh Janie..." I could not hold the moans back. I loved the twisting and sucking motions she was doing, and I could feel my balls tighten. "Baby," I tried to break the seal, with no avail. "I'm close baby." She pulled me almost entirely out of her mouth, and met my gaze with burning hot eyes. Smiling for a moment, then vivaciously impaling herself back on my shaft, sucking harder than ever. I braced myself on the towel bars on the wall, hoping I didn't lose my footing.

If there were some way to make this feeling last forever, I'd take it. I'd never get anything done otherwise, but her perfection makes me so hungry. I felt my balls pull into me again, and I reached down to steady her for what was to come. Knowing my body so well, she adjusted so my spray would shoot all over her beautiful chest and face... and that is exactly where I aimed. She grabbed my balls as hard as she could, and braced for my hot juice.

"OHHhhh God," I garbled out, as I pulsed all over her pretty face and on to her breasts. She held her smile while lapping up every last drop she could get out of me. I sat down slowly on the side seat, to give my body a minute to stop shaking from climax. She stood, and began washing herself in the shower.

"Thanks for letting me join you. I needed a shower, bad." she giggled, and turned back into the shower spray.

"I owe you big time, love. That was unexpected as ever..." I stood, and turned her clean-self back to my face. My lips consumed hers and our tongues were intertwined for moments. "And it was so, soo good." I smiled.

"Oh yeah, you owe me all right. I'll get out of your shower now. I'm going to do a bit of work this afternoon. I figured that would give you a few hours if you needed to get anything done." She switched places with me in the water stream, and began to climb out of the shower making sure to swat my ass cheek as hard as she could on her way out.

"Ouch! I'll definitely be repaying now." I heard her laugh while she was fiddling around with her bathroom accoutrements. "I may try and do some work, too. I've got to see what I have first. I don't really remember anything about last night. Can we plan to hook back up this evening? Say, living room, about 8?" I wasn't sure she was even still there, but I was hopeful.

"Sure, that sounds fine." Her head popped back into the shower, and she blew me a kiss. "Love you, Gabe." She smiled, and darted out of the bathroom. Still, to this day, I have no idea how I ended up so lucky. *You worked for it, obviously*. I finished rinsing the soap off, and stepped out of the shower to dry off. I noticed my phone was flashing, so I picked it up and opened the message.

>*Gabe, we need a run for L4. High priority delivery. Hoping you can do this now, and get it done. Let me know. D.*

I quickly texted back, now super thankful that Janie decided to work a bit, too. *An extra pay check?* I think so!

>*I'm good! Be over in a few.*

I threw on some jeans, and a black polo shirt. Since I'd started with James Industries, black seemed to be what I felt the most comfortable in. *And it makes you feel like a secret service agent. Don't lie.* Rolling my deodorant on, I spritzed a few squirts of body spray on. I was out the door and on my way to Don's in a flash.

I pulled the van into the covered loading dock, and was met by Donovan's finest loader, Talon Pierce. We exchanged idle glances, as I climbed out to grab the paperwork. This location seems to be picking up their order frequency, which I wasn't exactly thrilled about. This was a dark place, and the people weren't like the rest of us. Pushing my feelings of reserve in my back pocket, I headed back to the work van.

"What's up with this order?" he idly asked as he fitted the final box into the back.

"No clue man." I tossed the paperwork into the open door, and turned back towards him. "This is one of my least favorite locations. Anyway, all ready to go?" He nodded, and slammed both the doors closed.

"Be safe, G. See you in a few." Exchanging waves, I was back on the road. My cell started ringing almost instantly. Fumbling through my pants pocket, I managed to yank it out without swerving. *Ah, only the biggest hazard of driving with a full order.* Greg. I turned the radio down a bit, and flipped the phone open.

"Hello my good man! Long time no speak." His laughter filled my ears. "How've you been, Greg"

"Gabe! We're doing great, man! Life is just so damn busy with the kids and everything. But I know you understand. How's everyone doing?"

"The kids are away at summer camp, and Janie's business is doing great." This was always the awkward part. No way could I ever tell anyone about my job...not even my closest friends. It helped that they had met Donovan at a few local events over the years. The James' new Hammerhead boat line was top selling across the globe in pre-sales, and this gave me the best cover there was.

"And how about your job?" I could almost hear the wonder in his voice through the telephone.

"Oh, it's great. Don really keeps me busy, and we're still really benefitting from the flexibility." I heard Rylee squeal in the background. "Hey, it's been so long. You and Heather should come over some evening next week. What do you think?"

Since the events of our past, some of our friends haven't frequented our house as they did before. It didn't seem to matter that security was now that of the Pentagon, the memories were just too heavy for some. Both Janie and I tried to understand that over the years, but the loss of Heather's friendship really did it for her.

"You know, Heather and I were just talking about that. Sounds good! And we're actually getting a few days break from the kids while they go to her parents' house next week. Just a second." I could hear him discussing something in the background, but his words were too muffled to understand. "Hey, sorry about that. How about Wednesday evening? That work for you guys?" Off hand, I could think of nothing happening...but I knew better than to plan before consulting with the boss.

"Let me text Janie and make sure, but I think it'll be good. We'll say 7 o'clock for now, and I'll text you later to confirm."

"Great! Can't wait to see you guys!" I could hear him smiling, and couldn't help but wonder how long it had been since he had been free from the wife and kids.

"You too, we'll talk soon." I hung up, and turned the radio up. *Cocaine* came over the speakers, and I couldn't even try to hold back my inner Clapton. Plucking a few strings on my air guitar and driving with my knee went better than I had hoped. I turned on the GPS for the last few miles of weaving through city streets, but finally came upon Location 4's gates.

I came up to the gate and Saul, their "shipment unloader," came around to my passenger side window. He was the creepiest son-of-a-bitch you've ever seen, with jail-original tattoos around his eyes, and wearing more "gold" jewelry than was legal. His eyes were dark, and gave nothing away. For the most part, he was cordial. But having these gates close behind me each time, even for the ten minutes I was inside was entirely too much.

"Hey, Mr. Shaw. How's it rolling?" I smiled, and nodded across to the passenger window.

"Hey esse," he stuck his head in and around the vehicle, checking for bugs, scanners, or anything else that would locate him. "You've got our full order in here, si?" I nodded, and handed him the clipboard of paperwork.

"Absolutely. Just tell me where you want me to pull in for unloading." He rifled through the pages of paperwork, and seemed satisfied with the box count in the back.

"Go unload by that red Caddy, esse." He tossed the clipboard back into the passenger seat. "I think Hector wants to talk to you, too." He walked back around the front of the van and radioed of my arrival. I watched as the gate and the garage door near where I was to go opened slowly, almost at the same time.

I drove through the large, open lot. It was entirely fenced in with an eight foot tall chain link fence, with barbed wire two feet on top of that. There were empty buildings surrounding, with many of their windows completely broken out. Large pieces of wall were missing in some cases, and I couldn't help but wonder how things functioned in a place like this. Refocusing, I pulled around to back into my space.

As I pulled the handle and stepped out of the van, I was hit in the face with my own van door. It instantly cracked me right in the face, and I could feel the blood dripping down my chin.

"What the fuck?!" I yelled, and looked to see who the door basher was. *Oh shit, Gabe. What the hell is this!?* Looking up, I noted that Hector had four minions around him, and he looked really fucking pissed off. I put my hands up in defense. "Whoa, wait a minute. Your whole order is here, on time. Early even. What the fuck is the problem?"

He smiled widely at me a first. The stout, short, fat little Mexican man. It was obvious to most that Hector Reyes was a midget-kingpin Mexican drug lord. I still couldn't figure out how James' had ever started doing business with these people. Still

66

smiling, he took a few steps towards me. Before I knew it, I was getting blasted in the face repeatedly. I fell back against the van, where one of the minions held me to it while two others began to beat the shit out of me. I defended myself with my arms and hands as much as I could. Each punch alternated sides of my rib cage, and my eyes had almost swollen shut, making it harder to see. *Goddamnit!* Finally they let me fall to the ground in a heap to my knees.

"You tell your boss we'll stick with the current market prices." I looked up at him, squinting through the blood and sweat, shaking my head. He smiled again, and his minions backed away from us. I started to stand, still staring the sonofabitch in the eyes, just watching for him to make a move. "Ah, Gabriel. I do apologize to you and your lovely wife for hurting your pretty face. My issues are with Donovan. Retaliation is a bad idea."

Without saying another word I got back into the van, started it, and took off. I made it about a mile down the road, and stopped in a Meijer parking lot to give myself the once over. I pulled the mirror down to check out the facial damage. I could still see out of both eyes, thankfully, but the gash on the side of my head was deep. My eyelids were purple and extremely puffy. *Looks like you've been in a bar fight...*

"Fuck!" *I guess you should've listened to your gut on this one, huh?* I pulled out my cell and quickly dialed Donovan. Getting out of the van to inspect my rib cage, I noted quickly that moving my left side was extremely difficult. Lifting my shirt, my side was turning four shares of purple while I watched. These bruises were going to hurt.

"Hey G! You headed-" I wasn't going to wait to listen to him ramble.

"You're going to need to call in your nurses. Those motherfuckers just jumped me, and I'm going to need stitches!!" I could hear him rifling around.

"Oh Jesus, are you okay?! Where the fuck are you?!" He sounded angrily annoyed. I couldn't say that I blamed him. Donovan was a very fair, overly generous drug lord. "Looks like it's time for location four to be shut down. Come back here, and I'll get one of my on staff RNs to come fix this. Need pain meds?"

"Yeah, you'd better make it the whole package. I'm not feeling very well. I'll be there in about thirty minutes. God*damn*it Donovan! I am NOT dealing with shit like this." I hung up the phone, uninterested in anything Donovan had to say at that point. I was pissed off as hell. This wasn't something I should be dealing with. The only thing I was thankful for now was that we did cashless transactions. I'd seriously hate to think what I'd look like if there would've been cash on the premises...

8

I pulled into the James Estate hoping that Janie hadn't yet been notified. Checking the clock, it was already 6:45, and I hadn't checked in all afternoon. I parked the van in the back lot bay, and locked the gates. I turned to find Don on the golf cart, with a nurse riding with him. He looked me up and down, and shook his head.

"You look like shit, buddy. I'm really sorry..." he winced. "Hop on back, and we'll go get you stitched up, and home to that beautiful woman." Walking was getting harder as my muscles stiffened. My abdomen felt like hot pokers were stabbing me, but I still managed to carefully climb on to the cart. He whisked us all back into the warehouse, and straight to the back "sick room."

Helping me up on to the gurney, the nurse pulled my shirt over my head revealing my very purple rib cage. She took note of the size and shape of the injury, and put gloves on her hands.

"How's that feeling?" She gently touched my skin, which was radiating heat like fire. "How's breathing?" She listened to my heart and lungs, and didn't seem too concerned.

"It's fine. My head is killing me, and I'm sore as ever." I stretched a little, and every bone in my spine popped back into place. Reaching into her bag, she pulled out a syringe and some numbing balm for my rib cage.

"Give me your arm," she reached for my arm holding a shot full of something. I squinted at the syringe. "It's just pain meds to take the edge off. Nothing you can't handle." She mocked.

"Fine," I outstretched my arm to her.

"Here, keep this and use it on your ribs if they hurt. It's just an external analgesic." She shifted back to her bag, and pulled out a bag clearly marked "Suture Kit." She rolled out the kit before me, readying her area, and filling needles with numbing agents. "Now, sit still and I'll be done in a few hours. Probably looking at 30 stitches." She smiled, and squinted a little. I could smell the whiskey on her breath. "Mind if I time myself?" I shook my head.

"By all means, just fix it." She helped me lay back on the table, and it was nice to close my eyes and just chill for a few. The needle jamming through the thin skin of my forehead and temple didn't hurt as bad as I had anticipated. I could feel my phone buzzing in my pocket. She stopped sewing my eye long enough for me to adjust to grab the phone. It buzzed again telling me there was a message. I opened it up and hit play.

> "Hey Gabe, it's just me. I haven't heard from you, and I thought we were going to meet up tonight. Please call me... love you."

Her simple messages always got me, and it was how I could tell she was flipping out. Probably pacing the house, constantly frequenting the windows, checking for any sort of movement in the tree lines. I put my phone on my chest to let the nurse finish her task, and as perfectly as possible. There wasn't going to be an easy way to fill Janie in on this, and I figured at this point it would be best done at home. Donovan appeared in the room with a satchel, and his flashy smile.

"Hey bud, looking better, and much less bloody!" I smirked at his attempt at humor. He set the satchel at my feet. "This is for Janie, and you, I suppose. But really, more for her." We both laughed aloud, knowing exactly what was going to happen moments from now. The nurse finished the last stitch, and immediately looked at her watch.

"Hell yeah! 77 facial stitches in an hour! Not bad!" She smiled at us both, and handed me a bag of pills. "These are just some Tylenol with codeine. You can take some NSAIDs, too. Will take the edge off for a day or two. If you need anything else, just ask Don to call me. Those stitches will dissolve on their own. Keep them dry for 24 hours." She smiled at us both, and packed up her nurses travel bag.

"Thanks, Hill. I appreciate you services, and will compensate you well." He smiled, and patted her shoulder as she passed by him on her way out. Donovan closed the door behind her, and turned back to me. I was busily feeling the line of stitches through the gauze pad on the side of my head.

"Fucking cock suckers had that shit planned!! They didn't miss a beat!" I stood up, acquiring my balance again, and remembering to breathe shallowly for a while. The pain was excruciating, and collapsing seemed like a better idea. "I should've fucking known when Shaw was even in a decent mood." Donovan rubbed his chin as if in deep thought, with his thumb tapping directly in the center.

"Oh, my friend..." he began. "Rest assured Reyes and his gang will now feel the wrath in the worst way." His smile was wider, whiter, and bigger than ever. *Is he...beaming?*

"I don't know if I want to know." I said, recalling how I had spent the afternoon.

"You do want to know, and I want you to know. I've cut off their entire supply in this state. And when they try to move over state lines... Well..." he shrugged, and made a shooting sound with mouth, and a pretend gun with his fingers. "No one," he extended his hand to me. "And I mean no one, will ever get away with touching my right hand man. I promised you protection, and failed tonight. I'll make this up to you, Gabriel." I took his hand in a firm shake, knowing that my business partner was also my most trusted confidant, and friend.

"Thanks, Don. I know you'll take care of it. I'd like to review our security policy for deliveries, and I'd like you to consider a two man delivery system. I'll get a plan together, if that's okay, and drop it by soon." He nodded.

"Absolutely. I'm already in." He turned and motioned to the door. "Now my friend, time to go face our dear Janie." I sighed, and grabbed the satchel.

"Thanks for this." I started to walk out the door and my phone buzzed, this time a text message. "I'd better hurry...she's on to us, Don. Talk to you tomorrow." I carefully climbed into the 370z and started her up, rolling the windows down for some fresh air. While I was glad that we only lived down the road, I wished I had a little more time for blaring music to help ease my brain for the torment I was about to cause my wife. Reaching out to enter the code to our security gate my body seized from pain, and I was temporarily frozen in place. Leaning my head on the head rest, I took a few steadying breaths. I pulled into my parking spot slowly.

Within seconds she appeared in the driveway, almost sprinting towards the car. I braced myself for what I knew would be a hug tighter than I could handle.

"Gabe!!" her scream was half panic, and half relief. Her eyes were red and it looked like tears were streaming down her cheeks. As she approached me climbing out of the car, I saw her anxiety hit. Her eyes were wider than I'd ever seen, and she froze a foot in front of me as I came to a stop. "Oh my God... Gabe?" she cried again. "What happened, baby?" She took a step towards me and I took one back. She sobbed.

I took her hand in my own, and gently spun her for a reverse hug. I just couldn't handle hands on my ribs, and didn't want her to panic quite yet. I wrapped my arms around her and held her hands in my own.

"Calm down, Janes. I'm home, and I'll be fine." I kissed her head, reeling from the thoughts I was now having about what this would do to her. "Can we go inside and I'll show you my war wounds?" She turned back to me again, with tears in her eyes. The tears just made her more beautiful, and I was just so thankful that I made it home tonight.

Heading into the bedroom, she watched me wince and walk around in pain trying to find a moment of comfort. I set the satchel down on the table, but her focus was solely on me.

"Can I help you?" she softly asked, keeping her distance until I confirmed I needed her. There was no hesitation.

"I'd really like to take off my shirt, but I can't lift my arms much." She smiled, nodded and disappeared into the house. I heard her banging around in the kitchen, so I tried getting comfortable on the side of the bed alone. Sitting didn't bring me any relief, but once I was on the mattress, I was frozen in place. The pain throbbed with intense, immeasurable waves. Moments later, Janie reappeared in front of me with scissors.

"All right, while I cut this off of you, you're going to tell me who the *fuck* I'm about to *kill*." Her face told me she was sort of kidding, but the gleam in her eye told me she just made a lifetime enemy with strangers she didn't even know yet. I gestured. "First, anywhere I shouldn't touch?" I nodded again and pointed around my ribs, and again at my forehead. She smiled, acknowledging my pains. Kneeling between my legs, she pressed the surround sound button on to radio. *"Music always calms the beast..."* I heard her whisper-chant in my ears. The scissors started at my neck line and aimed towards my waist. Every movement of the shirts fabric felt like it was tearing at my skin.

"Location 4 had a drop off today. When I got there," I winced, and she winced. And apologized. "It's okay. Just keep going." She smiled up at me, and in a flash, all I could picture was her fabulous mouth on me. Anywhere. *Everywhere.* "When I got there, they jumped me. Upset about Donovan's prices, or something." Her mouth hung open, and her face slowly turned red. I put my hand up slowly, trying to calm her temper. "Donovan has handled it in the best way- he's cut off their supply chain in the entire state." She grimaced, temples still pulsing with her strong, angry heartbeat. The scissors cut through the last section of shirt, and it finally hung open like a vest.

"There. Now we can get it off." As it slid off, her eyes turned from a wide panicked stare, to being completely anguished and upset. "Oh my God, Gabe... this is *horrible*." Her warm hands barely covered my bruised and swollen ribs. I could tell the care she was taking not to crash into my sore spots and I loved her for it. "What can I get you?" she refocused, eyes trailing up my naked chest.

"I'd love some smoke, and a drink. Jack and Coke. Do we have that?" Smiling, she disappeared into the kitchen again. I slowly propped myself up with pillows on the bed, and managed to find a position that wasn't too bad for breathing. She emerged again holding a few drinks and the ashtray. *Oh man...* Moments like this the realness of Janie just hits me. *Over and Over.* Her smile was gorgeous, and her hair laid flawlessly on her chest. Pornographically outlining the perfect shape of her breasts.

"All right, here we go." She set everything on the bed, and handed me my drink. She pulled the chair over to the side of the bed so she could sit by me, without touching me. *She really loves you....cherishes you, even.* She plopped into the chair, and stole the ashtray back. "Let me get this going for you." Seconds later, we were passing our relaxation back and forth.

"Man, today really sucked." I said, as I looked down at my rib cage, and again felt the line of stitches on my head. She sat up in the chair, and reached for my head.

"I won't push, or touch hard. Can I feel it through the gauze?" She always loved things like this, and getting an up close view of bleeding wounds and the like. Squinting my eyes, I braced myself. Her fingers were soft and so gentle. She felt the entire line of the gash, and then ran her fingers across the bruised, swollen areas on my ribs. I slammed the last of my drink which was made ridiculously strong. I put my glass down and turned back to see Janie eyeing me, in a more than sensual way.

Very slowly she removed her t-shirt, revealing a thin tank top hugging her pert, and perfect nipples. She moved towards me slowly, as if assuring me she was not going to hurt me. Her hands laid upon my thighs, and crept towards my waist line. The instant thought of her touching me heated me enough to raise the pole. I tipped my head back, focusing on the sheer joy of her touch. The pleasure it brought, and the calm she laid upon my soul.

Her mouth landed on my thigh and her soft, delicate lips kissed their way to the crease of my upper thigh and hip. I yearned for her to touch me again, more and more. Her fingers slid up and down my leg, moving slowly to my chest, bringing a stilling heat over the entire area. I welcomed the numb, and my cock pushed against my pants. The smirk on her face told me she wanted complete control. That was just what I needed. She yanked my pants down at the knees, pulling them out of the way for her next planned move.

My cock bounced on my stomach, ready for her in every way. Her eyes burned into mine. My breathing was erratic, and my thoughts running wild. I wanted nothing more than to take her over and over again, on every available surface. Her warm lips were growing closer to my cock. I wanted to impale her with every inch, and make her feel me in ways she'd only dreamed of. But I couldn't move.

Her hands stilled me and she stood up in front of me.

"Relax, Gabe. Let me handle this…" her words trailed off, and she pulled the thin tank top over her head. Her breasts bounced with the removal, and fell perfectly into place. I longed to pull each one into my mouth, and suck each nipple to peaked arousal. She leaned into me, and kissed up and down my shaft. My grip on the table tightened, and I heard the wood shift. She engulfed my entire shaft, and her suck was fierce. I lost my breath, and my words. The pain was eased, and my entire body went numb. Her perfection overtook me, once again, and I was won ton at her feet. Releasing the suction on my shaft, she kissed her way up my sore abdomen, over my chest, biting my neck to my mouth. Her tongue dove into my depths, and I accepted by dancing with her tongue for minutes at a time. She tasted of sweet lemons, and vodka.

"How're your legs, cowboy?" she winked.

"Oh, they're ready for you, beautiful." My teeth ground together with the anticipation that was driving me wild. She climbed carefully on to my lap. Her thin white undies shown the fleshy meat she hid between her legs. The flesh she loved having manipulated, squeezed, and fucked. Her mouth moved back to my cock, and back down she slid. I could feel the intense throbs I was giving off, and wanted as much of her as I could get.

She backed off of my stick, and met my gaze. She stepped away and removed her panties, revealing the best treasure any pirate would seek. Slowly, I picked up my heavy arm, and laid it on my thigh. She repositioned her naked ass on my lap in perfect reach of my curious fingers. Touching her skin, she was burning hot. She was fire under my touch and I could tell she wanted everything I had to offer. I slipped my fingers into her tight slit, and she soaked my hand with her readiness for me. My cock throbbed with the constant want I had for her tight, bountiful pussy. I wanted to hammer her into tomorrow, and make her scream my name.

She began slowly dancing, twisting her way to me, spinning away from me at the last second. Putting her ass into my hands, she stepped over my legs and straddled me. I couldn't hold in my moan...she was just too irresistible. She carefully slid on to my hard shaft, and began moving up and down at a steady pace. Her hands gripped my thighs, fingernails digging into my flesh for leverage. Barely moving, I added the final few thrusts I needed to climax. I stilled her wiggling hips with my hands as I blew my load into her darkest corners. She rode out her last orgasm with me.

Moments later she was gently cleaning me off, and making me comfortable for the night. I couldn't help but smile at her. She knew me so well, she didn't even have to ask. Setting my drink on the table next to me, she turned wearing the most stylish sheet I'd ever seen.

"Need anything else?" Her eyes were open wide and glittery with the after-sex glow. Her cheeks were flushed, and her skin boiling hot. Her hair was a mess, but her smile so vibrant. *You know, you make her the happiest girl in the world...* I shook my head.

"Nah, just come back to bed. I want to cuddle." Her forehead wrinkled, and she bent down to kiss my forehead.

"I'll be right back then. I just need to get my own drink." She skipped out of the room adding, "And don't go to sleep yet, either!" How could I? I just wanted to be wrapped around her, and let her calm my body. No plans the entire weekend, so this was what it was. What I needed to do to heal my body after getting jumped. She came back to bed, and slid in next to me. Her skin touched my own, and her hair fell on to my pillow. It smelled so fresh...so feminine. She wiggled into me, curled up and closed her eyes. Pushing the intense, sexual thoughts out, I scooted myself next to her so I could lull to sleep feeling skin on skin.

9

I woke up Monday mid-morning, thankful I didn't have anywhere to report to for work. Standing up slowly, I headed towards the bathroom. I heard Janie leave hours before, and I slightly remembered her mumbling something about her day. My mind wandered while I took my morning pee, and I knew I needed to make a few moves at work. I sat down to my desk and began typing up a few new security procedures for James Industries. Not just for my own safety, but for everyone involved.

Beginning with the most basic procedures, I added in new rules about two man deliveries, and which specific locations would be safe to exit the truck and which would not. I also wrote in a special section about Tasers and brass knuckles, just in case.

It was nearly two when I looked at the clock as I hit print on the documents. While I threw on some pants, I dialed Sean on the cell. It rang a few times before he answered, and he sounded out of breath when he did.

"Hello?" he panted.

"Hey man, you dying?" I joked, listening to him chuckle through the deep breaths.

"Nah, man, I was doing some yard work. Being productive, you know?" He cleared his throat. "What's up Gabe?"

"I need you to meet me at Donovan's. Like now. I need to go over some things with you, as you'll be taking over a few locations."

"Great! Yeah, just give me fifteen or so and I'll be over there." I finished zipping my pants, and stepped into my flip flops.

"Thanks man, I'll see you in a few." I quickly hung up the phone, and opened a text to Donovan.

*I'll be over in a few...Sean too. New security plan &
handing over the locations I don't like.*

Pulling up to the code box, I entered my code, and
proceeded to park in front by the Beamer. I made a quick jog to
the front door and entered the code for it to unlock. I stepped
into loudly playing Marvin Gaye, and was instantly met by
Mylah, who was coming down the stairs naked. She quickly
covered up her chest, and turned away from me. Putting my
hands in the air, I averted my eyes away from her.

"Ah, sorry Mylah. I didn't think." She giggled and ran
back up the stairs. I headed into the office, shaking my head the
entire way. Opening the door, a heavy stench of marijuana filled
the air. "What the hell?" I let fall from my lips as his chair spun
around.

"Hey Gabe! You're looking much better." We shook and
he sat back down, fumbling with an ashtray. I motioned to his
activity and raised my eyebrow.

"I know, I know," he started smiling widely. "I said I'd
never do it. What can I say?" he shrugged, and slid another pre-
rolled joint into his case. "I caved." Laughing out loud, I took a
seat on the couch. "So, Gabriel... What've you got going on?" I
extended a copy of the new security policy to him.

"This is the new policy. I hope you can appreciate where
I'm coming from with this, and that I think it's best for
everyone's safety. Yours included." He took the copy and began
glancing through it. Nodding at certain things, and placing
asterisks by other points. This must mean it's going to pass
inspection? Sometimes Donovan was a hard read. He looked
through the entire document, and put it in the "IN" folder on his
desk.

"I love it, and I can definitely see where you're coming
from. I like the idea of two delivery men, and I'm all for dual
training who we have on staff now." He paused, and lit the half-

smoked doobie that remained in the ashtray. One quick light, and he drew a long draw. "Now, I'm not thrilled about losing you as my top delivery and sales man, but I'm fine with the changes. With your training, I know we'll have the safest, best men available." I nodded, smiled, and took the joint from him when he offered.

"Thank you, I appreciate it. I'm not sure I could survive watching Janie's face see 'what happened at work' again, you know?" The smoke scratched at my throat. I passed it back to Don, and if on cue, added his last bits.

"However, there is location five. I can't drop that account, because it's worth *millions*." *Ahh, fuck.* I forgot about Lizzie. "Location five demands you, and only you. I've avoided a few of her ridiculous requests, but Gabe... you're stuck on that one." He shrugged, making a semi-apologetic face.

"Shit, I didn't even think on that one." I nodded. There was a knock on the door, and Sean stuck his head in. I smiled, and waved him over. "Come on in man, Don and I were just finishing up some other business." I turned back to Donovan. "Eventually I need to be rid of that one, too. Look," my tongue swiped over my teeth. "I have a history with her. And she's fucking crazy." He nodded, and smiled. Eventually, laughter broke out and calmed the tense room.

"Welcome Sean," Donovan extended his hand to him, and they shook. "Gabe's been busy while he recovered from his ass kicking, and has a new policy and plan. You'll be taking over as our main deliverer." I felt Sean's eyes slowly turn and look towards me, his mouth hanging open the entire time.

"I know you'll be good at this." I nodded in his direction. "I'll be going over some pointers with you, and sending you out to meet your partner in crime here in a minute."

"Sean," we both turned back to Don. "So we're clear, Gabe is your boss. He asks, you do. As long as you're making him happy, you're making me happy." His smile said it all. A

81

warning, threat, and promise all rolled into one. *That was for Janie.* I just knew it. Deep down I was glad he still looked out for her whenever he could. Donovan was no longer a threat in my life. Admitting to myself years ago that Janie's interest in him was simply the attention he gave, I relaxed almost immediately. That was when I was finally able to fall into my role in James' Industries. That was when business sky rocketed.

"Absolutely. I'm ready to help make James Industries millions." He nodded first at Donovan, and then turned to me, and did the same. Standing, Donovan turned the music up again through the house.

"Excuse me, boys. Take your meeting to the foyer or front deck, please. I've got some ass to go catch in this house." He rubbed his hands together as if getting the best prize in the world.

"And a fine ass it is," I joked as I left the office holding the front door open for Sean, who followed closely behind. I took a seat at the table, and Sean sat down next to me.

"So, where do we start?" I handed him the new policy paperwork, and a sheet with the Location information on it.

"This paper is the new security policy." I pointed to the document, and rifled quickly through the pages. "Read over it, know it. It may seem silly in parts, but please read it all. If not for yourself, for me- the one who just got jumped." He smiled at me half-hearted, and chuckled. "And this one is the information on the Locations. You'll see the Location number, address, and contact person. In the "notes" section you'll find the specific directions, if there are any." I looked at him, wrinkled forehead, taking it all in.

"Okay, it seems pretty cut and dry, right?" I nodded.

"For the most part, yes." I couldn't help but pause. "It's going to be a lot safer with two people, instead of one. Oh, and you can go out back and meet your partner, Pierce, too." He nodded, and I checked my watch. Almost 5. "Any questions?"

"Not really, I don't think." He rolled up the paperwork, and put it into his back pocket. "I'll read this tonight, and let you know if I have any questions later. When will the delivering start?" I shrugged.

"I'm not for sure, but most likely in a few days. Give him a day or two to add you into the insurance policies and such." He nodded, and extended his hand.

"Thanks, man," we shook. "How do I go find this Pierce character?" I pointed around the side of the house, to a set of double gates.

"You'll recognize him when you see him. His piercing eyes are unforgettable, especially after you've pissed him off." He shifted uncomfortably. "I wrote your access code on your paperwork. Two codes. Memorize them, for your own sake. Pierce will be back by the loading docks prepping orders. Very intense guy. Super nice though." I waved at him, and headed off towards the filing cabinets. By the time I climbed in my car, he had already coded through the gates. It seemed like everything was playing out as it should. I headed for home, hoping I'd get some more time wrapped around my wife.

When I pulled into the driveway Janie's Jeep was already parked. I could hear Maroon 5 blaring on the radio, but not clearly which song it was. *Knowing that would surely help you understand what you're walking in to.* It was a very valid point, but moot. I was ready for anything. Entering the house, Janie sat hunched over the bar, clinging tightly to a large glass with ice and something.

She turned to see me, and an instant smile plastered across her face. Her arms fit around me, and her face nuzzled into my chest. She inhaled sharply, and her fingers pushed into the center of my back.

"Rough day today," she muttered into my shirt. Her hands fell around my neck to my collar. She pulled me closer to her mouth, so our lips were almost touching. "Want to go grab

83

a few drinks and dinner?" She smiled into my lips as I kissed her, and nodded into her mouth. Her tongue was needy, and gentle. Her mood was still off and I still couldn't tell why.

She disappeared into the bedroom, and reappeared moments later in a jean miniskirt and a white tank top. It looked stunning against her tanned skin, and golden blonde hair. I grabbed my keys, and we headed out to the local bar. We took our usual table next to the jukebox, and I adjusted myself in the booth to get comfortable. The waitress knew our orders, and gave a thumbs up across the bar.

"MMmm," she moaned. "I hope the jalapenos are extra hot in the poppers. I've been craving them so bad." Our drinks appeared on the table, and Janie was quick to down one with Ericah before she went back to work.

"Oh, I love ya, Janes! Your food will be up shortly, hun." We'd gotten to know Ericah over the past few years. She was a beautiful woman, with a huge boisterous personality. She was working her way through college at Indiana University, supporting her daughter all the way. Janie giggled, and turned back towards me.

"She's so cute. Wanna do a shot with me?" Smiling, I caught a glimpse of that twinkle in her eye. We threw the shot back, and another, and another. Our food came out, and Janie speedily devoured her poppers, and stood to program a new song into the jukebox.

Out of the corner of my eye, I could've sworn I saw a familiar blonde on the other side of the bar. I shook the thought off, as Janie returned and sat at the table. She flipped her phone open, and turned it to show me the picture of Lilah and Galen at camp. Her smile beamed, flipping back to look at them. Lost in her phone, I quickly glanced around again. *Nothing*. No one out of place, and no new faces. I couldn't shake the feeling. Janie turned to put her phone away in her purse, and the face appeared next to our booth, entirely too close to my wife.

"Well, you're looking much better now, huh Gabriel?" Her smile was devious, and I could tell by her tone that this wasn't going to be pretty. My mouth hung open, and my eyes darted from her, and back to Janie, who now looked perplexed, but smiled regardless. Lizzie's face turned back to Janie, and then to me. "Going to introduce me, or what, Mr. Lazarus?" She extended her hand to Janie, who took it hesitantly, obviously more confused than ever.

"Janie," I tripped over her name, and she looked at me more fiercely than before. "This is Lizzie St. James. She is a client of James Industries, and one we frequently deliver to." Lizzie laughed aloud, almost cackling. *Oh Jesus, not here Lizzie...* Janie smiled, nodded, and shook her hand.

"It's nice to meet you, Liz-" She cut her off with her loud laughter.

"Yes, I'm a client of Donovan's, and an old flame of Gabriel's." She nodded her head in my general direction. "That's funny, Gabriel. Definitely not how you use to introduce me." I couldn't help but look away, and swallow the ever growing lump in my throat.

"Yeah, everyone's got a past, Lizzie. It's no big news. I'd like to forget most of mine." She pursed her lips at me, and turned back to Janie, and I could feel myself tense.

"Well, Janie, it was nice to meet the woman who stole Gabe's heart. Maybe we'll see each other again soon." As quickly as she appeared, she was gone. Looking across the table, I knew I was in for it. I could see the wheels in Janie's head turning. All I could do was hope to make it home before the shit hit the fan when she pieced it all together.

10

Walking through the side door she still had barely spoken to me, and it had been hours. I had a sneaking suspicion that she knew I had history with Lizzie, and that I might've left out some of the details. All these years I had gotten away with leaving out the bits of my past that I knew would be an issue. Janie's past was lively enough for us both, thusly leaving mine to rest. But now... I could tell what was coming.

I watched her move around the house silently, and into the bedroom. She came out wearing a bathrobe, and her hair pulled up into a messy bun. She carried the tin with her, and stopped briefly at the bar to grab a quick drink. She poured the vodka in carefully, and spritzed it with a fast squeeze of a lime. She headed over to the couch, and fell on to the cushion. Catching my eyes as she sat, she smirked a little. *Oh shit, you're in trouble.*

"So, are you going to make this easy on me? Or am I going to have to ask millions of questions to just get the basics?" Raising her eyebrow, I could feel her tension. I sighed deeply, and headed over to the couch, nodding.

"Of course I'll tell you. I wasn't sure if you'd be able to remember things, and connect the pieces, or not." She wrinkled her forehead in obvious thought.

"What do you mean, 'connect the pieces?'" She thought again. "Should I know her?" Her face contorting in disgust as she asked. I tried to remember the last time she'd ever come up, and I truthfully couldn't. I shook my head.

"No, you don't know her. I think you've only seen her once or twice. The last time you saw her, you got pretty upset back in days of the Phoenix." She squinted, as if trying to place her face. Her eyes slowly fell back to mine, and I knew she had it.

"She's the chick I saw leaving the break room that day? The one you were arguing with?" I nodded, and watched Janie swallow hard. "You never really told me about her." Her voice and confidence shook. I sighed, reaching for the tin.

"I wasn't really sure *what* to tell you about her. We were friends, fuck buddies. She lived in a world that, back then, I had only dreamt of. She was completely different from any woman I'd ever met, and I fell quickly into that trap." Janie downed the rest of her drink, and sighed. "I found out when I tried to end things with her, that she had had other ideas of our relationship the entire time."

"So, I don't get why it matters so much now. Is she really a client? Or are you..." she looked away from me, and I knew exactly where she was going.

"Yes, she's a client. However, I didn't know that until recently, and neither did she." I paused, and thought it over. "At least, I don't think she knew until I knew." Looking over to check the damage meter, her eyes were squinty again.

"Then why the off feelings? Why are you acting like she's about to take your life?" I swallowed hard again.

"Because I think she's up to something. I have no proof, and no idea what it is." She smiled suddenly, as if catching on to the game. Her tongue was pressed into her cheek, and her jaw was clenched on top of that.

"She wants you, doesn't she?" I nodded, and Janie's head bounced up and down seeing a dimmer version of the full picture. "She's made you deliver to her extra, I bet, too, hasn't she?" I nodded again. She turned away from me, and shook her head. "Does Donovan know your past history with her?" I shook my head no. She sighed. I reached for her hand, and surprisingly she didn't pull away. I could tell she was thinking in her worst way- silently. She always had the worst thoughts when she couldn't find the words.

Figuring she needed a minute, I stood with my glass to get a quick refill. She moved forward, grabbing her empty glass, and handing it to me for a fill, too. I smiled at her, and headed over to the bar. *Better fill those up a little more than normal, buddy.* I took a quick glance at my cell, on which I had one missed call. It was already almost 11pm, so callbacks would have to wait. I picked up the glasses, and headed back over to the couch. She took her glass from me, and repositioned herself facing me on the cushion.

"Tell me about her. And you." Sipping the drink, she waited for me to situate myself next to her. "And please don't leave anything out." *One steadying breath is all you get...*

"Well, years and years ago, maybe a year before I met you," I had to take note of the look in her eyes. She was so eager to hear about my past, so open to whatever it was, that it made no sense as to why I felt awkward in this moment. "I met her at the Phoenix. I was coming off of a long term relationship that ended sort of harshly, and she offered up exactly what I wanted." Without looking at her, I took a swig of my bourbon.

"Keep going," she whispered, and rested her hand on my thigh. I nodded, and pressed on.

"To me, she was a safe place to lose myself. There was a lot of sex. I mean, wow." Glancing at her, she winced and frowned at me. Her glass was to her lips, and the vodka seemed to be flowing straight in. Wiping her mouth with her arm, she smiled and relaxed into the couch again, nodding. "I was comfortable with her, but never fully invested. She was an endless pit. Had nowhere to go but down. A few times through the year before you I tried to break it off with her, but she'd just appear wherever I was." I quickly looked at her. "She was *my* stalker."

She looked down, nodding again. I knew she'd understand that part, and I'd hoped it would make it easier on me. I could feel the bile in my throat rising. *Tell her, Gabe.* It was an instance, and with explanation...*she'll understand.* I hoped the voice in my head was right. I put the glass to my lips, and tipped it back with my head.

"After the day you saw me ending it with her, she appeared at my house. There were demands, threats, and I..." I couldn't even say it. I could barely breathe, let alone swallow. Suddenly, it felt like the walls were closing in. I felt my heart start to race, and there was Janie's hand. She took it within her own, and gave it a squeeze.

"You had sex with her?" I watched her swallow hard after realizing what was up, and having the balls to ask anyway.

"She made me, Janes." I sat up on the edge of the cushion with disgust. "I wanted nothing to do with her, and she knew that. She used my feelings for you to get what she wanted from me. I'm so sorry I didn't tell you then..." Thumbing her hand that was still holding mine, I gave her a brief squeeze.

"This whole time," *Oh shit.* I braced myself for the wrath. "*You* had a past, too? A crazy one, that stalked you?" She laughed out loud, completely taking me off guard. "And here I was thinking I was the only one!" She sighed, and melted into the couch...and my right side. Sitting completely still for what seemed like minutes, I had to stop and make sure I wasn't dreaming. *Was she really laughing about this?* I shook my head.

"Yeah, I guess so. You're not mad?" I pulled away from her so I could see her face.

"Not at all. How can I be?" She squinted at me, and climbed on to my lap, very ungracefully. Nose to nose she sat with me, lips almost touching. Her lime scented breath was warm, and landed in the perfect spot. "I'm not mad. Not upset." Her hands trailed down to my chest. "I am curious as to her motives...but I'm really more turned on by you right now." Her teeth clenched, and a hiss escaped her lips. Her hands encircled my neck, shoulders, and then she headed to my waistband. I stopped her hand midway down.

"You sure?" She nodded fiercely. I could tell she had it bad, and I decided to make this last. There wasn't much hesitation in her drunk body as she opened her robe, and threw it to the side of the room. She stood before me, perfect in most every way... I just wished I could clear my mind.

"You're worried, aren't you?" she pushed, and stepped towards me. "Don't be worried. I'm not afraid of her. It just really feels like she's forcing her way back in to your life." She pulled me to standing so our bodies were touching. The truth was that I was worried. Lizzie never stopped until she got what she wanted, regardless of anything or anyone else. She took my hands, and ran them down her chest. The feeling of rough skin falling over her nipples was amazing, and brought me back to the present.

Fast as I could manage to move stitched, bandaged and bruised, I slung my arms around her, and we walked back into the bedroom. I loved how her breasts squished into my chest, and overflowed all around her sides. I pushed her on to the bed, and I saw her eyes light up. Without a second thought, I raised my hand, and let it come crashing down on to her left ass cheek. She panted heavily, begging for more with her eyes. I winced from the tugging pain in my rib cage, gritting my teeth to enjoy the pleasure in the moment. Alternating arms, I raised my hand again, this time colliding with her right cheek. Raring back, she failed with pleasure, moaning and clawing at the sheets for more.

In that instant, the flashback was intense and dark. The chains were tight against my wrists, and her fingernails dug into my flesh, drawing blood on each nail. She was dressed in leathers, and held the cane high in her hand. I closed my eyes, and shook the thought out. *Certain things about the past must remain secret, huh?*

Janie's hands enclosed around my wrists, and she gave a stern tug. Pulling me down to her mouth, she pushed inside, probing even the darkest corners. Only the need for air broke that kiss, and my insanely intuitive wife.

"Hey, stay with me. Stop going wherever you're going." She grabbed my face, and pulled me to her again. "We'll deal with that crazy bitch later, all right?" Smiling, she slid her hands into my pants. Her soft, warm hands were quick to circle my shaft, and tighten. I could feel my eyes rolling back in my head, falling into the trap that was Janie. "I need you, Gabe. I need you now." Our eyes met just long enough, and I could see and feel everything she needed.

I couldn't hold myself back if I tried, engulfing her mouth with my own. More than ever, I needed to possess her. She was mine. Sliding my pants down my legs, I tossed them to the side. Pushing her on to her back, I slowly began spreading her legs. *I've often wondered how many times you've gotten to open this amazing prize over the years...* Without much second thought, my head fell into her waiting lap.

So soft, warm, and wet, my tongue knew exactly where to go and what she liked. Feeling her flesh twitching under my tongue, because of my power was unnerving. My cock throbbed with the mere thought of her tight walls hugging securely around me. Kissing up her abdomen, I stopped on each nipple biting and squeezing, making her wiggle even more underneath me. Dipping my fingers into her, I stroked myself with my right hand. She was so wet, so ready to take it all.

Piling up a few pillows, I lifted her ass on to the pile. *Perfect.* I palmed my length, and lined up with her hot pussy. Dipping the head of my cock barely inside of her made her go wild. Her eyes got glassy, and she desperately grabbed at everything around us, including my skin. I loved it when she got rough with me, and squeezed my flesh as hard as she could. I pulled out of her again, this time moving my hand and thrusting inside of her fully. She took every inch, with a gasp when our skin touched below. I could feel her walls pulsating around me, and could feel her juices flowing like a waterfall. Her nails dug deeply into my skin, forcing the electricity to push through my body.

"Oh God!!" she yelled over and over. "Gaaaabe!" There it was. My name. My favorite of all of her screams. That scream meant I had found the spot, yet again, and I could now drive her wild with constant orgasms. I pushed deeply into her again, riding out each wave of pleasure that struck her. Every clench was tighter than the last. I couldn't take much more of this intense squeezing. I could feel myself getting close.

Pulling out one last time, I rubbed my head all over her swollen, red hole. Her heels dug into my ass, pulling me back into her trance. Spanking her swollen clit with my hard dick, I jammed it back in. The smallest amount of friction set her into another tantric orgasm, and that was it for me. I pushed into her as deep as I could go, feeling my shaft tense to the point of explosion. Each pulse of come sent her into even bigger convulsions.

But the smile smeared across her face told me she was more than thrilled with the performance.
As we lay in a pile of skin, sweat and fluids, there was a certain unmistakable peace that came over the room. Over us both. She pulled the blanket over herself, and readjusted on her pillows. When she patted the pillows next to her, I didn't object.

"She makes you nervous. She makes sneaky, idle threats, and communicates in code. She's forced you to do things in the past. Your relationship with her years ago, was dark. Secretive. Heavy." She leaned in, and kissed my cheek. "Am I close?"

Looking at the ceiling, and into our reflection in the mirrors, I smiled at her. It was amazing how much she could read me, the old me. The one I worked so hard to change before I met her, without the need to know any of the details. God I loved this woman in ways she'd never understand. *And you already know that she feels the exact same way about you.*

"Yeah, you're about dead on." I could tell this was by far, the best news she had gotten yet today. Smirking, she nuzzled into my naked chest. Looking back up at me, dead in the eye, she smiled the most devious, hateful, ferociously serious smile I'd ever seen.

"You know, if she hurts one hair on your head, I'll fucking kill her." I smiled nervously, because I wasn't sure I'd ever seen my wife so serious, or so scary. *Feel that feeling in your gut? Yeah, she's serious All right.* She buried herself back into my chest, and we both curled up for the night.

11

When I woke up the bed was already empty. I could hear Janie out on the phone, laughing and chatting with what

94

sounded like one of her employees. Lying in bed, I checked my email and messages on my phone through squinted eyes.

> "To: Gabriel Lazarus, VP
> From: Donovan James, CEO
> Date: 06-15-2010 05:12:26
>
> Morning Righty,
>
> Just checking in to see if everything is under control for Janie's work party on the 17th. I wasn't sure if you had enough security, or could use a little more? Also, I've got a package for you two. Come and get it when you can.
>
> Don."

Stretching, I finally got out of bed. The air was light today. Janie had opened the windows, and the flow through was nice. Heading out to the dining room I was met by bacon tasting lips, with a cup of coffee.

"Good Morning," she began. "Plans for today?" she asked as she handed me the coffee mug.

"I didn't have any plans, but Donovan emailed and said he has something for you, and we can come get it whenever." She smiled widely, and tapped her chin with her finger.

"I don't have any plans *either*. Everything is done for Saturday, really. I've got a caterer setting up, and leaving. The bartender is you, if that's okay." She smiled again, and I nodded. "So, can we head over and see what he's got? I'm curious!" she slid on her sandals, and grabbed her purse.

"Let me throw on some shorts, and I'll be right out." She nodded, and I headed into the bedroom to put some clothes on. I heard her start the Jeep. *Guess that means she's driving.* Putting a rush on things, I grabbed my cell, wallet, and sunglasses on the way out. Thankfully Don didn't mind my choice of clothing, or lack thereof. Basketball shorts, flip flops, sunglasses, and a cell phone. *Who needed more?*

We parked, and Janie bolted out of the car. As if on cue, Donovan opened the door as she approached. His timing was impeccable. *And obviously planned.*

"Hello Janie!" he shouted and held his arms open to her. Of course, she jumped right into them.

"Hey, Don!" Their hug was brief, and he invited her inside. Holding the door open for me, too.

"Hello, Sir." I said in passing. He closed the doors behind us, and entered the security code.

"Head on into my office there guys. Mylah is around here somewhere...don't let her sneak up on you." He chuckled under his breath. We both took a seat on the leather couch. This couch held many memories for us both. Donovan headed behind his desk, opened a safe, and pulled out a large box. Spinning around in his chair, he put the box on his desk, and smiled directly at Janie. "I've got a bit of a proposition for you, Janie."

I turned to see my wife not shocked, but instead smiling wide, as if she had been waiting for this moment for quite some time. Oblivious that I've caught on to this, whatever "this" really was.

"Well, let's hear it then." She said bluntly. Donovan nodded, and opened the box. Inside there were packets of green pills, hundreds of them. She looked into the box, and nodded.

"These are the THC pills I was telling you about. When we talked, you were thinking these would be a good 'mom-market' seller." He put his hands together into a fist. "Do you still feel that way?" I almost couldn't believe what I was hearing. *What was I watching?* This wasn't what I wanted for my wife, but I also wasn't the husband that was going to hold her down. *Fuck.*

"Of course! I think those would sell like wildfire!! I also think that it would be easy enough to distribute between my employees. I don't think they would mind because it's only a THC pill, nothing like meth or heroine." *My mouth fell open.* They had really talked this through already. I checked my watch. It was only 4 o'clock. My mouth was dry, so I stood quickly to hit the bar. A few ice chunks later, my glass was full of bourbon, and I was back to listening to this new, crazy idea.

"Well, then why don't you take this box with you for Saturday, and sell it? Let's just see how it goes, okay?" She nodded, and reached for the box. "Set your own price, too. Just see how our market is." I took a drink.

"I know of one market that it will excel quickly in, and I think it will do equally as well in the businessman groups. I think they're great for travel!" She winked.

"You okay, baby?" She smirked at me and I wondered if I had turned pale. I couldn't help but wonder how long this had been planned for, and when exactly this planning had taken place.

"Yeah, it's fine. I just don't want you putting yourself in harm's way. At all. Ever." I lingered on the 'r' in 'ever,' hoping to emphasize my point. Donovan nodded in agreement.

"Gabe, she's not delivering, or selling. Only refilling the stock for her employees." He grunted, and leaned on to his desk. "You think I'd put her in danger again?" He shook his head.

"No, Don, I don't. Just caught me off guard I guess. So, what are these things?" Janie reached into the box and tossed me a packet. "Forget-Me-Not Caps." I inspected the package, which only claimed the same high as smoking a joint. The pills were green capsules, and looked innocent enough. "Do they work?" Donovan smiled, and stood to head to the bar.

"Well, Gabriel. There's only one real way to find out, don't you agree?" Just then Mylah strolled into the room, wearing a figure hugging sundress. "Do you all want to stay for a bit? Do a little product research with us?" Janie all but jumped out of her chair, her excitement oozing from her skin.

"Absolutely! My boss' parties are always the best!" I joked with him. The music turned up slightly, and 'Stairway to Heaven' came over the speakers. He put two pills in front of me, next to a glass of water. "What, no more bourbon?" He shook his head.

"I wouldn't. This stuff is heavy." I nodded, and turned to Janie, who was already downing both pills. "Give it about ten minutes." Janie climbed back over the couch to take her seat next to me. The room fell silent as we all waited to feel or see what this newbie had to offer. Looking around at everyone, mellow seemed to be the mood of the moment. Janie's fingers started to mingle with my own, and I could see the glassy look in her eyes.

"How's it?" I smiled at her.

"I don't have many thoughts, that's for sure." Her eyelids were getting visibly heavy.

I could feel it taking ahold of my head in the same way. I welcomed it. The numb was taking effect on everyone, and the giggles were pouring out of us all. Suddenly, Janie stood up and began to dance. As if in slow motion, Janie stumbled, tripping mindlessly over the large ottoman. As if special effects were happening, Mylah came out of the air, and scooped Janie's head up before it bounced on the ground.

"Gotcha." She smiled at Mylah, and her hand caressed her face.

"Wow, Don…" I couldn't even explain the heaviness these brought. Happiness, calm, and utter numb. I turned my head and caught his smile, confirming my feelings on the new pills. Donovan's expression changed suddenly, and I slowly turned my head back to see what had caught his eye.

Holy Shit. Is this real? Mylah's tongue was probing into Janie's mouth, and their hands were kneading, pulling, and grabbing on to anything around. I could feel my eyes bulging out of my head, and my heart beat sped up. They were oblivious, and in their own little drug induced world. Checking back with Donovan, we both had the same plastered grins, staring blankly into the pile of female hotness.

The noises they made while rubbing on each other were perfect, and watching their hands linger on certain parts made my cock start to twitch. Janie's sundress had ridden completely up, and her pale teal, lace bikinis were in clear view. I couldn't take my eyes off of the faint line showing through her panties that was the entrance to heaven as I knew it.

Mylah's eyes caught mine, intently looking into my wife. Her fingers crept down Janie's stomach to the hem of her undies. They lingered around the lace, feeling the details. I pulled my eyes to Janie's face, which was waiting for my own, smiling big as ever. Mylah shifted, and so did my eyes. Her fingers dipped underneath the elastic band of Janie's panties, and my dick throbbed hard.

From my angle, I could see the exchanged glances and facial expressions both of the girls were passing back and forth. *Did they plan this?* Mylah pushed into her, and she let out of low, deviant, carnal noise. I couldn't help but shift in my chair, and saw that Don was already palming himself. *Just like old times*. Mylah was really getting in rhythm with Janie, and my cock was twitching all over the place. Her eyes met mine, and at that moment I just wanted her.

Mylah pushed her sundress up even farther, exposing Janie's perfect breasts, bouncing with every thrust. I bit my lips trying to control my own tongue that wanted nothing more than a quick lick of my delicious wife. Mylah withdrew from her, and climbed to her face, planting one last kiss on her lips.

"This stuff makes me really horny," she said as she stood, turning to seek Donovan out.

Janie only laid on the ottoman for a moment before she threw herself at me on the couch. Her breasts pushed into my face, and I tried relentlessly to catch her nipple for a bite. It took my hands to steady her wiggling tits so I could suck her. While I nibbled her nipples, she found the one spot on my pants that rubbed her clit and my hard on at the same time.

She backed off of my lap, reaching to unbutton my pants. She unzipped while licking her lips, it was as if time was slowing down. My dick throbbed for her mouth, my teeth gritting together in anticipation. Pulling them down to my thighs, she began kissing back up to my abdomen. How wrong would it be to push her head on to my cock right now? I tipped my head back, trying to enjoy her tease. Instead, I was welcomed into her warm, wet mouth. I could feel my balls pulling, and tried to acclimate to the perfect feeling of tight, wet walls.

Her hands fell around my balls, and began to squeeze, knead, and pull. Releasing me suddenly, she turned around in front of me, and backed up over me. Lowering herself on to my lap, I slid easily into her wet slit. Grasping my balls again, she pulled them while she fucked me like she was on speed. She cried out over and over, tugging harder with each wave of pleasure.

Looking to my right, Donovan drove deeply into Mylah on his desk, paperwork and everything falling and crashing to the floor every few thrusts. She pushed into me hard, and I felt her walls cave around me. Over and over leaking all over me.

Wrapping her long hair around my hand, I pulled her backwards so I had a tight hold.

Hanging on tightly to my balls, I fucked her as hard as I could, pulling out entirely, and ramming back in. She loved penetration. Craved it. *Begged for it*. She was dripping wet, taking my cock over and over again like a champ. I thrust into her at the same time she twisted my balls, I felt everything constrict, and my eyes rolled back into my head. I came into her harder than ever, and it just kept coming, and coming, and coming.

She fell next to me on the couch, and we both attempted to redress. Donovan and Mylah were all giggles and secrets cuddling in the corner. I stood to button my pants, and box up the package.

"Well, I guess we can all agree that these will be our best sellers." I chuckled, and handed Janie her underwear from the ottoman. She took them, and put them into her purse. Offering her my hand, she took it to stand, readjusting her sundress on the way up.

"Oh Donovan," she headed over to the two of them. "This has been a fun visit...reminds me of old times." She reached out to hug Mylah, who instantly engulfed her in a hug, running her hand down her side, and kissing her cheek. "Love you, My."

"We'll see you guys in a few days at my party, okay?" I picked up her purse, and the box. "Come on Gabe, I'm famished." I laughed aloud. *Oh God, she's got the munchies*. We turned and headed out the door, back to the Jeep. She tossed the package under the compartment in the floor board, climbed in her seat, and buckled up.

"So you're hungry?" I could almost see the drool dripping out of the corner of her mouth. Her eyes lit up with the mere mention of food. And I couldn't exactly deny that my own case of the munchies was peaking, too.

12

"Hell yes. Can we stop and get some take out from somewhere?" She rifled through her bag, pulling out her phone. She laughed at a text message, and tossed it away.

"Anything good?" I joked.

"Nah, just Bradley RSVP'ing for Saturday." She smiled, her mouth falling open. "Tacos! Let's go to Taco Bell." I nodded, as that was usually the pit stop when one was insanely drunken or drugged. We quickly snagged a dozen tacos and proceeded to devour them in the parking lot. Sauce was dripping down her cheek. "Oh my God, these are so good." She was ravenously eating. I loved it.

"An excellent choice." I crumpled up my trash. "I'm exhausted. What're you plans for tomorrow?" She cleaned up her area picking tiny shards of lettuce from her lap, and wiped the sauce off of her cheek.

"I'm just going to prep for the party on Saturday. Hoping for some booze, cooking, and music and cleaning." My eyes darted to hers. *Cleaning and booze?* "You got it... My favorite things." We both giggled and I reached across the Jeep and put my hand on her thigh.

"I have to make a trip with Sean tomorrow to train him on a run. I should be done by mid-afternoon." I pulled her hand to my mouth while our fingers were interlaced, and ran her knuckles under my lips.

"Sounds good. I'm going to check in with the kids at camp tomorrow, too." I pulled in the driveway as we both yawned wider than ever. "I'm going to bed now. Stuff really makes you crash after a few hours, I guess."

"Ok, I'll be right in." Turning back to the Jeep I collected the package, and as much trash as I could carry. I was having seriously mixed feelings about Janie stepping into the business like this. Above all else, her safety was the most important thing to me. Heading into the house, there was a trail of Janie to the bedroom. Flip flops. First one, and then the other. Her purse, and then her sundress. Stopping in the kitchen I threw the garbage away, and put her purse back on the table.

She looked so peaceful that I couldn't wait to be under the sheets next to her. I slid the package carefully into her desk, and deftly climbed in bed behind her. Her skin was still quite warm, so pulling the sheet over us seemed appropriate. It took minutes to calm my mind, until I felt our bodies breathing together.

~

The alarm rang out early, almost screaming into my ears. Moving as stealthily and quickly as possible, I turned the alarm off trying not to stir Janie. Sitting up on the edge of the bed, I stretched and looked back at my wife. Her blonde hair fell all over our pillows, in a tornadic mess. Her face was totally calm, lips perfectly parted. Her breast was squished on her side, seductively peeking out at me. Wrapped around her foot, the sheet fell down her tanned back revealing her hips as she adjusted her legs.

Gritting my teeth together, willing myself to get up and ready for work, was rough. Peeling myself away from her was getting harder and harder to do. I jumped into the shower, quickly rinsing off the crazy intense night before. As I buttoned my James Industries polo, my phone rang.

"Hello?"

"Hey Gabe, its Sean."

"I'll be over there in about 30 minutes or so."

"Sure, no problem. I just got here and was wondering if there was anything I could get started on?" Checking the time, it was only 8:06 in the morning. I wasn't sure if Lonnie would be in yet, or not.

"If you can find Lonnie in the back building, you could probably help him load up the hauler for the runs today."

"Okay, sounds great man. Oh, is Janie coming in?" I grabbed my keys off of the table, and headed out the door. I climbed in the car wondering what in the hell he wanted to know that for.

"No, she doesn't work there." The annoyance in my voice rang out loudly. "See you in a bit." I hung up, and turned out of the driveway. I still couldn't quite figure out why that had mattered and it put a sour taste in my mouth. I pulled into the lot, and parked in my space just as Donovan was heading out the door, paperwork in hand. We exchanged nods.

"Sleep well last night, my friend?" I couldn't hold in my laughter.

"Shit, yes! I haven't seen Janie sleep that soundly for months." I wrinkled my face at the pile of papers in his hands.

"Oh, these are the new plans for the Hammerhead raft line you've thought up! Development approved your ideas, so I'm off to the branding and patent boards!" He smacked the stack with his hand, seeming to be very excited. "Great idea, man! This is going to be extremely lucrative for you." I smiled knowing that this solidified my place in his company, and felt assured we'd never hurt for anything again. I was truly excited to hear my design had passed development, and couldn't wait to celebrate with Janie later.

"Thanks man! I truly appreciate the chance to grow with James Industries." We shook hands, and he climbed into his Beamer. Before closing the door completely, he added one last thought.

"You and your wife were the best decisions I've *ever* made." He smiled, and revved the engine to life. Waving him out of the drive, I turned and headed for the back building. Entering my code, I was met with the loud music of Pink Floyd, and it was obvious that Lonnie *was* here.

"Hey Lon!" I yelled over the music the best I could. I saw a stack of boxes walking towards me, and an arm jutted out with a wave.

"Hey boss!" he yelled, setting the pile of boxes into the back of the truck. Glancing over his shoulder, checking to see where Sean was, he nodded in my direction. "You goin' to 4 and 6 today?" I nodded. "Trainin' the new guy?" I nodded, and his face grew pained.

"How's he been doing this morning?" The look of pain turned to strain. I could tell he wanted to say something important. "Fine, tell me. What's going on?"

"I'm not sure, but that guy rubs me the wrong way." I could feel myself pull back, slightly shocked, but still listening intently. "He's askin' questions 'bout things that don't matter, constantly. Personal questions 'bout schedules, timin' on deliveries..." His hand rubbed his forehead. "I'm just not sold on this one yet. He's just not like the rest of us."

Staring blankly now at Sean, watching him work and smiling and random things, I was completely lost in thoughts. The feeling in the pit of my stomach normally didn't mislead me, and I wasn't sure I could ignore the feelings I was having. These weren't the things that I was hoping to hear first thing in the morning, immediately after he's asking about my wife.

106

Watching him again, he barely noticed my stare. He was diligently stacking the boxes Lonnie had told him to move, and was following directions. I shook my head a bit.

"Thanks, Lon. I know you wouldn't of said it if you didn't really feel it." He shook his head in agreement. "And I've learned enough from life to know that nothing is ever as it appears, and no person is ever as they seem." He smiled.

"You're right on that one, boss. I'll get back to it so you can get on the road." I patted his back.

"You're a good guy, Lon. Thanks for the heads up." Heading over to my desk, I sat down with my phone for a moment. Logging in to my secret app, I made the notes of what Lonnie had told me about Sean. *Glad you're being a little safer, than sorry.* As I was hitting save and locking it back up, Sean appeared on the other side of my desk.

"Truck's ready man. How long you think we'll be out?" Again, more questions.

"We'll take off here in a few, and head to location four first. I'd like you to drive, so you can get a feeling for the truck, and so I can see if you suck at driving or not." I chuckled, and smiled at him. Piling up some paperwork I needed to work on for the raft project, I headed over to the truck and hopped in. Sean climbed in the driver's side. He glanced at the address, and punched the button for '4' on the GPS system.

"Oh wow, this makes finding places easy I bet." I smiled, wondering if he was being truly serious. GPS had been out for years, and I'm sure he'd used it himself on his past traveling jobs. *Too many nuances to ignore...*

"Yep. So, no excuses for late deliveries," I added. "Ever." He smirked a bit, driving through the city to the location. As we grew closer to location four, my anxiety began to grow. I hadn't been back since I was roughed up, and truly had no desire to see this group of Latinos again. We were down to blocks. I was busily taking notes, when Sean's phone rang.

"Hello?" he sounded perplexed. "Oh, Hiya! Yeah, it's all good." I couldn't help but wonder who he was talking to. "MmmHmm..." he chuckled to himself. "Just as it should! That's why it's planned!" He laughed loudly, almost throwing his head back. Looking back towards my paperwork, I shook my head. "Oh, I don't know. Let me ask." He turned to me.

"Are we going to be on time for everything today? Deliveries, and back to the base, I mean?" I checked the clock and it was just after 10am.

"I don't see why we wouldn't be." I said smiling.

"Hear that? All on time. Great. Let me know. Talk later!" he hung up, seemingly more pleased than before he answered. He signaled left and turned into the alley. Slowing at their gates, he pulled next to the guard office. As he rolled down his window, he turned and gave me the strangest look. "This is the place, huh? The thugs that beat your ass?" Raising my eyebrow, I nodded idly.

"Good Morning esse, who are you?" Sean looked displeased, and I leaned over. Suddenly, the guard's smile widened, "Oh, it's you, G!"

"Yes, Shaw. Let us in." The gates opened, and I pointed to the back corner of the yard.

"Head that way. New procedures here, we don't get out of the truck." Sean nodded, and pushed his lips together.

"No problem," he said, backing into the bay doors. I handed him the clipboard, and paperwork. Leaving his window down he waited for one of the minions to approach. "Hola!" I heard him say as he handed the papers outside for signing. This interaction was going much faster than before, thankfully. The truck shifted as the back door was opened, and they began to unload their product. We bounced around for a moment, and then felt the doors close. Pulling out my phone to log the time, I opened the missed text message.

Checking in... Loc 4 done?

At least he was a concerned boss. I quickly texted back, as Sean gave a wave and we exited the locked lot.

Just finished, heading to 6. Want me to say hi to Whendi for you?

"So, that wasn't so bad." I nodded in agreement.

"Not going to put anyone in that position again." I shook my pointer at him, "Safety first!" We both laughed. The day seemed to lighten the feelings I was having towards Sean. We chit chatted through the day about the kids, so I couldn't resist asking about Delaney.

"How's Delaney doing?" his face sank a bit and he exhaled deeply.

"She's all right. I guess. I don't really see her much anymore, but for when I pick up Dominic." He shrugged, looking forlorn as ever. "She's dating some big businessman." Sighing again, he slammed his hand on the steering wheel. "I really, really ruined that one." He looked out his window.

"I'm sorry man. Maybe you'll get lucky in love again soon, and find someone new." My phone buzzed again. "Take that right, right there." I pointed at the side dirt road.

"This is where it's at??" Sean was perplexed, and searching the open corn fields. He seemed lost.

"Yeah. Whendi prefers solitude, and nature." I smiled widely at him. "She's a *wild* one." He nodded and fell back into singing the Cranberries on the radio. Opening my phone, it was Don again.

Yes! Holy Shit... Invite her! MMMmmm...

Laughing out loud, Sean turned at my reaction.

109

"Everything ok man?" Chuckling still I pointed at her parking lot, and we pulled into *"Feffer's Flowers & Fancy Things."*

"Absolutely. Donovan's just at it early today." Checking my watch, it was now just before one. "Just pull over here, and we'll carry it all in." He nodded, and took notes of carrying in the delivery at this location. As I exited the van, I heard her Minnie Mouse voice reign over the sounds of the outdoors.

"Gabriel!!" she cooed. "Oh, I've missed your presence... and body." She slunk towards me, walking like a gypsy. "You've got it *all* for me, honey?"

"Hello, Whendi. Of course I do, and I'm also delivering a personal invite and hello from Donovan. He misses you," her face flushed. "And would love for you to attend our party in on the 24th." She took the invite from my hand and wandered back into her building, holding the door for Sean and I. Motioning us towards the backroom, she hustled us down the hallway, away from her few customers.

"Well, boys," she took the top box off, and ripped it open. She leaned far into the box, and her low cut hippie dress revealed everything she had to offer. I caught Sean's smirk, and gaze down the loose valley of the tits. She sniffed the product like a bouquet of flowers, and groaned with its fragrant aroma. "This is perfect, and my customers love the quality." She sauntered back around the table towards Sean, poking him in the chest with her boney pointer finger.

"Care to test some out with me?" Her long skinny fingers dug into the stash, filling up a pipe she had close by for sampling. I could see Sean's eyebrows raise as he thought of staying to hang out with Miss Fefferkorn. *He's got no clue what she's about, you know...*

"Thanks Whendi," I patted Sean's shoulder. "Unfortunately, we have to hit the road and finish our deliveries for the day." She looked displeased, but very understanding.

110

"You tell your boss I'll see him in a week or so. Thank you, boys. As always, you do deliver in every way!" Her peppiness rang out as she hurriedly headed back out towards the lobby and greeted her customers. I held the door open for Sean, and caught Whendi's last wave. *What a whack job*. We climbed back into the hauler, and headed back to the base.

My phone began ringing, so I tried to dig it out of my pocket to answer it, but just missed the call. *Shit*.

"Gabe? Gabe is that you?!" *What the hell?*

"Yeah, what's going on Don?" I could hear the franticness, and voices everywhere behind him.

"Location four was just hit, took everything, and set it on fire!" My mouth fell open.

"WHAT?!" Flipping back to my record log to see what time we left, we were out of there by 10:30. "We were gone by 10:30, Don. What're they saying?" My head was spinning with thoughts. These people didn't take lightly to any changes, and if for one second they thought we had something to do with this, we'd all have just signed our death certificates.

"Reports in to me so far sound like it was someone else, another rival. He's only just contacted me to see if we can refill it all once things calm down." My mind whirled, and glancing at my driver, who seemed all too calm. "I just needed to check in, as I hadn't heard from you. Where are you?"

"Almost back to base. Whendi will be attending the party on the 24th. She seemed…. Hungry. Needy, even?" My voice now questioning the upfront suggestions and pictures playing through my head of our stop at *Feffer's Flowers & Fancy Things*. I heard him chuckle, and sigh.

"Thanks for the good news, let me know when you're back so we can do damage control."

"Absolutely, be there in a few." I hung up, and slipped my phone back into my pocket. Putting my travel bag back together, and my papers in all of the correct folders, Sean finally took notice.

"What was all of that about?" I shook my head.

"Something happened at one of our Locations. We're still trying to get all of the details, and how it will affect us. If at all." Seeming to be pleased with my answer, he rolled down his window entering his code to pull back into base.

"Well, I guess as long as it's not too important. After we park, what should I do next?" Checking my watch, it was now almost 2.

"Go find Lonnie once the hauler is checked back in, and mileage is logged. You can help him shift orders for the rest of the week for your last hour or so." I turned to make sure he had gotten all of it, and he extended his hand to shake.

"Sounds great," we shook. "Did I do okay today, boss?" He asked half joking, yet semi-serious.

"So far, so good, Sean." Grabbing my things I headed out of the truck and into the main offices, where Donovan was busily pacing back and forth, listening to something on his ear piece. Catching me out of the corner of his eye, he motioned me over to his desk quickly. Muting his mouthpiece and covering it for safety sake, he leaned into my ear.

"You're not going to believe this." He paused, listening in his ear again. "Their camera footage shows these vehicles watching their facility, and making repetitive drive-bys. Best part," he paused again. "One camera showed a woman driving."

Instantly shocked, I pulled my head back almost in disbelief. It wasn't typical for women to be in this business, especially as driving deliverers.

"A woman? Do they know who might've done this?" I locked my paperwork up in my safe, and tossed my travel bag under my desk. "I mean, as long as they know it wasn't us.... I don't want to deal with those people any more than I have to." He smiled and patted my back once.

"We're good, G. They know we're not enemies...they were just pissed off at me, which I have since rectified." He took note of something on the paper. "They've got it narrowed down to a few places, but are being very tight lipped about how they're going to handle determining who exactly made this call." He looked at the clock and back at me. "Why don't you go ahead and head home to help Janes prepare for tomorrow. I'll update you on this crap in a few hours." I nodded, and turned on my heels.

I couldn't wait to get home to her, and help her with her party plans. My head was a little cluttered, worried even, for the breech at our Location. If there's one thing I've learned in this business over the years, it's that everyone action has many unforeseen consequences. AC/DC blared on my radio on the way home, and the air blowing in from the sunroof and open windows were doing just what the doctor ordered-instilling a nice calm over my brain.

13

Climbing out of the car, I noticed that somehow Janie had managed to set up the extra tables all on her own. I shook my head at her determination, wishing she would've waited for my help. The side yard was looking festive as ever with all of the party decorations set up. Sneaking into the house, McLachlan played loudly on the radio. Squinting a bit, I could hear Janie's voice singing loudly from the bedroom.

The day hadn't gone as I had hoped, and I wasn't sure that filling Janie in now would do anything but worry her. I decided before walking in the house that she didn't need to know this minute if she didn't ask... and I really hoped she'd be too busy to think about it.

Quietly I headed in, seeing if I could accomplish a little surprise. She was busily singing away folding towels for our bathroom. Her version of McLachlan's 'Adia' was far better than even the original. Being that she was so into the song, she nearly jumped out of her skin when I jumped behind her and grabbed her hips.

"Ahh!" she jumped away from me, turning around like I had cornered her in the wild. Her breathing slowed once she saw me, and her fist came crashing back into my shoulder. "Ass! What the hell?!" she was smiling now, but I had a feeling still ready to box in my face.

"I'm home from work, baby. Don sent me home to help you for tomorrow." Her smile grew wider, and her eyebrow raised pretty high. "Uh oh, what's that face for?"

"Well, I've got most everything precooked and in the fridge. I just have a few things left to do outside, and I could probably call it a night." She folded the last towel, and carried them into the bathroom. She reappeared, flinging her arms lightly around my neck. "If you can check the hot tub chemicals, and set up the chairs, I'll make us some dinner. Dinner and a movie maybe?" I nodded and bent to kiss her lips.

"All right, I'll be outside if you need me." I took off my work polo, and threw it on the bed. I caught her sneaky eyebrow raise, taking in my naked chest. Her desire was so palpable. I headed out to the shed, the last place I remembered seeing all of the chairs. My phone dinged, which meant I had missed a call. *Odd. The phone never rang, Gabe.* Unlocking the shed and simultaneously listening to the message, I couldn't place what I was hearing. The machine voice replayed over and over, repeating the same message.

"Hello, Mr. Lazarus. We took care of that for you. You're welcome."

I looked back down at the phone to check the number it came from, and I didn't recognize it. Saving the message, I dropped my phone back into my pocket and began hauling chairs over to the deck. My mind spun around a few ideas on the message, but got me nowhere. I didn't recognize the voice, either. *Maybe a solicitor?*

Walking over to the shed, I pulled the test strips, and chlorine additives. Dipping the strip deep into the water, it was nice and warm. The water was perfect, barring the chilly wind blowing occasionally. I opened the chlorinator and poured a little chlorine in. Back at the shed, I turned the heat up a few degrees, and ran the hot tub on cycle, too. *Very efficient.*

Heading back into the house my phone rang. I answered as I entered.

"Hey Don, got more info?" I was eager to hear all I could about this mysterious robbery.

"You know, they are being SO tight lipped...it's like torture. All I know now is the woman from the van video has light hair, and looks white. All that was lifted from their warehouse was our shipment, plus the rest of their stock." I felt my brow wrinkle.

"That's odd. Where was the fire?"

"Only in their storage area for the product." He sighed. "This really sounds more like a specific targeted hit than anything else. Don't you think?"

"Yeah, it really sounds that way." Janie entered the kitchen, and was now feet from me.

"I'll just update you tomorrow on anything else that I hear, all right?"

"MmmHmm, that works." Janie was busily making dinner, and it looked like it was going to be worth waiting for.

"Well, tomorrow then. I'm out." We hung up, and I headed over to surround my wife with warm arms. Stirring what appeared to be sauce, she fell backwards into my chest and embrace.

"Everything okay at work?" I smiled, and kissed her hair.

"Everything's great. Don was just checking in on you, and making sure you were good to go for tomorrow." I released her and spun so I could see her face. "Everything ready for tomorrow?"

She thought while she stirred, and tapped her fingers on the counter she rested on with her left hand. She shook her head.

"No, I think we're good. I'd just like to relax tonight, I think." She smiled. "Why don't you go grab a shower? By the time you're done, I'll about have this chicken con carne done, and we can dig in."

That was by far the best idea I'd heard yet today. I couldn't resist stealing one more kiss from her before I went though. Not even my kiss could derail her from her intense cooking sessions. She'd really been excelling at most everything in the kitchen she'd been working on. The new classes she'd taken were really paying off for all of us, even the kids appreciated her work.

Forty minutes later, a few scrubs, and some scalding hot water, I reemerged to find a candle lit couch dinner all set up for us. Dinner looked amazing, and I couldn't wait to dive in. I was starving. And then she sat down opposite end of me. She wore a silky, almost see through nightgown.

"How's dinner?" she asked coyly, meeting my gaze over the candle light. I took a bite of the mouthwatering chicken, and moaned in appreciation.

"It's perfect, just like you." She smiled, and I thought I caught a bit of flush cross her cheeks. We shared a few bottles of wine through dinner, and she updated me on who was going to be in attendance from At Your Service, LLC the following day. She was so excited about this party, for everything to be perfect. Still to this day she doesn't realize that everything she does *is* perfection.

We finished our meal and sat down to watch one of our old favorites, *Chasing Amy*. I couldn't help but sing along to the songs sung by Joey Adams in the movie. Half way through, Janie was fidgeting so much, I couldn't take it anymore.

"Care to follow me to bed?" I held my hand out to her as I stood from the couch. She willingly took it, nightgown clinging to every part of her I wanted to be buried in.

~

The alarm clock went off at 10, and she bolted out of bed faster than ever. Her guests were to arrive about 1 o'clock, and I knew she had food to get back into crock pots. Begrudgingly, I got up and headed out to the kitchen for a pot of coffee, or two. I stood in front of the kitchen window, staring blankly out into the yard.

"All right, I've got the food under control. Could you just work on shifting a few things at the bar?" I had no idea how she was this peppy already, after last night. Wine just messes with your head.

"Yeah, of course." She took off again, this time carrying crock pots out to the patio table. Setting my coffee back on to the counter, I reached for the emptier bottles of liquor from the upper shelves of the pantry, and headed out to refill the stock. Stepping out on to the deck, I found Janie giggling, smiling, very pleased with herself. The serving table I'd made her a few summers ago made hosting parties so simple. Filling the middle container with ice kept anything cold, and the base behind was deep enough for her roasters and giant crocks. *Pat yourself on the back there, buddy.*

"Do you think it looks okay?" she asked, almost disheartened.

"Looks great, baby." I walked towards her, extending my arms to her. She cheerily climbed in, and nuzzled into my neck. The scent of her hair alone boiled my blood, and made me hungry for her. Running my fingers through her hair, I tipped her head back to meet my own. "Everyone's going to have a great time." I whispered on to her lips. She smiled, and my heart sped up.

"Thank you," she leaned up into my kiss. It seemed that time would stop every time our mouths connected in such a sensual way. I could taste her desire, but I knew there wasn't enough time to get what I truly wanted. I dipped my tongue into her mouth one last time, and I broke our kiss.

"You're never going to get anything done with me out here nagging at you. I'm going to head back inside and watch some television for a bit." She nodded, seeming to understand I needed to chill out for a while.

"No problem, I'm going to turn on the radio out here and get myself changed for the party! Your cheeks are red, are you feeling okay?" She stopped finally, looking perplexed, and put her hand on my forehead. She winced a little. "Yeah, go rest up. I'll check on you on my way through." She rubbed my arm as I went around her.

I just couldn't shake this uneasy feeling I'd had since I had woken up this morning. The feeling where you know something is going to happen, but you just don't know when. I laid down on the couch, turning on some old reruns of Cheers, and relaxed my eyes for a bit. I was overtaken by sleep before I knew what had hit me.

~

Janie.

"Does anyone need a refill while I'm up?" Kiara asked everyone in the tub. Bradley held up his glass, as did Caty. "So, these pills... they're only THC?" I nodded, and sipped my drink.

"Correct. They are quick release pills that allows the drug immediately into the system. The high is amazing, and potent." I watched as everyone checked out the packaging, and chatted amongst themselves.

"I'm game. I think these are going to be a hit!" Darrel agreed with him.

"Yeah, I love weed, but I'd rather not carry around a bag in my pocket. These are so much easier to travel with!" Darrel had finally spoken up in our group in the past few months. Only took him a year to trust us, and know that we were on their side, too.

"I think you're right. And they're very low on the "illegal" side of things, because these pills are not regulated, or known about yet." I leaned back on the lounger cushion, and pushed the button to increase the flames on the fire.

Everyone seemed pleased and very willing to try the new sell. Their commissions from sales would be extreme because Donovan believed in taking care of his own. Especially with a new product that could end up sweeping the underworld markets.

"It's time for me to head out! This was so much fun. I really needed the relaxation." Caty was collecting her things. Her boyfriend had come to pick her up so she wouldn't drive drunk. She came over to me on the lounger and sat down. "Thank you for being a great boss." She leaned on my shoulder, and patted her pill-filled brown box. "These are gonna go quick!" she slurred.

"Thanks for coming girl! I love hanging out with you guys!" I stood first, and helped her back to an upright position.

119

"Let me know how sales go!" She climbed in the car and I waved to Andy. He said hello, and laughed at Caty's disposition. *Ooops. She's a tad drunk.*

Heading back up to the deck, the level of drunkenness had subsided slightly, but the crowd was louder than ever. Kiara came out of the house from the bathroom entrance, and the door slammed loudly on the wooden frame. *Shit.*

~

I was stunned awake by the sound of slamming doors and insane laughter. I checked the clock and it was 8:34pm. *Oh shit!* I had slept the entire day! I slowly stood up and headed for the bathroom. I grabbed a drink on my way through, although just an ice cold water bottle. I stepped out on the deck and was greeted with a few smiles.

"Hey Gabe!" Bradley yelled from the hot tub. "How're you feeling, handsome?" This guy has always called me "handsome," and I've never really gotten over, or into it. *Cute enough, I guess.*

"Yeah, I'm feeling a bit better. I'm really sorry I didn't get up on time Janes." She was smiling, happily drunk in her chair. Only a few of her employees stuck around this late, and it dawned on me I didn't see Donovan.

"Get yourself a drink, Gabriel." She said sardonically. "Come join us for a little bit."

They were all gathered around the hot tub, some half in, all in, or just lounging. Janie had her legs in, and was wearing the hottest bathing suit cover up I'd ever seen. I pulled up a lounger beside where she was sitting, next to Darrel Diquee. Darrel was Bradley's significant other. From what I understood, they were quite serious.

120

"Did Donovan show up?" I asked leaning into her bare shoulder. She shook her head.

"He sure didn't, I haven't heard from Mylah, either." She shrugged. "Figured something came up, or they just got hammered and forgot."

I could read her body, and I could tell she was a bit squished. Mylah had become her second in command for the most part. Except for times like these. The big events, both her and Don seemed to disappear for.

"Janie, this has been a fine company summer party!" Bradley squelched. "Your food was SO good... you should really think about that route, girl!" He pulled himself from the hot tub in the smallest speedo you've ever seen. I couldn't stifle my laughter. He caught on to my humor, and came and shook off next to me. "Take that, you!" he said, running back to Darrel's side. He'd really grown on Janie over the years, so my tolerance is a little higher with this dear man.

"Oh Brad, always the party animal!" I stuck my hand out to him, and after putting on his pants, he shook it hard. I escorted the pair to their car, and saw them off our drive through the gates.

"I should probably be going, too," I heard Kiara say from behind me. Turning, I saw Janie embrace her, and shoot me a look over her shoulder. It wasn't just any look, it was *the look*.

"Thank you Kiara, for everything. You're a wonderful woman, and a fabulous employee." The girls fell into one last conversation before ending the night, and I couldn't help but think of all of the things that Janie gushes on and on about regarding Kiara. The only complaint she ever had was that Kiara wouldn't ever fully follow the security rules, like most everyone else would. Janie understood to a point, and tried to see her side of things. Everyone grows up differently she would always remind me.

Kiara walked down the drive past where I was standing. She turned on her way, and waved at me. I gave a wave back, and entered the code for her to pull out on to the street. Heading back up the path to the patio, Janie was already cleaning up, and throwing things in the trash. She smiled as she saw me approaching.

"Don't you even think about touching that stuff. Just relax. You were out to the world earlier, and in my experience over the years, that usually means you're trying to fight some sort of germ." Maybe she wasn't as drunk as I'd first thought. "Please, just let me. I don't want anything to do with your devil germs." Grinning she went back to cleaning up the mess.

I took a seat on the lounger, and watched her clean up. A mere fifteen minutes later, and she sat down gently on the cushion next to me, cuddling into my side. Nuzzling her hair, I inhaled her scent deeply.

"I'm really sorry honey," I began. I still couldn't believe I slept through her entire party. I pulled her closely into me, and stroked her arm. I could feel her face pull into a smile against my skin.

"Gabe," she turned and met my eyes, shaking her head. "It's really okay. My work parties aren't quite as wild as your work parties, so I promise you didn't miss anything crazy." She adjusted in her seat, lifting her bathing suit cover up under her armpits more. "Actually, I was just waiting for you to get this party started." She winked, slipping her bathing suit off from underneath the cover up. I gasped.

"Waiting for me, huh? Well, I'm here now..." I gently placed my hand on her exposed thigh, and ran my fingers slowly up the lengths to the hem of the cotton cover up. Dipping my fingers underneath, I could feel the crease of her leg and her hip. Following the crease, and watching her thoughts turn lustful and greedy, I could tell she was heating up.

122

She leaned in again so I could feel her chest pressing into my side. With each shift, her cover up slid further south, finally exposing the bouncing prizes for my starved hands. Fumbling with her nipples, I finally latched on to them, and twisted them with my pointer and thumb. Her breath hitched, and without a second guess, she was up and pulling us both into the bedroom. There was no looking back from that point.

14

"Hey Love," she kissed me awake, trying not to startle me. "I'm heading off to work now. I'll meet you at Don's this afternoon." I opened one eye long enough to catch a glimpse of my lady all dressed in suit for work. She must have a new client on board.

"Have a good day," I managed to garble out. Yawning, stretching, and getting up to pee, I finally headed in for my coffee. I wasn't sure how I had survived all the years of my life without coffee. *What, was that from birth to twelve?* As I poured the hot, steaming goodness into my cup, I had to give it a real good inhale. *All that French roast really perked up the ole brain!*

Staring out the front window, the tree line was beautiful. Midsummer, everything was in bloom, full, and lush. Over the years the trees have really filled in around the house, providing an excellent barrier around the property line. Looking around just reminded me how glad I was to have gotten this house from the landlord years before.

Straightening out my sports coat, I finished my orange juice at the counter. Today was to be my first day in office all day, with no more runs or deliveries. I hadn't been this nervous since being promoted to vice president. I opened my phone to send a quick text to Janie.

Morning Love. Can't wait to see you later. Have a good day.

I noted to myself that I needed to find out how Janie was so motivated in the mornings all the time. I needed more of that shit. Pulling into the base, I took the spot marked "VP." The lot was completely full, and I wasn't sure I had ever seen it like this before.

"Good morning, Gabe!" Don's voice bellowed from his office as I walked by.

"Hey Don, how's it?" I stopped, and leaned against his door frame.

"It's going good, I think. You'll find the next door to your right now has your name on it. A bit of an upgrade for you." He smiled, and patted my shoulder. Leaning back, I checked down the hall and noticed the old conference room door was closed, and seemed to have a plaque on it.

"Oh man, what did you do?" I asked coyly. I all but skipped down to the office door, beaming to see a gold plaque reading: GABRIEL LAZARUS, VICE PRESIDENT. *Whoa, official!* "This is great, Don." I glanced him over my shoulder with his arms crossed, still in his own office doorway.

"Go on in, buddy." He said almost mysteriously. Now I was intrigued, and couldn't wait any longer. Opening the door, I was met with deep blue walls with crisp, white trim. Bright silver fixtures adorned every wall, with brightly colored paintings coming from every side. The couch was a dark grey color, and the jet black tables were stellar.

"Holy shit man," he joined me in the office. He nodded.

"They did do a fabulous job, didn't they?" He smiled again, and I couldn't help but wonder who.

He pointed into the corner, "That's your mini-fridge, and pantry. They're coming to stock your bar later on this afternoon. I need to get back to it, lots of conferences today.

124

Buzz me if you need me, and welcome to your first full office day." He laughed and cleared his throat.

Walking into the office, it was a lot to take in. But it all looked so comfortable. The couch was perfectly cushioned, and relaxing to lay on. *Knew you'd try that out first, man*. The bar looked amazing, I couldn't wait to get Janie in here to see all of this! The TV was huge and took up the entire wall in between the windows.

As if on cue, my phone buzzed, with the familiar ring tone of Janie. After she saw Crazytown in concert, *'Butterfly'* became her anthem. *Appropriately so though, don't you think?*

So, do you love your office?

What?! She knew?! Wait a minute. My fingers couldn't go fast enough on the keys.

How did you know about this?! It is amazing! Can't wait for you to see it!

I took a few moments to take it all in, and sit in my new huge desk chair. It was a truly powerful feeling to sit behind such a grandiose desk, and such a strikingly beautiful, and steady chair. Her ringtone buzzed again.

Honey, I've already seen it! I designed it! SURPRISE! I love you, and I hope you love it! Be there soon!

I couldn't wipe the smile off of my face if I tried. Looking around the office again, I could see both of our tastes in this room. She made it warm and safe, and fun and sexy. Jumping on to my computer, I entered the secure system. There were a few emails from the design teams about the Hammerhead raft

125

plan, so that's where I started. It seemed like so long since I had sat down and created the plans in the first place.

Hours later, my desk phone chimed in. "Hey Gabe, this is Don. Could you pick up?" I raised my eyebrow, as I was pretty sure he could've just walked over.

"Yeah?"

"I have a slight problem. Lizzie is here, and she's demanding to see you. If she doesn't see you, she's going to call her boss, who will pull their entire account, and most likely kill us." I swallowed hard. The memories that came with her weren't wanted, and I didn't want Janie to get involved with this nonsense. "Can you see her?" I sighed, and rubbed my forehead. *Is it worth risking your lives for?*

"What does she want to see me for?" The words rolled out of my mouth before I could stop them.

"She says to discuss the new drop off procedures, and new delivery man. Says she'll be twenty minutes or less. But Gabe," he paused, and I could hear him shuffle. "She only wants to work with *you.*"

This was everything I didn't want, but again, there went the words. "I'm sorry, G. I haven't figured out what to do yet."

"Yeah, I guess. Send her in." I slammed the phone down without second thought, and checked my watch. Janie was due here at any time, and walking in on this could be catastrophic. Resting my elbows on my desk, I put my head in my hands.

It seemed that time stopped, and I was stuck thirteen years before. Her house like a dungeon, and those that went in, didn't come out the same. She was the pushiest blonde I'd ever had the pleasure, and subsequent turmoil, of dealing with. Sighing loudly, I lifted my head to see that she was standing in my office doorway.

She smiled at me the same way she used to, and I felt the sideways grin creep across my face. She walked in as if something were indeed on her mind, and closed the door quietly behind her.

"Gabriel," she cooed, taking seat on the comfortable couch in the middle of my office. She extended her arms to lay across the top of the couch, and rested her head along the back pillows. She looked around my office, taking everything in. "Love your office. It's so…" she paused, almost searching for a word, but stopping once our eyes met again. "Hot." Her nose wrinkled when she spoke.

"Yeah, it's pretty great. My wife designed it all for me." Her eyebrows rose, and I knew that she knew where I was going.

"Yes, your wife. How's she doing?" I felt my brow bend, and I wondered why she was doing this.

"She's great, and should be here in a few minutes." Almost excited by the thought, Lizzie was on her feet heading towards my desk in a breath. Leaning over my desk as far as she could, revealing what she hid behind her shirt, showing me what I had willingly given up years before.

The smallest chest, and perkiest nipples I'd ever seen. Smirking again, I turned my entire chair from her, and gazed out the window.

"Oh Gabe," her heels began clicking their way to my chair. She stood in front of me now, kneeling. "I know what you want. What you've missed." She bent in front of me, and I could feel the terror coursing through my veins. My heart was beating out of my chest, and the terror was now mixing with lust. *Shit. I'm only a man…* Her hands gently landed on my knees, and began to trail up my thighs.

"What do you think you're doing?" I sat up quickly, and grabbed her hands on my thighs, stopping them as they climbed almost to the gold. "Lizzie, just don't. It's not like that." Her eyes met my own and her face changed.

"I'm doing this, Gabe. I've been given a task, and I'm going to see it through." I felt her hands push farther into my lap. Doing my best to hold them back, I shook my head. "You'd be smart to let this happen, or you'll be down one of your biggest accounts." She said it so matter of fact, I was taken back by her answer.

"What?!" I adjusted again, pulling myself back in my chair.

"I'm going to blow you. Because that's what I was sent here to do."

"And if I don't let you?" I couldn't believe this, and Janie was racing through my mind.

"Then I'll report back that you didn't allow it, and my boss will most likely order the hit on you, and then your pretty wife, considering all he's done for you." *What??* My jaw clenched together. The same type of idle threats that she used to sport, while she tied me up and drove pins through my balls.

"Lizzie, this is utter shit! My WIFE will be here ANY minute." She shrugged.

"Guess you'd better fix that then, huh?" She smiled, trying to play the innocent role. In all the years we've delivered to location four, I'd never met her boss. Lizzie and her minions had always dealt with us. Now I was starting to see the bigger picture, and couldn't help but wonder how they had discovered our services years before.

Looking at the clock, I knew I was running out of time. Glancing at Lizzie kneeling before me, ready to finish her task, it pained me knowing what I was about to do. I picked up the office phone, and rang into Donovan's office. He picked up quickly, thankfully.

"Yeah, I need you to intercept Janie when she gets here. I don't care, keep her the hell out of this office until I text you." I glanced back to Lizzie, unable to hide the look of tortured disgust on my face. "Twenty minutes maybe? I don't know.

128

Don't screw this up, Don." I slammed the phone down, and turned back to Lizzie.

"You have twenty minutes." Reaching down, I unhooked my pants and zipper, and sat back in the chair again, folding my arms over each other. She looked contrite, and pleased.

Readily hopping up on her knees, she folded the corners of my pants back exposing my boxers. She ran her hands up and down my thighs, obviously trying to relax the tension that had built. She exhaled suddenly, and I could feel her hot breath on my skin. *Fuck.* I was losing control. Blood slowly filled my shaft and it was growing to explode out of my boxers.

"That took longer than I remembered," she said as she grasped my shaft, leading it into her mouth. Gritting my teeth together, and staring at the ceiling, I couldn't help but remember all the times we spent together years before.

Our relationship had never been much more than what she was doing now- pure sex. Any feelings I thought I'd had for her were blown to bits when she got possessive in our 'fucking only' set up. *But oh God, it was good when it happened.*

Her teeth gently ground up my shaft. This felt so wrong, yet so familiar. Her tongue was rough, and I couldn't help but wondered how many cocks she'd been on since I'd last dealt with her. Pushing all the thoughts out of my head, I looked to the window again to find my escape. To hide my self-disgust, as I'd have to face my wife in minutes.

She broke suction, and began frantically stroking my hardened length. I knew that she understood I was not going to come easily, and give her the satisfaction. Her hands suddenly tightened around my shaft, and she dug her nails into my sack. Groaning loudly, there was no denying the pleasure that brought, still, after all these years.

"Give it up to me, G." She smiled, and stared directly into my head. Forcing my eyes to close and look away from her, there was only one way I was going to come. *I cannot believe you're doing this right now...* Now was no time for my conscious to start in, I just needed to finish, and get her out of here. I pulled her back on to my lap, and pushed her violently back on to my shaft. Feeling the back of her throat choking on me, and seeing the tears pour from her eyes, I was satisfied delivering my own message.

Holding her forcefully on to me with my left hand, I could feel my load building, and readying to explode. Cutting off her breath, I made sure to empty myself into her throat, gagging her repeatedly. Moving my trash can closer to her with my right hand, I waited until her face began to turn pretty shades of red.

Finally letting her off to breath, she was gagging hard enough to vomit. Breathing heavily after each upchuck, she looked up at me with mascara stained tears dripping down her cheeks.

"Jesus," she managed in between breaths.

"Tell your fucking boss that's it! I don't want you dirty ass near me again. I'm NOT doing runs, and I'm NOT doing you." I grabbed her forearm, pulling her into my face. "Do you fucking understand me?!" For the first time in our lives, she looked terrified of me. *Well, that's something, I guess.* "I mean it Liz, no more of this. I don't care what he orders of you. If you have any self-respect left, you'll abide by what I'm saying."

I could feel myself breathing heavily, angrier than ever. Her smile turned ornery once again, and she stood up, adjusting her clothes. Walking back around to the front of my desk, she opened her purse to withdraw an envelope, and her makeup compact. She first began fixing her makeup, and clearing the smeared mascara from her face. Snapping the compact close, it was the loudest noise in the room. *Except for your beating heart.* She handed me the envelope.

"This is for your boss, please see that he gets it." She turned towards the office door, and opened it slightly. "I hope you've enjoyed our meeting for today, Gabriel." Taking her pointer finger, and running it over the corner of her mouth. "Some things only get better with age." She exited the doorway laughing the entire way down the hall.

Standing to look out the window, I watched her get into a fully tinted, black hummer, with a driver. Clinging to the window, I punched the wall a few times next to me. Glancing down, my pants were still unbuttoned, and I looked like I had just been worked over. *Uhm, you were...* Pulling back up my pants, readjusting myself, and re-buttoning, I glanced again out the window, and caught Janie sitting in the garden with James. *Fuck. FUCK!*

15

After about twenty more minutes, I picked up my phone and texted Donovan. I had no idea how I was not going to tell he or Janie about this. I felt so strangely used for little more than my boss' profit, and his desire to never lose a client.

She's gone. Envelope for you. I'm coming to find you and Janie.

Locking up my office, I headed towards the garden where I had spotted them moments before. Opening the doors outside gave me the fresh air I was so obviously needing. I saw Janie in deep conversation with Donovan, laughing so hard her head was falling back. I couldn't help but time-trip back a few years to their relationship, and how sexual it had turned. I froze, and fell into the trance of memories.

In the grand scheme of all of this, I was more worried about what Lizzie's boss had in store for us than what would happen if Janie found out. I knew there were other motives for this, and I was determined to find out.

Walking up on their conversation, Janie stood to wrap her arms around me.

"Hey stud!" she said happily. "You done with work yet today?! I want to go see that awesome office!" *Oh no, not the office.* I felt my face pale.

"Oh, I just locked up. I figured we'd take off now, as I've finished all of my work for today, baby." I smiled at her, then glanced over at Donovan, who was more than perplexed. "Would that be okay, Don?" I asked, innocently extending the envelope to him, nonchalantly as ever.

"Yeah, of course! I love early days!" he took the envelope, and checked his watch. "And it is almost 4! I'd say we can call it for today." He paused, raising his hand. "But I will need a rundown of your client meetings today, ok?" I nodded, and smiled.

"You'll be getting those very soon. You'll be very enlightened, I think." He raised his eyebrows, and looked concerned. I nodded again, adding "Yeah *that* would be a good feeling for this one."

We both glanced at Janie, whose eyes were now bouncing between the two of us, trying to get a read on whatever we were talking in code about. Her eyebrow raised higher and higher by the second.

"You men! I swear." She rolled her eyes. "You could just come out and say it. I'm sure I'd be all right..." she trailed off. I took her hand, and began walking towards the cars.

"All right Don, I'll check in with you tomorrow, okay?" He nodded, and threw us both a wave. I could tell by the look on Janie's face that she was on to us, and now I'd only wondered how I was going to keep this to myself until I had a better grasp on what was really going on. "Let's go home, baby." I wrapped an arm around her shoulder, and escorted her to her driver's side door.

Leaning up to my mouth, she kissed me deeply, sucking in air through her lips as we broke apart. Her hands were hungrier than my own. My tryst event from an hour ago seems to have made me hot and fiery for her, in a carnal-claiming sort of way.

"Seems like you're all geared up..." she looked down towards my crotch, which was already growing at the mere thought of her naked before me. I nodded. Her hands ran down my chest, brushing over my hardening length gently. "Then let's get you home." She smiled, and fell into her seat. Thank God she was cool enough to wait for home. I needed a shower, very badly. I waved, as she rolled down the window.

"Meet you in the shower." I smiled, and winked. *Perfect, I think she would be proud of your deceit. Very sneaky, very old-Janie... don't you think*? Nights like these I was thankful that Donovan's house was so close to ours. He'd often called it all "destiny" that we'd met up, work together, live a few miles apart, and are essentially best friends. *Damn, you lost her on the highway!*

Turning into the driveway, I let out a chuckle seeing the clothes strewn from the Jeep, in to the house. This was going to be a good night. And of course, as if on cue... the phone rang. I picked up Janie's jacket off of the ground, but didn't recognize the number.

"Hello?" I cautiously asked. There was a ton of noise in the background, what sounded like hundreds of people talking.

"Dad?!" Oh, it's *her*. I could pick that voice from anywhere.

"Lilah! How're you, honey!?" I could feel the pep pick up in my voice, and my smile was spreading from one side of my face to the other. "How's camp so far?"

"It's great, Dad! Galen and I are having so much fun! I still don't like the bog, but I'm learning to help with the wildlife!" It wasn't until I heard her voice that I really felt the pain of missing the kids. "Oh, here Dad...Galen wants to say hi. Love you!"

The phone shuffled through the air, and again I heard the hundreds in the background. I wondered what Janie was in the house doing, and if she was already naked, or waiting to be stripped. After the day I'd had, I wouldn't mind ripping everything off of her, one shred at a time. *What? Old habits resurfacing, Gabriel?* I felt my jaw clench.

"Hey, Dad?" Galen's voice was slightly unsure, not really appreciating the phone yet in his young life.

"Hey buddy! How're you doing?"

"I'm all right. I really like camp. The best part is the stars at night, reminds me of home." *Aww, dude.*

"That's awesome bud! You know, I've looked at the stars these last few nights, so, I'm pretty sure we're looking at the same ones." His giggle spoke volumes. It was happy, with a side of heavy, and I could tell it wasn't just me missing him. We were all missing each other.

"Ok, well, I've got to go! It's almost supper time, and it's our turn to help set the tables. And the line for this phone is SO long." He laughed again.

"Okay buddy. I love you, Galen. So does Mom! Tell Lil, too! Have too much fun!" I was smiling ear to ear again, shaking my head.

"Yeah, you too. Bye!" Inhaling slowly, I sucked in a big breath of air. Reaching down as I stepped in to the house, her skirt and shirt were next to be picked up. I could hear the radio in the bedroom on, and the shower stream was steady.

Heading over to the bar, I poured myself some brandy, and a glass of vodka on the rocks. *Ah, are you trying to get your wife drunk? Or are you just trying to forget about this afternoon?* Either way, the first few sips went down pretty smooth.

"Gabe?" she beckoned, almost questioning if I was even here. Filling my glass again, this time I downed it quickly, and refilled before I joined her. My head was swirling with thoughts of the day. I was confused by what had happened, and I still wasn't sure of the point. I wasn't the key to their drug supply. I wasn't the boss that set the prices.

I sat on the bed, carefully setting both glasses on the side table. I took off my shirt, and threw it on to the floor. My mind wandered back to the afternoon, my perfect office... *and her.* I didn't want to revisit these parts of my life, or any part before Janie. I didn't want to waste time on what was, nor did I want to go back. Lizzie needed to be out of my life, and I had no idea how to push her back out.

"Gabe?" her voice shook, and she was dripping wet, frantically trying to dry off. "You didn't answer me." I felt my forehead wrinkle, and patted the bed next to me. She sat slowly, her towel parting open right at the apex of her thighs.

"I'm sorry, my head is just flying everywhere." I needed a distraction, not an excuse. "Guess who called me right as I pulled in tonight?" Cocking my head, I smiled at her coyly, smelling the fresh, clean scent of her soap. Her brows wrinkled, as if not knowing what to expect. "It was Lilah, and then Galen for a few minutes."

Her hands covered her mouth, and tears sprung to her eyes. Her head darted from side to side, and she bolted off the bed, out to wherever she left her purse. I heard it hit the floor, and she reappeared in the doorway, looking ever so defeated.

"I missed their call." Tears filled her eyes again, and she closed them tightly, pushing one tear to fall from each eye. *Well, if that doesn't break your heart in half, I'm not real sure what will.* For a moment, all I could do was take her in. Janie had a few chinks in her armor, and her children were definitely two of them. *I think you're another, Gabe.* I stood, wrapping my arms around her while she leaned against the door. Only a few tears fell, and she smiled again.

"Maybe we could just watch some television or something?" I could tell that my lack of attention in the shower,

136

and the kids missed call had done her in for today. *Damn.* I nodded, and fell back on to the bed. She piled up her pillows in a way that only Janie can do, and turned to find me holding the glass of booze.

"I made this for you earlier, before I checked out." She took the glass, and smiled a little. "I'm sorry, baby, my head's just full from work." *What a literal statement. Shit.* She nodded, and sipped at the condensation covered glass.

"I know," she drank again. "I've noticed since we left Donovan's earlier. Whatever it is," she turned to lay next to me, curling into the side of my body. "I figure you'll tell me when you're ready." She took another small sip, and relaxed back into the pillows, and me.

Time seemed to be slowly going by. Janie had fallen asleep half way in to the *Lost* episode, and I couldn't help take note how perfectly she molded into the side of my body. Raising my arm a bit from around her, I had the perfect picture of her. Her long blonde locks were trussed messily around her face, only outshined by her obviously waterproof mascara, which had somehow made it through the day, the shower, and a two hour nap. I nudged her gently, repeatedly, until she woke.

"Oh man," she rubbed her eyes, still half asleep. She had absolutely no idea how beautiful she was during these moments. How lucky a man am I to get to spend the rest of my days like this? "Did I fall asleep?" she giggled, knowing she'd been out for hours.

"You sure did, and you know what?" She sat up playfully, looking wild eyed as ever. She shook her head no. "You slept right through Kate kissing Jack!" Her mouth fell open, and her hand landed on her forehead. Dramatically, she fell over on to the bed, bouncing us both.

"Did they fuck?" I couldn't control my laugh. "Well?!" Now impatient with me, I fell over next to her mimicking her silly. She was having none of it, and climbed on top of me, still demanding answers. Grinding my hips into hers, as she was now in the best position ever, I shook my head.

"Nope, I don't think they're going to fuck, baby. I think Sawyer's taking this one home." She scowled at me, and reached far over my head into the stash. Her breasts were suddenly bouncing directly over my mouth, and I couldn't resist taking a small taste, even through the cotton t-shirt. Her strong dislike of Sawyer didn't fool me... She hated any male with blonde hair and blue eyes, still to this day. I just knew better these days than to question it.

"I hate it," she began, fumbling with the pipes. "I hate that those two would be so perfectly hot together, and they're keeping them at fingers distance on purpose. Killing my fucking libido." Our beaming smiles met in mid-air, and we both let out a cathartic laugh.

"Can I tell you something?" She inhaled deeply, smiled, and nodded. "You're so beautiful, all sleepy," I ran my finger through her hair, down her shoulder, and across her thighs. I took instant note of the goose bumps that flushed her skin. Our eyes met almost in a panic. She noticed, too. Her eyes squinted, and she inhaled again. I could see the days stress and worry falling away from her, and she was opening herself to me.

"You know sometimes your words make me blush." She rested her pipe on the table and took the last shot of now watered down vodka, making sure I saw her licking her lips when she was done. She leaned into my space, our lips mere inches apart. "Your words," she spoke with the sweet smell of the lemons in the vodka. "They make me extremely hot." Her hands swiftly took mine, and moved them under the giant t-shirt she had adorned. She was overflowing with heat, and had obviously been anticipating this, just as I had.

"Oh Janie," our mouths were fierce, probing into each other quickly. She was needy, and I could taste it. *Can she taste your need for calm?* Our tongues fought to be dominant, and eventually she caved to me. My fingers dipped inside of her, and she pushed herself on to my fingers over and over again.

Leaning back, I unbuttoned my pants and began to pull them down. Suddenly, I was frozen. I hadn't showered. *She is all OVER you, Gabriel!* I was disgusted by myself, and tried getting up. Janie's hands were warm on my chest, pushing me back to the bed.

"No way," she stripped the shirt off of herself. She wrapped her hand tightly around my shaft, and I melted into her hands like putty. *Worse. Butter. You're just greasy.* Closing my eyes to push the voice out, her hand was all I could focus on. "Please don't go," she began, and her mouth slid down my shaft before I could stop her.

"Oh God," My thoughts were so twisted. I wanted her to stop because it was wrong, and dirty. *But her perfect mouth, oh dear God...* I just couldn't stop her. And now, as my balls pulled into me and my cock throbs into her mouth, I want to come all over her tits. She stopped rather abruptly, and looked up at me, confused. Worried, almost.

"When did this happen?" her eyes pained. My heart stopped, and I sat up to see a scratch mark on my shaft. *Oh Fuck! What in the hell is THAT, Gabe?!* The memories of the warm walls, and wet mouth... the bitch left her mark! My breath was ragged, my heart uncontrollable, so much pleasure, and mental torture... so much like the past I couldn't take it. Janie's hands were softly holding me, mouth so close to my sensitive skin.

"Who knows, come on, please let me inside." *Distract her.* Pulling her towards me, she didn't push much farther on the wound. Staying on top of me, she opened herself to let me in. I dove in to her depths without much further thought, and was quickly lost in the welcoming, wet walls of my Janie. They pulled and pushed. They quivered and fluttered, tightening on me constantly. Every hug squeezed the blood in my hard shaft, pulsating through my body. Inside of Janie was the best place to be. *Ever.*

She rocked on my hips, taking me entirely in to her deepest, most sacred places. She moaned loudly, and I could feel her clenching again. Her tantric abilities were astounding, and I loved watching her come all over me, again and again. After the third orgasm, she fell open, ready for the primal taking. Flipping her over, I spanked her labia lips a few times to liven her nerves. She lost her breath from my surprise assault.

Beginning slowly, I gave her one fast, hard thrust. Bouncing her hard up and down, she smirked- the true sign she wanted it all. I steadied myself on my knees, and used the wall for leverage. Pulling completely out of her, I danced around her labia, and dove tip-only a few times. She wiggled and waggled over the bed for more, and at that point, I fucked her like my mistress. I built a quick, hard, steady rhythm, and she whimpered with every push. She clawed at my hips when I pulled away.

The sounds of sex were abundant. Her pussy was dripping wet, and there was now lube all over the place. Her moans were enough to set any man over the edge. Her voice took on a throaty, raspy edge when she was really into it. Anyone could absolutely tell how passionate she was. *And that was so fucking hot.* The sounds of my balls driving into her ass over and over, mixed with my grunts and moans... these were the nights I lived for. I felt her clench on me again, and there was no stopping myself now.

Pulling her hips as far on to me as I could, she gasped with the fullness of my entirety. Her mouth a perfect circle, coming around me over and over again. I felt my balls pulls, and my shaft tighten. Yanking out of her quickly, I shot my load all over her beautiful breasts. Dripping with my ooze, I used her shirt to wipe us both off, while she caught her breath.

"Thank you," she said breathlessly, stroking my arm. I leaned in and kissed her hard. Opening my eyes while we kissed, her pupils dilated with my touch. *How hot is that?* "I needed that." She mustered out.

"Any time, baby. I mean that." We lay in our post-coital bliss, drifting in and out of sleep. Her naked body still pressed against my own, laying peacefully. The memory flashes, then the image of the wound on my cock. This was hitting too close to home. As I drifted to sleep, I couldn't help but wonder what was in that envelope she gave to Donovan.

16

I entered Donovan's office promptly at nine. His smile was bright, albeit looked like he was hiding something sinister.

"Now," I folded my arms, feeling my anger setting in. "What was in that envelope?" He scratched the back of his neck, and spun to face me in his chair. The silence in the room grew heavy, and I could tell he knew more than he was saying. "If you're going to keep putting me in this spot, you'd better fucking tell me what's going on." He folded his hands in front of him on his desk.

"Her boss says this has to continue, or they're going to have us raided. If we're raided," he paused, trying to read my face for some sort of response, he continued. "We'll lose accounts, and essentially the money makers for our business. I've been trying to get you out of this for months, because I do get that this is going to end badly for someone." I nodded, and felt the anger set in. Donovan motioned for me to sit in one of his chairs. I shook my head.

"I can't sit. This is insane." I began to pace the floor. "I'm disgusted with myself, and now I'm hearing you say this is going to happen again?!"

"Yes and No. I mean, I'm trying to get this off of the table. You, off of the table. But it seems you're a really good bargaining chip for these people because of your past with her." He stood up, and walked around the desk, sitting on the edge. He sighed loudly, and I could feel the weight of his emotion. He looked up at me again, this time nodding his head ever so slightly. "I know you don't want to do this, and I know this has to be the most difficult thing in the world." I nodded. "I just need to get information on their company... something to take back the upper hand."

He said this to me like it was an unassigned, quiet job to handle. His squinting eyes confirmed my theory. I shook my head and sat in the chair. He was obviously milling over some big decision, making twisted ideas inside of his head.

"You think she's going to slip up once while she's here?" I scratched my forehead, almost in disbelief. "She's so focused on me, it's the worst feeling in the world. Back in the day, for me, it was a friends with benefits sort of deal, gone haywire." I met his eyes. "For her it turns out, we were building a foundation for the future. Except, I missed that memo, and I started my future with my wife, instead." I shrugged, and Don smiled, as if finally understanding more of the history.

"One of those, huh?" He exhaled, falling back into his chair. "I think you could pull something out of her. The way she is around you, I think you're underestimating how much of hold you still have on her." Thinking back to the times we'd been around each other again, I could see how he may have a point. *A disgusting point, however much of one it is.* "The next meeting is set for Friday, the 23rd." I gasped at the quickness.

"Don, I'm not going to carry on like this for long. This woman is like a disease, and the longer this is going on, the more likely it is she'll poison my life. Been there, done that." His brow turned sour, and I held out my hand. "I'm not saying I won't try, I'm willing. But I hope you understand the risk, and danger I'm putting my family in." I shifted in my chair leaning up on to my knees. "And you never told me, what was in the envelope?"

He pulled out the envelope, and slid it across his desk. It was open, and the contents were barely peeking out. It looked of nothing more than paper, or something thin. Motioning towards the envelope, Donovan pointed at it.

"Look if you want to, but it's going to make you uneasy. And as I've said, I'm working on it. Now that we've talked, I understand where these pictures came from." My eyebrows raised, and I could feel curiosity taking the place of my fear.

"Pictures?"

"Oh yeah, of you and this Lizzie girl from years before. A few of you and Janes, but they seem to be older." I couldn't hide my displeasure. Snagging the envelope, the pictures fell into my hand. I was instantly taken back to the long, dark nights in the Goth clubs. The heavy smell of leathers, sweat, and sex filling the air of the clubs. *Pictures. Again.*

I was looking at myself a dozen years younger, dabbling in things I knew nothing about. In some of the pictures I donned the full black leather Dom suit. In others, I was chained to the wall, with multiple women clawing at my flesh. In more than one I was locking some body part with Lizzie, or some other random woman. In another I was the third wheel of the threesome. We frequented more swingers clubs for belt notches than I care to admit. I closed my eyes tightly, and shook my head. *What am I going to do?*

"Does Janie not know about this?" He looked confused. "I mean, you guys have been through much more than some old pictures and past lovers." I shook my head.

"She doesn't know anything about my past. She has, however, seen Lizzie in the past, and recently. She accosted us while we were out at the bar last week." Donovan's face dropped. "Exactly. I won't let them hurt her, and the road we're going down something is going to end badly, I know."

"We'll keep everyone safe, I promise you that. We won't have a repeat of the strip mall." He shuttered, as if remembering the state of Janie as they pulled her through the vents. He took a quick drink of the scotch that had appeared on his desk.

"All right, I'll deal with Friday when it gets here. What about the estate party on Saturday? Were all Locations invited?"

"Yeah, for the most part. Should be a good turnout, and I'll need you all afternoon and evening, for sure. Mylah is hoping Janie is coming so they can tub together, and run the bar." My head throbbed suddenly, and pains shot through the backs of my eyes. My hands came to my head, and I leaned back in the chair. "You all right, man?"

Squinting through the pain, I tried to nod. Reaching for my phone, it fell to the floor.

"Hey Gabe," Donovan began, steadying me with his hands. "How about I take you home? I'll drive you, and have security follow to take me home. You're not looking so good." He pushed me back into my chair. "Relax, bud. Let me help. It's going to be okay." I closed my eyes, and heard him pick up the phone. He pushed a few buttons, and the wave of pain flushed across my face again. "Hey Janes, its Don. No, no, everything is okay. He's sick, a migraine, I think. So I'm bringing him home.

145

Just didn't want you to panic. Of course, yep. Ok, be there in ten."

He threw my arm over his shoulder, and steadied me down the hallway to the parking lot. Stopping quickly, he carefully slid a pair of sunglasses over my eyes. Someone pulled up my car, and helped me in to the passenger side. *Fucking stress! Fucking migraines!* There was silence in the car on the way home, and it was so incredibly loud. I was thankful Don understood the headaches, and knew to get me home to Janie.

Pulling into the driveway, I felt the distance and knew he'd be breaking to stop right by the front door. I heard the gears shift to park, and I reached out for his wrist.

"Thanks, man. I appreciate this, and I'm sorry I blew the work day." His other hand patted my own.

"Absolutely not a problem. Now, hang tight, and I'll help you in the house." I fell back into the car seat doing my best to keep my eyes tightly closed. The migraines I get were unhuman. From another planet, obviously. It felt as if my entire head was opening up from ear to ear, splitting right across my eyes. The car door opened, and Don's hands pulled me up and out of the car. Guiding me into the house, I could hear Janie running to greet us.

Her hands were like cold ice touching my burning hot skin. My hands instinctively reached for her.

"It's okay Gabe, Shhh," she quieted the room, and my mind again. "Don, can you help him to the couch? I've darkened the room." She whispered quickly. Moments later, I was falling into a soft pile of pillows and couch cushions. *Thank God.* The shuffling of feet was throbbing so loudly in my head, and I heard the side door open and close a few times. I could faintly hear them discussing something, and it sounded like business. *What now?*

Her hands were tenderly on me again. Silently, she lowered a cold compress over my face, and gently stroked my temples as softly as she could. Moving slowly down my body, she unbuttoned a few buttons on my shirt. Even with my eyes closed, I could feel her moving lower, and loosening my belt and pants buttons. My shoes slid off effortlessly, and I felt myself restfully sink into the cushions. Her hands rested over my abdomen, and she touched me gently as she walked away.

~

I awoke suddenly from an overly active dream, where I was running from something that seemed dangerous. *Gee, I wonder why?* Cautiously opening my eyes, I hoped the worst was over with the migraine. The room was still darkened, except for the kitchen light over the counter. Janie was curled up sleeping in the oversized lounger, looking peaceful as ever.

Slowly I began turning my head checking to see if the movement was still an issue. My head wasn't pounding immediately like it had been, and I could still see. I sighed a little and tried fixing my pillow so I was sitting up a bit more. Checking the time on my phone it was already after 9pm. Stress always induced these massive headaches, and over the years, they continue to get progressively worse.

I steadily stood, heading over to the counter to grab an apple. Sitting at the bar, Lizzie was still swirling through my head. I just needed to do this long enough to get the upper hand, and get myself out of this horrible hole. *Literally, huh?* I watched Janie sleep, and replayed certain parts of conversation with Lizzie through my head.

I thought of her now, and back then. She was the same sort of withdrawn, mysterious person. She hungered for the same things, obviously, and I could see no real way to penetrate for information in that way. I would have to be more creative with the methods I wanted to use, and sneaky enough to get what I needed to save us. Taking a large bite out of the apple, I couldn't help replay all the times we'd have to save each other, Janie and I. Surely she would understand this, if she did find out.

I stood to find more snacks, as not eating all day hadn't helped the migraine, either. I grabbed my notebook, made a sandwich, and took my seat again at the bar. I was glad Janie was asleep, this was nothing I wanted her to be a part of. I opened the notebook, jotting down everything that had happened the day before. I wrote as many things down about her as I could recall from our past, and as many of the memories that I could clearly recollect.

As I continued, my list looked less like business, and more like a list of things one would be interested in to seek out the oddest, most unusual type of pleasure there was. I chuckled to myself as I crossed off certain things, like hitting up our old BDSM group meeting places. *Oh good. Just not worth it.* I came to her sister's name on the list, and remembered a broken, pretty shattered relationship between them. Then my pen stopped on her parents. *Eureka, maybe?* I felt the smile creep across my face.

Years ago she hated the idea of her parents finding out about our sins, and disowning her from the family. As prominent Christian figure heads in their church, this news would be catastrophic. I fiercely scribbled my notes and plan on the paper, leaning back, admiring it. It was now nearly midnight, and I was creeping across the hardwood floors to my computer, trying not to wake Janie. *Yet.*

Passing by the bar on the way, I couldn't help stop for a bourbon on the rocks. A celebratory drink for nailing down a plan to get Lizzie and all of her counterparts out of my life. *For good.* The cold glass against my lips was relaxing, and the fiery beverage relighted my spark. I opened my email to message Donovan.

"To: Donovan James, James Industries

From: Gabriel Lazarus, JI, VP
Date: 06/21/2010 12:10:26 AM

Subject: Plans

Hey Don. Just wanted you to know I think I've found the crevice in which I'll be inserting myself to get what we need. I'm almost positive it will work, I just can't rush it. Set up Friday's meeting in my office around 10am. Hopefully by this time next week, this will be a thing of the past. One thing: I'd like to keep this from Janie as long as I can. (You and I both know she'll find out one way or another.) My migraine seems to be going away, but I'm going to work from home both today and tomorrow. I'll be in Friday morning ready to face hell. That will most likely be wearing heels.

Gabe"

Glancing back over my shoulder, Janie was beginning to stir in the chair. I turned off the computer, and began waking her to move in to bed. I couldn't help but watch her sleeping. Slowly inhaling and exhaling, barely moving except for the occasional twitch or smile. As gently as I could possibly be, I ran my fingertips down her arm, and thigh. The soft cotton she wore clung tightly to her skin, and she smiled at my touch.

Her eyes opened briefly, and she stretched her arms above her head, pushing her already pert nipples even farther through the thin material.

"Time for bed?" she asked huskily.

"Sure is," I took her hands and pulled her to stand. "Let me help you to bed, my lady." She giggled, and I pressed my nose into her fragrant hair. Turning her to sit on to our bed, she wrinkled her brow and reached for my forehead.

"Your head feeling better?" It was hard to will myself away from her sleepy, messy beauty...but she was too tired for the taking.

"It's only better because you took care of me." I kissed her forehead and I pulled her to my chest, while we situated ourselves in bed. "I love you, Janie." She moaned, wiggling into me again, falling into the arms of Mr. Sandman on her way out. I closed my eyes knowing I had things in control, and my blood pressure was a little bit calmer as I drifted off to dreamland tonight.

17

"You did WHAT?!" Her laughter was uncontrollable, and almost contagious. Working from home definitely had its perks. Watching her slink around in a t-shirt all day cleaning and working, had me entirely too geared up. I was ready to take her. Pent up aggression, anger, and resentment had left me craving her more than the usual.

"Oh no! I think that's hilarious! I'm glad you told them off, they absolutely deserved it! There's no reason for those small town bitches to be concerned with you or what you do anymore, Kiara." Her laughter rang out again, even over the Doors, who were blaring on our house speakers. "That's so tacky. Don't they understand what defamation is? Sometimes walking away is the best thing to do, and I think you're right to do what you did. Walk away, close the doors. Burn the mother fuckin' bridge!" She glanced in my general direction, and made the "talks too much" sign with her hand.

Smirking at her, my distraction took a heavy turn. Janie sprawled out on the bar, wearing only the socks she continues to slide around the kitchen with. I could imagine myself biting her nipples, and tasting her core. I felt my eyes roll back into my head, and a slight convulsion roll through me when I thought too hard about her quivering hot flesh under me. Opening my eyes, she stood inches in front of me and quickly covered my lips with her own. *She pulled away too soon!*

"No way, Mister. I've still got a little work to finish up!" She squeezed my cheeks with her fingers, and headed back to her side of the kitchen. Each step she took gave me a peek up her shirt to her red underwear and perfectly shaped ass. She picked up her phone, quickly dialing. *As if she thought I'd really be deterred because she was on the phone!*

"Hey Bradley! Tell me about it all." She giggled, and started clicking through her email. Give her five minutes. "Yes, I got that one. Your totals, and notes, are impeccable." She nodded as she agreed with him, and her brow wrinkled deeply if she didn't. It was amazing how much work I hadn't gotten done because I'd been so focused on my beautiful wife today. *Maybe working from home isn't the best fit for you, Gabe?* "She was a 'Juicy Lucy' huh?"

Her laugh hit my eardrum, and surged straight to my cock. It pushed at my sweats, begging to be freed to seek out what it so desperately wanted. *Janie.* Her words sank into my head, just as they use to, and I wanted nothing but her. Again, the laugh. My cock pulsed, and I sucked my breath in through my gritted teeth. My eyes darted to her, and one glance was all I needed. "Greek salad?! Eww, no way!! You're a crazy man, Brad! All of your customers love you for it, too." Her giggle dug into my veins, pumping my blood faster still.

Her body started to turn, and her eyes looked over and met mine. She smiled demurely, almost sideways, and as if on cue I threw my chair across the room and headed straight for her. Her eyes widened, and her voice shook. "Brad, I need to go! Something has come up, and it needs to be handled immediately. I'll email you once I transfer your pay. Bye!" *That giggle is contagious.*

I wrapped my arms around her, and pushed her in to the wall a few feet behind. My tongue dove deeply into her, dancing with her tongue in the most erotic of ways. Her warm, wet mouth was more than receptive, and my hands slid easily under her shirt, feeling her magnificent tits. She crashed herself into me, tugging at the hem of my shirt.

Before my shirt was even off, her mouth skirted around me and she was clawing and biting at my chest. Her terminal beauty struck me at that moment, with the sun beaming in on her long blonde hair and sun kissed skin. I ran my hand down her sternum, and over her belly. Without hesitation, she whipped her own shirt over her head and tossed it down at her feet. She sank to her knees before me and I braced myself against the wall.

"Looks like you need me," she panted, hot breath landing on my taut cock skin. Her hands slid into the elastic, and encircled my shaft tightly. I gasped with the heady feeling, and pushed myself further into her hands. She moaned, and I throbbed. Her eyes flashed to mine, the most beautiful hazel shown before me, and she wrapped her lips around the head of my cock.

Her tongue hit my flesh perfectly timed with every throb she felt. I could feel my balls pulling in to themselves, readying to blow, so I steadied my thinking to draw it all out. She broke the suction she created with a popping noise, and climbed back up my abdomen, kissing the entire way. Our mouths met once again, hungrier than ever, and we clumsily fell over to the bar. *Ah, your dreams are coming true.*

Taking her cues, gently laying her on the bar, I pulled her red panties down slowly, unwrapping the best present I'd ever gotten. She was recently waxed, and perfectly smooth. The tiny heart island of pubic hair needed explored, so I dove in to the patch, and down to the wet flesh between her legs. Pinching the meatiest part in between my first and middle finger, she moaned and writhed around on the bar. Sinking inside, the warm, tight walls screamed my name.

My cock throbbed and I pulled her over the edge of the bar. I needed to rub myself against her wet flesh, and work her up with the tip. Her fingernails dug into my arms leaving me desperate for more.

Even her nails were no comparison to the exquisite feeling skin on skin brought. Or the electric nerve feeling rubbing myself all over her brought me. Marking her as mine, over and over again.

"Please," she begged, panting, needing me inside of her. She positioned herself over me, and I impaled her as deeply as I could. She cried out with garbled words, and those nails dug in even harder. "YES!" she screamed again. Lowering myself to her she latched on to my earlobe, making me throb even harder in steady surges. I felt her walls clench, and her body went rigid. The flow of warm come dripped out of her, and all over me. Rubbing myself in her juices, I needed more.

Bracing her with my hands, I let my tip dance around her clit. In and out of her tight, hot hole. Finally, taking me all the way in, I set a steady rhythm, pounding my hard flesh into her welcoming opening. My hands wandered around her body,

154

stopping finally on her fine ass. Spreading her apart even more, I slipped a finger inside and she gasped. The instant clench that came was mind blowing, and so tight. She hugged, tightened, and got wetter in a repeated pattern that was making me lose my mind.

She ground herself into my hand, coming over and over again all over me. Our eyes met momentarily and she looked so turned on. Pulling out of her, she flipped over on the bar, placing one leg up on a bar stool. Her hands slid around to her tight, swollen pussy, and she dipped a finger inside. I lost my breath with the mere image of her fingering herself, and then she smacked her ass. *Hard.*

"What're you waiting for?" She opened herself up more, and I knew exactly what that invitation was. I lined myself up with her rear, and pushed my way in. I slid my fingers into her pussy, and pumped away at her. I could feel the electric pulses squeezing her insides over and over again. She pushed herself into me more, taking me as deep as she possibly could. I could feel every quiver, every muscle spasm, and her every moan were all *mine*. I was close. I pulled out of her quickly, and she turned and looked at me like I was Satan.

"Just a minute baby," I headed to the sink. "I want to come in your pussy, that's all." She smiled, repositioning herself on one of our barstools. She threw one leg up on to the bar, and I throbbed hard in my hand while I washed myself off for reentry. She moved the other barstool, and threw her left leg over that one. Completely spread eagle and open for me, she wiggled on the stool. Her pussy glistened with come.

"Please." She reached for me. Without much thought, I walked over and crammed my massive cock into her tight hole. She squeezed her nipples while I fucked her, and they bounced in perfect rhythm with every entry. I loved watching her take all of me inside. Pulling entirely out of her, and ramming back in, full length, top speed always made her come. I dove deeply inside of her, and circled my hips around changing up the pattern a bit.

She tightened again, and I couldn't hold back any longer. I pressed into her as deeply as I could, and pulled her lips to my own. The kiss was passionate, sexy, and intense. My come pulsed into her for what seemed like five entire minutes. The throbs and touches were exquisite, and my skin was on fire. Her hands settled on my shoulders, and they were cool to the touch.

Up and down my arms she rubbed, both recovering from our escapade. I finally pulled out of her, and come poured from her on to the floor. She smiled and shrugged. I tossed her a hand towel, and sat down on the barstool.

"Want a drink?" I asked, sort of sarcastically. *Not drunk enough?*

"I do." To my shock and astonishment, she was going to join me for my afternoon drink. "I'll be right back." She headed off towards the bathroom, most definitely to pee, and clean herself up. I poured her a vodka with ice and lemons, and more bourbon for myself. I slipped my pants back on, and sat back at the bar. She reappeared standing instantly by my side, and gently kissing my shoulder. "I love you." She said nonchalantly as ever, sitting down again next to me at the bar.

"Love you too, Janes." I handed her the drink, and she took one long gulp, wiping her mouth off with her arm. She pulled her laptop over to her, and opened up her email.

"So, tell me about who's all coming to Don's party on Saturday?" I smiled at her, and took a long sip of my drink. If I said too little, I could really set up trouble. If I said too much, I'd be hashing out my plan and what was coming for hours. Thankfully, the CD player shifted, and Zeppelin came blaring through the radio. Janie was singing 'Black Dog' before I could stop her.

"Most all location contacts will be there, and all of the staff. He's going to have some new customers and employees coming in and out, so I'll be working on selling our brand and name all evening." She wrinkled her nose, and nodded.

"Will Mylah be there?" Nodding back, I smiled.

"Yes. She's looking forward to some bar time with you." I got two thumbs up to that. Janie loved spending time with Mylah, and sometimes Donovan and I were lucky enough to watch. "I know Sean, Pierce, and Lonnie will be there, too." Now was my chance. "Do you remember the chick from the bar? Lizzie? She'll be there with her bosses, too." She nodded, and sent the email she was typing.

"Oh, wonderful." She closed the lap top, and finished off her glass. "No worries, I'll be working the bar." She held up her glass, and tinged it with her fingernail. "Refills? How much are refills?" Pulling a joint out from behind her ear, she lit it quickly.

"Don't be a hoarder, Janie." I teased, jokingly. She passed the doobie over, and I took a long hit. It had been longer than I had liked in between my highs, and this was a welcomed calm. Checking the time, it was already after 10. Working from home days were highly enlightening, and very exciting. We passed the joint back and forth until a nice warmth overtook us both, and we headed to the couch to watch some television.

~

Friday morning seemed to sneak up on both of us, as we'd enjoyed each other quite constantly over the past few days. *If making yourself into a sexually spent blob of goo was the point, you have definitely succeeded!* We were both in the kitchen for breakfast at the same time for once, and it was quite amusing.

"What're you up to today, beautiful?"

157

"I'm going to deliver a few pay checks, and sign a new business for cleaning services for Kiara. Word of mouth is spreading about the naked cleaning." She smiled, winking. "How about you? What's on your agenda?"

"I've got a client meeting this morning, and then I'll probably end up shopping for the booze for tomorrow or something. Want me to text you after my meeting, and you can come with me on the booze run? I mean, only if you want." She looked at her watch, and back at me.

"Sure, that sounds like a plan!" She came over and hugged me tightly. "Thanks for the past few days, Gabe." I kissed her forehead, and wrapped my arms tightly around her.

"Thank *you*, love." I swatted her ass as she leaned past me to grab her purse and keys.

"All right, text me. I'm off! Have a great meeting!" she threw her hand in the air, beaming. I waved back, and mustered out a half smile. The next few hours would be difficult, dirty, and wrong. But I was ready to take the steps I needed to.

18

Entering my office, I opened all of the windows, blinds, too. If she wanted to play games, I could play with the best of them. I turned on the computer, and set the internal camera to begin recording right at 10am. I put a condom in my desk drawer just for safety's sake. I felt like I was as ready as I could be for what was coming. I checked the clock and it was 9:56am. Minutes seemed like hours, seemed like days. I tried to distract myself reading some company emails, but my focus was too scattered. The knock on the door took me by surprise, even though I knew it was coming.

"Hey, Gabriel." She said idly, standing in the doorway, obviously waiting for a personal welcome inside. Her tan coat was tightly closed with a belt.

"Lizzie. What a coincidence meeting you here today." She wrinkled her brow, almost confused.

"Yes, I'm right on time. Like always." She entered the room, and closed the door behind her. "Now, I'm here to collect." She instantly opened her coat, revealing a dingy pink negligee. *Ugh, pink.*

"I guess the idle chit-chat is a no go for today then?" She pursed her lips together, and moseyed over to my desk. *Slide your chair back so she gets in camera range!* I wheeled myself back a bit, forcing her to take a few extra steps to reach me. "Come on, Liz. Don't you want to talk? Like the old days? I remember we had some pretty deep conversations." She crossed her arms.

"This isn't like the old days, Gabriel. I'm here on business, and my boss says *this* is my job."

"Really great boss then, I guess." I shrugged. She looked distantly out the window, as if she was close to responding. *Close to changing her mind?*

"Look, if you'd just do this, we could get it over with." She reached out for me, and I ducked out of her grasp. "You always liked it enough, come on Gabe. I'm not that bad...am I?" *Oh God, you've got no idea how cold, and bad you are.* Sighing, I shifted in my chair.

"What do I have to do this week to appease your cowardly boss?" I cocked my head to one side, and waited for her answer. She bit her tongue between her teeth, trying to hold back her smile.

"Well, I told him last week I blew you. This week, he wants us to fuck." I knew it, and nodded. Shrugging my shoulders, almost cartoonish.

"I won't argue, I guess. If you're going to make me, what choice do I have? Oh, one. I will be wearing protection." She nodded, looking petulant as ever, and I reached into the drawer. She slid off her coat, and I glanced to make sure the tiny recording box was going in the corner. "I really think this is ridiculous, treating you like a prostitute, and trying to make a mockery of my marriage. Your boss must be a *real* winner." She sat on my desk, spreading her legs open revealing her flappy lips, attempting to pull off the "sexy older woman" vibe. *Fail.*

The instant disgust rolled through me, and I held back heaves. She fingered herself for a few minutes, watching my reaction intently. Waiting for something that I was going to keep to myself as long as I could. When there was no reaction on my face, or in my pants, she grew impatient.

"Come on, Gabe!! Just fuck me. It's that easy." I winced, and shook my head.

"It's not really that easy when I'm not into it. Or you. I haven't been for years." She positioned herself over me, and began rubbing the crotch of my pants. Locking my hands behind my head, leaning back in my chair, I could tell it was finally starting to get to her. "Even if you get it up, I hope you understand it's only a biological reaction. No feelings. Except disgust." I caught her expression flash to despair, falling quickly right back to anger, and completing her mission.

For the time being, keeping my erection at bay wasn't an issue. It was easy. All I had to do was fall back to the horrible memories of finding Janie in that bathroom. Or in the back of

161

the ambulance after her entrapment. I'd think of Michael, or the Visitor, and even Sean to some extent. *Wait a minute, where the hell has Sean been?!* Damnit, I couldn't keep my thoughts in focus, and I felt the tingling sensation in my crotch.

After a few moments, the blood flow picked up, and my dick was hard enough for her to sink on to. She moved quickly when she noticed, not leaving much escape room for me. Having her bouncing up and down on my lap, in my face wasn't any better. *There's no going back now. Here's hoping your plan works, G.* She rocked back and forth, and tried squeezing my shoulders. I was suddenly thankful for the condom, removing most of the "good" feeling that would ever come with this encounter.

"Come on, Gabe. Make it worth it..." she panted, as if having the time of her life. I raised my eyebrows, and shifted my interlocked fingers on the back of my head. I was almost sure that there was nothing harder in the world than trying to ignore the feelings, both physical and mental, that intercourse in general brought. I was starting to have second thoughts about the entire plan, and if I could really get the information needed to put us on top again.

"I would've preferred just talking for a bit. But you had to have it your way." This was growing old, and I was getting angry. I rested my hands on the arm rests of my chair, tightening my grip a bit. Forcing my hips up into her, she screamed loudly with my counter pressure. I could feel the shift in her body, and that she was very close to the edge. Ramming in again, gritting my teeth in disgust, I did my best pump fake ever. I moaned, and tried to block the visions of her orgasm, and thrashing around on my stick.

Looking past her, I saw the Jeep pull in to the parking lot. *Oh my God. No.* My heart stopped beating. I closed my eyes to hide the new turmoil all over my face. Planting my feet on the floor, I gave a shove backward. This not only separated our

162

bodies, but gave a few feet distance between us. She adjusted quickly, and looked around, as if someone was watching her.

"Here, give this to Mr. James." She extended a slip of paper this time. She buttoned her coat closed, and headed to the door. "You really need to work on your hospitality, Mr. Lazarus." Swinging her purse over her shoulder, she almost looked hurt. "Maybe next time you'll-" *Oh no.*

"Next time?! No. I don't think so, Liz." She smirked, completely oblivious to my plan. *Thankfully.* I pulled the condom off, and pushed it into my pocket. I zipped my pants as I walked towards the door, pushing her out faster. I glanced at the piece of paper, and it was simple: "Double it, Saturday."

"Regardless, we'll see you tomorrow at the party." She leaned in to kiss my cheek, and I darted out of her way.

"Don't think so, Liz. See you tomorrow." I had no idea if they'd pass in the parking lot, or in the building. All I knew was I needed an immediate shower, and I felt ill. Rushing into Donovan's closed office and into his full bathroom suite, I locked the door behind me. Leaning on the door, I tried to calm myself. Why was Janie here? *She must've just come instead of waiting for a text*!

Pushing myself off of the wall, and over to the shower, I quickly stripped off my clothes and jumped in. I'd never scrubbed so furiously and feverishly in my life, and the friction on my shaft after having sex with Lizzie was giving me a semi. I turned off the shower, put my clothes back on still wet in some places, and towel dried my hair. *What're you going to say to Janie!? Why you're wet!?*

I opened the door, and because karma hates me, there stood my smiling wife a mere few feet from me, talking with Donovan's secretary.

"Hey babe!" she was beaming, so she must've gotten the new client, I thought. "Did you take a shower?" I nodded nervously, feeling my lips trembling as I pushed out a smile. And then I felt the words trying to come out. *What words are they?!!*

"Yeah, I got really dirty in the warehouse. Just washed up quickly!" There was a sharp, louder pitch to my voice, and I couldn't seem to control it. *Jesus Gabe, get a grip on your emotions.* I used the towel to cover my face, and continue to dry my hair. A few deep breaths, and I thought I had regained control. I wasn't good at secrets, and when I looked back up to Janie's face, my brain squished again. She was looking at me like I was lost, or had gone crazy. Her nose wrinkled, and she poked me in the arm.

"You ok? Getting another migraine? You're acting weird." She glanced at Dorothy, and back to me. My head felt so heavy. Full of everything it shouldn't be. My wife was standing in front of me, and for whatever reason, I felt frozen. *How do people keep these secrets?* I shook my head, and desperately tried to focus.

"I'm sorry. Yeah," I turned, and pointed down the hall to my office. "Let me go grab my keys, and stuff. Still want to go on the booze run with me?" She smiled widely, and nodded. Walking down the hall, I could hear her infectious laughter spreading through Dorothy's office, and the entire front waiting area. Swallowing hard, I tried to calm my thoughts. I sat at my desk, first ensuring there were no signs of the escapade around. Then I checked the computer file for the video, and made sure to save it to three places on my computer, and on the secret USB drive I had in a locked drawer. *See? You've got some of your proof now.*

Listening down the hall, I could still hear the ladies talking exuberantly. I opened up an email to Donovan, and typed as quickly as I could.

"To: Donovan James
From: Gabriel Lazarus JI, VP

164

Date: 06-23-2015 12:56:45 PM

Subject: Burning Hands

I've got almost all of the information I need to follow through with my plan. Tomorrow I'll get the rest. Attached is the video blackmail on Liz. You'll need to send this to Veronica and Edgar St. James. This is the most insane thing I've ever done for work, FWIW.

Heading out to order the booze to have delivered tomorrow, and then I'm out with Janie. We'll be back over tomorrow about 2, and can help with whatever else needs done. Janie's girls thoroughly cleaned up the place, and the decorators Janie hired are finishing up the setup of the pool area. Looks good, so far.

Gabe"

I sent the email, exhaling with relief, and remembered I hadn't heard from Sean. Turning off the computer, and sliding the USB drive into my pocket, I opened my cell and shot him off a quick text.

Sean, where are you today?

I locked up, and Janie was walking down the hall towards me. Extending my arm to her, she escorted me out of the building.

"Should I just keep the Jeep here? Or should I drive home?" I mulled it over quickly, but knew that tomorrow we'd be driving together.

"Let's just swing it by home, first. I'll pick you up there." I winked, and sped down the driveway and out of the gate,

165

leaving her in the dust. My phone buzzed as I pulled on to the back highway.

Home today, sicker than ever. Should be okay for tomorrow, what time do I need to be there?

Oh, well, that makes sense then. I'd have to text him back when I stopped in the driveway. I checked my rearview mirror for Janie, but no one was behind me. I turned on to our driveway, and stopped to enter the code. I hopped out of the car, and sat on the trunk waiting for her.

Feel better. 2 tomorrow. See you then.

Just as my nerves started to misfire, she pulled into the driveway. I smiled at her, and walked around to the passenger side of the Jeep. She looked so beautiful. Her long skirt was pulled up around her thighs- she had these fears that skirts would get tangled in the pedals while she drove. Her tan skin shown boldly against the light colored material. Her hair was windblown, and her sunglasses reflected my steamy gaze at her.

"Well, are you getting in this Jeep, or you just going to stare all day?" she asked impatiently, bringing me back to reality. I climbed in, and leaned over to her. Our lips were only inches apart, and I could smell her sweet cherry lip balm. Her giggle gave me goose bumps that covered my body.

"Let's hit up Cap N' Cork, and then maybe we could do an early dinner? Drinks, maybe?" She looked excited at the idea, and nodded, steering the Jeep towards the closest liquor store. My cell vibrated again. Opening the text, it was short and sweet.

Video sent. And so it begins. We will prevail.

The afternoon passed by quickly, and we managed to get enough booze for tomorrow's extravagant event. After signing the paperwork for deliveries, we were ready to head back home again, but decided that stopping in to the Hi Ho Tavern on our way was a better choice.

19

By the third shot, I had finally numbed and stifled the voices in my head, falling into semi-drunken conversations with my wife. My very sexy, very hungry wife. I sat across the table from her, watching her devour breadsticks faster than I'd ever seen. In between bites, she'd dip the breadsticks in a little farther into her mouth than she should. Every dip caused my pants to shift.

"You didn't want one of these, did you?" She sardonically asked. I shook my head.

"No actually, my hunger is definitely for something *else*." Her cheeks flushed, and her tongue rolled across her bottom lip.

"A few more drinks first?"

"Yes, a few more drinks." I took another sip of my bourbon, watching her closely. She picked up another of her shots, and put the cold glass to her lips. Her head tipped back, and the clear liquids disappeared. Her eyes opened with a deeper burn and she wiped her mouth with her arm.

"Good, because I'm havin' fun!" She stood up and danced around in her area. Glancing at her, doing the "cabbage patch," I couldn't hold in my laughter. Her skirt flowed between her legs, clinging to them in all of the right places. Her low cut tank top gave the perfect view every time she bent over to grab her knees to steady herself while she laughed.

"Are you excited for the party tomorrow, baby?" She spun again, stopping herself quickly on the table.

"Whoa, dizzy. Yes! I'm excited to run the bar with My, and get to see some of these oddball clients that you guys deal with." She took her seat, waving for the waitress. "Are there any that I should avoid?" I felt my head pull back before I could stop it, or the perplexing look that followed. *You know what she meant.* "Oh, I meant no offense. There's just been some shady things happening, and I didn't know if the people who hurt you, or any other "bad guys" would be there." She smiled a bit, as if to soften her question, making quotation marks with her fingers.

"I know what you meant, I just had to think about it." I smiled back trying to ignore how my instant defenses turned on. "There will definitely be shady people there, but no, not the ones who jumped me. Donovan withdrew their invitation." I leaned in to her. "And anyway, you'll be with Mylah. She'll tell you the dirt on everyone." I winked at her and leaned back, finishing the rest of my bourbon. Our favorite waitress, Ericah, appeared.

"Hey Janie, what do you need, hon?" She smiled, and cleared the table of our empties.

"Just to give you this, and tell you to have a fabulous night!" She slid her a twenty, and downed her last shot. Ericah smiled, and hugged her.

"Thank you! You just made my night! Love you guys!" She waved us out, and I nabbed the keys from Janie's purse.

"This time, Mr. Lazarus." She balled her fist, aimed it right for me, and shook it in my face. I smirked, and felt my eyebrows raise towards her.

"What does 'next time' entail? I mean, I'm *all* for whatever is it." She climbed into the car, with cheeks flushed yet again by my words. Closing our doors, our hands then met buckling our seat belts. The heat we were both radiating was steamy, and held so much promise. I heard her moan, and I almost lurched at her across the car.

"Take me home," she panted, oozing with desire, want, and need. I took her hand into mine, and intertwined our mutually sweaty fingers. She gasped for a breath, staring deeply at our conjoined hands. She swallowed hard and her eyes slowly turned back to my own. Focusing on our highway turn off, I steadied us on to the road home. *Oh, minutes more and you'll have her...*

Her hand pushed my arm higher, and she sank into my lap. First the button of my pants, and the sound of the zipper lowering was more than I could hold back. My crotch throbbed. Her hot hand was fishing for my cock. She took a tight hold, and I gripped the wheel as tightly as humanly possible. Glancing up at me again, she had a deviously sexy smile spread across her face.

"I'm hungry *now*... I can't wait for home." The last thing I saw was the twinkle in her eye turning back down to face my cock, and taking it in entirely down her throat. Focusing on the road and the darkness, the warmth and wetness was amazing. The suction, pressure, the sheer determination to continue driving while getting head was so distracting...and mind-blowing. *Literally. Almost home, Gabe. Keep going.*

Her tongue flittered across the head of my penis, and I felt her humming while she sucked. Listening to the rhythm and the song, it sounded a lot like the *Eagles, Life in the Fast Lane.* The low vibrations were shaking me at my depths, and I almost missed our driveway turn. Brining the car to an immediate halt, I parked outside of the empty guard station and code box.

"I want you in here." I said plainly, pulling her off of my cock. "Come on, let's go in." She scurried out of her side of the car, and met me at the station door. I found the key on my key ring after trying a few others first. We stepped into what can only be described as some sort of CIA headquarters. Inside was a dark wooden desk, twelve televisions, telephones and computers lined the walls. A large chair and a mini fridge were in the corner near the window. *Perfect.*

I stepped in and over to the corner, letting my pants fall to the floor. She immediately fell to her knees, and began fiercely pumping my cock into her deep throat. She was making my knees shake, and I needed inside of her. Pulling her back up so we were face to face, she threw herself at me in an instant. Our lips crashed together, teeth clanking, desperately hungry for each other.

I ran my thumb over the shoulder strap of her tank top, revealing her very contained chest. Reaching around her, I unhooked the lacey number with only two fingers. Her nipples tensed when the cool air hit them, and I took the opportunity to taste her, bite her, and suck on her pert perks of perfection.

Picking her up, I carefully set her on the desk. She pulled her skirt up around her waist, exposing the only thing I'd been thinking of for the past few hours. Palming my length, I stepped back to view this amazing picture, and hope to save it in my memory bank forever. Janie, sprawled out on the old wooden desk, with the moonlight glowing in next to her... *Irresistible.* I sucked both fingers so she could clearly see my intentions, to which she smiled.

"Yes," she moaned in a whisper, grinding herself forward on to my fingers. She was ready for me, and felt like sheer heaven. She held her knees open, and watched my fingers assault her over and over. I pushed into her entirely, pressing our chests together. She bit my earlobe, and the intensity that blew threw me was extreme.

Quickly withdrawing my fingers, I wiped her wetness all over my tip. Her smile was now a grin, as if she'd been waiting for this all day. Teasing her with the head of my cock, I pushed in and out of her a few times. I could feel her trying to suck me inside, screaming for me to really give it to her. *Not this time?* I inched my entire self into her, slower than I'd ever gone before. She wiggled and writhed around on me, but I held strong.

Dropping my hands to her ass, I squeezed her cheeks with force. I slipped my fingers down to where our flesh was connected, and began to push on her holes. Sliding my finger quickly into her ass surprised her, and she instantly came all over me. It was the heaviest, headiest feeling in the world feeling those walls, getting wetter by the minute, squeezing and coming all over the place. She steadied herself on the desk by grabbing on to a shelving unit, and the window.

While I enjoyed the slow fuck, I needed to own her now. Scooting to the side of the desk, she laid down on it completely opening herself to me. Immediately thrusting my cock into her tight hole, I found a hard, steady rhythm. I could feel my balls smacking her with every thrust, and her pussy was wet with both of our bodily emissions. It felt like her whole body was angulating around me.

I felt her tighten again, and I couldn't hold myself back any longer. I could feel my testes ascend inside me, and my balls constricted. Moments later I was pushing deeply into Janie, staring her in the eye, repeatedly releasing my load into her womb.

"Oh God," she panted and gasped. "So much throbbing." Every time my shaft pulsed, her super-sensitive nerves would fire, making her clench and squeeze all over again. She collapsed on to the desk, covering up her flushed cheeks and big smile. "Welcome home to *me*!" she giggled.

Catching our breath, we both finally stood, adjusting our clothes back to a decent state. Janie continued looking around the station, making sure no one had witnessed our indecent encounter moments before. She checked her cell phone and it was nearly 11 o'clock.

"Hop in babe, " I opened her car door, and she closed the station's door tightly. She smiled as she sat down, and I jogged back around to my door. There was a certain level of drunken exhaustion that overcame us both, and after the long workday, I was ready for bed. Driving down the driveway to my parking space, I parked and got out to open the door for her. She had her keys out to unlock the side door, and we headed inside the house.

"I'm just going to check my messages, and head to bed. Tomorrow's going to wear me out." She yawned, tossing her purse on to the counter. I headed to the sink, and filled a glass of cold water. I drank it in a few gulps, and headed over to the desk where Janie now sat at her laptop. Planting my lips on her forehead, she squeezed my arm with her hand.

"I'm goin' to bed, I'm exhausted. And you're very right about tomorrow, so don't stay up too late."

"I won't," she yawned again. "Just a few emails. I'll be there in a few minutes." Turning to go to bed I passed by our wedding picture on the wall. The smiles on everyone's face were contagious, all these years later. Getting comfortable in the sheets, I closed my eyes trying to picture that entire day. It had gone so wonderfully, and the weather was perfect. July weather was always so unplannable, but somehow we lucked out with cooler, sunny weather. I rolled over so I could smell her pillow, listening to her typing frantically through the quiet house.

Her hair glistened in the moonlight, and even though she swore against wearing all white, she looked so perfect. So crisp. So clean. So... *mine*. I can still picture her walking down the aisle with Paul, and the tears that rolled down his cheeks. The kiss...that first kiss in front of hundreds of people. Amazing. Her soft lips, and the applause of the audience, I'd never been so high in love. *That night. Oh my God, that night.*

That night it was like our first time all over again. *Jesus Gabe, settle your thoughts! You were tired a few minutes ago!* I smiled at the voice. Butterflies were so easy to get with Janie, so natural. Her ease with life, the way she confidently carried her flirtation in every relationship she had, that was how everyone always fell in love with her. As if on cue, she appeared in the doorway, stripping out of her skirt and climbing into bed.

"Love you, Janes." I sleepily mustered out, snuggling into her back, inhaling the indulgence of her hair one last time before I passed out. Her hand rested on my thigh, and we drifted into peaceful oblivion.

~

We woke up to the alarm blasting at noon. Sitting straight up, I slammed the button as hard as I could. Hangovers and loud alarm clocks were a shitty way to start any day. My phone started ringing, and I fell back against the pillows before answering.

"Awesome." I muttered, checking the caller ID. "Hello, Don." I already knew he'd be freaking out about late deliveries, and the minor details.

"Gabe! Hey! How's it going?" he sounded very upbeat and peppy, which was a good thing for this stressful of a day.

"Good, just waking up. We had a late night." Donovan chuckled in the background.

"What time do you think you'll be here?" Looking to my left was my half-covered wife, who looked tastier than ever. *Damnit!*

"I can probably be there in thirty minutes or so."

"That's great! You can deal with the booze delivery then, okay?"

"Sure, I can do that. I'll see you soon, Don." Tossing the phone into the chair, I took another gander at the wife. Holy hotness, some days I could just go at her constantly. I think this may be one of those day. I gently nudged her awake, and she opened one eye slowly.

"Morning, beautiful." I smacked her ass. "Don needs me to head over now. The alcohol is running later than he'd like." She grunted, and gave me the thumbs up. I headed into the shower, quickly washing, and throwing on my pool day attire. Janie had found a reasonable navy suit, with a button up white James Industries Polo shirt. On my way out, I wrapped my arms around her.

"I'll see you in an hour or so," she leaned into my kiss.

"Okay baby, will you bring my extra bag? I packed some special stuff in there for you later, thought you could keep it behind the bar?" she nodded.

"Of course, you'd better go. I know him, and he's probably running through the house screaming. I'll try to be a little early, too."

"All right, see you in a bit." I opened the door, and as I exited I felt a hand smack me hard on the ass. "What the hell?" I turned around and stuck my tongue out at her. "Paybacks, Janie. Paybacks."

20

Janie.

I keyed in my code at James Estate and parked next to Gabe's Nissan. The parking team looked like they had the front lot open and ready for guests to start arriving. Walking through the house, I locked the front door behind me, knowing I'd be the last one in through this door. The music was blaring, and all of the windows were open creating a perfect breeze through the house. The house was pretty dark, but for the kitchen lights on in the back of the house.

Heading that direction, I heard commotion. Pushing through the kitchen bar doors, Mylah was on the other side, digging for something.

"Hey Mylah!" I said enthusiastically. She scowled at me. "What's going on?"

"I can't find the fucking punch bowl. And of course Don wants it for his special drink." She growled, all but climbing back in to the cabinet.

"I'm going to head out to the bar. What needs done out there?" She pulled her head out, now caught in thought, squinting her eyes a little.

"I think we just need to line the bottles on the back table, and write up some drink menus." I smiled, and nodded.

"All right, I'll head out there. Good luck with that punch bowl," I winked. Weaving through the dining room, I stepped out on to the back terrace through the sliding door. I immediately headed over to the bar, which was essentially a giant shed gutted and refilled with bar parts, bar stools, and a tiny bathroom in the corner. Mylah had gotten most of it ready, and the booze was all stacked in the back in alphabetical order. I already knew Gabe had done it, as it showed his truly OCD tendencies. *He'd always had a thing about alphabetizing everything...* I tucked my purse and bags underneath the counter, and closed them into the drawer.

Behind me, I began lining up the multiple bottles of rums, vodkas, bourbons, gins, and every mix under the sun. As I peeled the plastic off of the Captain Morgan's, I looked up to see Gabe across the pool, gawking at me, waving like a stalker. *Ha-ha, you love it!* My phone buzzed seconds later, and I checked it quickly.

You're beautiful. I love you. Be over there soon.

I could feel his eyes on me, even across the yard. Meeting his gaze, I smiled and waved at him again. I slid my sunglasses back over my eyes, and continued with the bar prep. My mind wandered around in circles about how he'd been acting in the past few days, and I could come up with no solid reasons. *Maybe Mylah will know?* Maybe I didn't want to tell her... Stepping back to check my work, the line of colorful bottles was ready to go. Tapping my chin, I decided to start on the menu signs. Donovan and Gabriel made the drink menu over a month ago while we cooked out, sampling all of the different flavors.

"Looks great in here Janes." Mylah slammed the punch bowl on to the bar, giving me "the face" as she did. "Look, a punch bowl." She awkwardly pointed at the bowl with a spindly finger, speaking in some crazy voice.

"Was it even in the kitchen?" She shook her head, and closed her eyes. Smirking a little, she bit her bottom lip.

"No, you know," she put the rest of the box she carried out on to the ground. "It was in the laundry room. On the top shelf, in the corner." I wrinkled my forehead, and held up the sign.

"Do you like the sign?" She nodded, reading over all of the words.

"Blue Lagoon, Sex on the Beach, the Zombie..." She giggled. "Earthquake and Hanky Panky...whew, that one was a strong one!" I nodded in complete agreement. Weeks before that drink made us all forget an entire night. "Ahh, the Prickly Firecracker. And the punch. Looks great to me!" She took one end, and we moved in unison to hang it on the sign hooks.

"Looks great! Big letters are easy for those impaired to read."

"Pierce should be around to fill our ice in a bit. In fact, there he is now." I turned to see Pierce rolling in a giant cart full of ice. Sean followed closely behind him. He wheeled the cart around the side of the shed, where a door opened up. He pushed the cart into the wall, where it fit perfectly, and would allow us to dispense the ice all night. Sean leaned over the bar towards me, handing me the lid for the ice cart.

"Hey Janie," he began, smiling bright as ever. I carefully took the lid, and placed it over the cart of ice. Turning back towards him, I smiled. Pierce helped close the doors, and gathered the paperwork.

"Meet me up at the main house in fifteen. We've got to move a few more things." Sean nodded at him. Pierce checked his watch as he marched off over the small grassy hill.

"How've you been, Sean?" He shrugged, glancing over his shoulder.

"All right I suppose. Staying busy with work, and Delaney took Dominic to the lake for the summer with her parents. I visit sometimes, but honestly it's awkward as ever with her new fiancé." I guess it had been some time since I had run into Delaney.

"He a nice guy to Dom, at least?" He nodded.

"Oh yeah, treats him like his own." *Ah, I see the problem then*. "And he's always cordial to me, as well. I don't know. It's just one of *those* situations." I understood.

"Oh, that sucks. Staying out of trouble, for the most part?" He laughed out loud, grabbing on to his belly.

"Come on Janes, you know me." I raised an eyebrow at him. "What's that for? It's true."

"I disagree. I don't know you like I use to." He looked to the ground with disheartened eyes. His eyes rejoined my own, with a new smug smile.

"Looking forward to this evening?" I nodded. "Me too. Who knows? Maybe we'll get to spend a little time together catching up." *What the hell?* I wasn't sure I wanted to do that, but didn't want to let him on to that fact.

"Oh, sure, if there's time. I'll be working with Mylah in here all night. And I know Gabe's going to be floating around doing all sorts of business stuff." I stacked up some plastic cups while we chatted, if not to seem busier, to keep myself distracted on other things.

"All right, cool. I'll see you later on then." He tipped his head to Mylah, "Mam." He smiled, and disappeared around the corner of the bar. That entire interaction seemed off. *Forced, maybe?* I quickly turned around and locked eyes with Mylah.

"Yeah," she read my own thoughts. "That was weird." I shrugged, trying to remain neutral, remembering all of the good times over the years. Albeit the bad times did cast quite a shadow over everything else.

"It's just been a rough decade for some of us." Looking over my shoulder, I could see certain guests starting to pour in over the hill. I pointed, and Mylah moaned. "Are you changing?" She winced.

"Not entirely sure. It gets super-hot in here, but I didn't want to wear my suit the whole time, either." She looked at me, indecisive as ever, and tucked her purse underneath the counter.

"Want to jump in really quickly with me?" I smiled widely at her, motioning for her to follow me in. "Just for a few, then we can lock ourselves in the bar. "I'll just change in the bathroom once we're back inside." Her eyes darted around, as if

179

testing the idea in her head. Suddenly she nodded, and stripped off the clothes she had on over her suit. We both sprinted to the still-watered pool, and jumped straight in.

The splash drew attention to us from all sides of the yard. When I surfaced from being underwater, most all eyes were on the two of us. Donovan waved from the upper deck with two men who looked like they must be from the mob. They were also waving. And clapping. Lots and lots of clapping. Mylah laughed, and we both headed over to the hot tub.

"My?" I asked, leaning over the side of the hot tub, letting the jets massage my tired hips.

"Yeah?"

"Tonight, while we're being wenches... can you make sure to introduce me to the people you know here?" Her eyebrows frowned, and she quickly downed a bottle of water. Donovan had water bottles put sporadically around the pool. *Hydration shall not be a problem tonight!*

"Of course I will. I don't know everyone though." I nodded. She had to know more people than I had been privileged to know about. And I knew someone here tonight had the potential to ruin my husband. *How did you know?* Just that ever-so-correct women's intuition.

The water jets felt so wonderful, and I almost couldn't will myself to get out. But, with so many guests now taking their seats at the tables, I knew we needed to get back to the bar quickly. Climbing out of the hot tub, we both towel dried of, and headed back into the bar. Mylah closed the side entry doors, and locked us inside. I climbed into the bathroom first, taking my suit off, and stepping off into a long skirt and tank top. I brushed and side braided my hair, threw on some lip gloss, and headed back out.

"Perfect timing! Wait one second, Janie?" Mylah's voice was questioning, and professional. I turned to see her talking to a nice looking woman, who was smiling at me.

"Janie, this is Whendi. She's one of Don's old friends, and also a Location owner." She extended her hand to me, and I took it to shake. "I'm going to change, be right back." I turned towards Whendi.

"It's lovely to meet you, Janie." She sipped on her Long Island Tea, and I noticed her near perfect nail job. "Gabriel is always the most professional, and wonderful man." I couldn't hide my smile.

"Oh yes, he's a great man. Takes his work very seriously." Another person came to the bar, and I extended my finger to Whendi for her to hold on for one minute.

"What can I get you?"

"Ah, let me get three Hanky Panky's." I winked, and nodded, quickly going to work on the three festive beverages. I made sure to open the tiny umbrellas for the upmost amount of excitement. Handing the drinks up together and setting them on the bar, he slid a ten into the tip cup.

"Thanks! Have fun tonight!" He raised his hands to me, and wandered back over to his table, hands full of liquid confidence. I turned back to Whendi, who was finishing her tea. "Would you like another?" She nodded with excitement. "How about a double?" Her eyes grew larger.

Turning my back to mix the liquors together, I could hear his voice in the distance, coming closer and closer by the second. Gabriel. *Finally.* I gave her a new cup, a special James Industries mug with a lid. I wiped off the cup just as Gabe took a seat at the bar, resting his head on the ledge. He reached down into his bag, and pulled out a bowl filled with what looked like mints.

"Don wants these on your counter. These," he lifted one up, as Mylah was coming out of the bathroom. "These are *the* pills, in a suck-able candy form. Please stay away from these. You both know what they can do." Mylah and I exchanged a quick glance.

"Oh my," Whendi began. "That sounds like I should take a few for later. Are they free? New stock? What *is* this?" I smiled at her, and at Gabe, while she inspected a package more closely.

"This is something you'll definitely like, and your customers will crave. Take some, and if you have questions," I slid her my business card. "Just shoot me a text. This is something I've been working with Donovan on, and it seems like he's finally accepted my ideas!" She smiled widely. "I own At Your Service, LLC. We do the party planning, and offer a multitude of other services, too."

"A business woman! Good. We need more strong creative women in this market! All right dear, it's been wonderful meeting you. I can't wait to touch base in the near future regarding your Forget-Me-Not mints here. I'm off to mingle and schmooze." We shook hands again, sealing our freshly built relationship.

"I've missed you baby." He leaned over the bar, and I stretched on my toes to reach his lips. He was hot and sweaty, and looked like he was ready for bed.

"Whendi seems really nice. Do you deal with her often?" He nodded.

"Just once a month, normally. She's Don's old high school friend. They've got a history that sometimes drips into the present, too." He winked, and reached into his pocket. Pulling out the smoke pack, he pulled out one joint and blazed it to life. *Well, probably not her. Zero reaction.* I reached for the smoke, and he passed it over the bar. After a few hits, I passed it over to Mylah, who took one long draw.

"Thanks guys," she smiled, heading over to fill bar orders. We were starting to get busy. I inhaled a few more times, pushing my lungs to the ultimate point.

"All right Janes," Gabe reached for the smoke and snuffed it out. His lips quickly found mine, and with a few words

182

of love exchanged, he vanished into the afternoon heat. I joined Mylah at the bar, and we continued to sing throaty renditions of the oldies that played on the radio, and kept the glasses of the rich mobsters filled to the brim.

A few hours in, you could tell the mood of the crowd had changed, and many of the guests had adorned their swimming attire, and some of it was just horrendous. Visuals that one just did not need to carry with them, and the ones that would stay with you for a lifetime. A large man appeared at the bar, and Lonnie was stumbling up with him.

"Heya, Janie!" Lonnie slurred. "Could we get a few of Don's spec-uhl-pun-ch-es?" He smiled, just happy he'd managed to push all of the thought out. I nodded and quickly filled the cups. Handing them over, I checked my phone, and it was after 8 o'clock. I hadn't seen Gabe cross the pool path for a while, so I searched the crowd up on the deck. Nowhere. *Humph*. I tapped my fingers across the bar, as if impatiently waiting for nothing.

Turning back to take an order, I was surprised by Sean's toothy grin.

"What can I get you?" I asked, simply enough.

"How about a walk? Can you take a break for a few?" I was pretty tired, and a quick drink and smoke break couldn't hurt anything. A short walk would get me out of the steamy hotness of the bar, too.

"Yeah, I suppose I can. Just a second, and I'll be out." I turned to Mylah, and told her I was taking a break, and would be right back. "Just keep the doors locked, I'll go over the bar." She laughed at my insanity. Bunching my skirt together in the middle, I threw one leg over the bar first, and swung myself over to the bar stool.

"That was awesome to watch." Sean said in a monotone voice, with his head cocked to one side. "Come on," he motioned to the gardens. "Let's go for a walk." I nodded, taking a swig of my water on the way. My phone was awkwardly hanging in my skirts' side pocket, bouncing off of my thigh every time I took a step. I followed Sean's lead, as he seemed to know where he was going. The farther we got into the garden, the quieter the party got.

21

"Yes! This is him! *The* Gabriel Lazarus!" Donovan was definitely showing his true colors tonight, ensuring I met every business contact he'd ever run across. "Gabriel, please meet

Rocco Kartier. He's the owner of our Location 2." I extended my hand to him. He looked like some sort of Greek god. Perfect tan, perfect tailored suit that was most likely hiding the most perfectly ripped body you had ever seen. *Don't let him smell your jealousy, Gabe.*

"Hello Mr. Kartier, it's wonderful to meet you in person after all these years!" Donovan sat down at the table, and we both took a seat, as well.

"Tell me Gabriel, what is this new product line Don's been raving about? Your new idea, I've heard." *Ah, Thank God.* Finally someone who wanted to discuss some real ventures, and not that of the illegal side of our business. I spent the next forty five minutes covering all the bases of our new product line, trying to solidify my first client before the product was even out for test markets.

"So, overall, you'll see why I'm so passionate about this line. I can't wait to be able to devote myself to this project, and fully help with the first assemblies." Kartier was impressed, and took nearly a page of notes from what we had discussed.

"This sounds fabulous, and it's something I'm truly interested in. Can you keep me in the informational loop on this? I'd like to see this immediately once the first models are completed."

"Of course, that's no problem." I quickly took out my cell phone, and programmed his name and Location number in, so I would remember after tonight that he wanted to see the models. "You're all programmed in. I'll make sure you get the emails." He pushed his chair back to stand, and I stood with him, extending my hand again.

"Well, I'm going to go socialize, and attempt to find my date. I believe she was heading to the hot tub- could you point me in that direction?" I smiled at him, and directed him to the balcony.

"The hot tub and pool areas are right down there, and if you take this sidewalk here," I pointed next to where we stood. "You'll be down by the pool in no time." He nodded, and waved as he headed down the winding walkway. *Finally.*

Taking the long way around to the bar, I headed into the kitchen of the residence to use the bathroom. I opened the door to find Lizzie standing in front of me, with one of the henchmen from her Location. I rolled my eyes as dramatically as I could muster.

"What the hell are you doing here?" I could think of nothing better to say. Of all places to try to corner me. *This was a new low.*

"Oh, always so nice to see you, too, Gabriel. I was wondering if you had seen Donovan?" I shook my head, and shrugged my shoulders. "Well then, I guess you'll have to do." I crossed my arms over my chest.

"No way. Not me, not here. You're badly mistaken-" Her slender finger raised into the air, asking me to hold my thoughts.

"You will want to come with me. See, at this moment, your wife isn't safe." *What? How could she not be safe? A ploy?* I glanced towards the bar, but none of the windows in the kitchen gave an appropriate view. As if on cue, Vayne stepped forward, offering a hand to guide me wherever they were going. I put my hands in the air, giving up on causing a scene in the middle of this huge party.

"Fine, what do you want?" She frowned listening to the tone of my voice.

"You know, you use to be much better at accepting the whole one-night-stand deal. Man, what has that woman done to you?" She chuckled, and I stopped dead in my tracks. I could feel the tension and heat pouring off of my body. My fists were clenching at my sides, and I hoped for my better sense to kick in.

"You're right, I did change. I grew the fuck up because the lifestyle I was living was deplorable! It made me cheap, and useless." Staring directly into her empty eyes, I needed to make sure that she knew my words were meant for her. "That lifestyle cut me off from my family, and everyone who ever really loved me." She broke our stare to look at her feet. The mention of her family must've tripped the memories. "So, no. It's nothing *she* has done to me. It's what I did for *myself*."

I took them to the front porch of the property, doing my best to keep them out of the Estate. Vayne took a seat off to the side, picking up his phone to make a call. I sat in the chair closest to the front door. I had no idea what they wanted, or what Lizzie's plans were this time around. Janie flashed through my mind. I pictured her back at the bar, working away with Mylah. I felt my forehead wrinkle.

"God, Liz..." I rested my forehead in my hands. "What are you doing? What is the point of all of this?" I sat back in the chair, desperately waiting for her answer. Any clue how to make this all end. "This isn't the woman I remember. Even when you were fucking me, you were so checked out."

"Well so were you!" She shifted in her seat. I had obviously struck a chord. "You were nothing like years ago. So cold, distant, and angry."

"What the fuck did you expect?!" I couldn't believe that she was this dense. This obtuse. "You forced me to touch you. To have sex with you. To be intimate with you." I spat to my right. "I didn't want to do anything like that with you again." Finally looking back to her, tears filled her eyes.

"I didn't think you would have as much of a problem with all of this. Considering everything, it just seemed like it would be handled, and forgotten. We thought this was how things played out between you and Janie." The sound of her name falling off of Lizzie's lips burned deeply.

"*We*? Your boss?" She nodded. In our almost two years with her Location, the boss had always remained behind cover. "Who is your boss?" Her eyes slowly widened. Her mouth dropped open, and I waited for the words to follow.

"I...I can't..." She covered her face with her own hands now. *What in the hell is going on?* Where was the fierce woman who was determined to take me over and over to get whatever her boss wanted? She was faltering. She was questioning something. She was hesitating.

"I need you to. This is insane!" I whisper yelled in her direction. Glancing back over my shoulder, Vayne was still on the phone, smiling and laughing with whoever the lucky caller was. I turned back towards Lizzie, and our eyes met for a split second. "Please, Liz. I'd never, ever drop myself into your life like this."

"You would if someone was forcing you. You would if someone knew things about you, and was holding them against you." Watching her facial expressions become more depressed as she spoke, suddenly, it all clicked. I rested my hand on her knee.

"And someone is doing this to you. You're stuck in the middle." She nodded, and tears burst out from her eyes. Relaxing into my chair, I clung to my steady thoughts. She grasped for any hope of calm, quieting her sobs the best she could. "I don't even know where to begin. I have so many questions. What can I do to make this all stop?" She swallowed the large lump that had grown in her throat.

"They want you out of the business." My jaw crashed on to the floor. *Out of the business*? "They see Donovan as a street threat, and they're ready."

"Ready?" Both feet were now tapping on the porch. "I just need to know what that means. And who it is." If Lizzie wasn't behind these instances and these weren't her petty ideas on how to gain business...or fame...or me... *Who is doing*

188

this? Someone who wants to hurt me, specifically. My head was spinning violently out of control. *Janie. "Your wife isn't safe."* My head snapped back towards her, and I sat on the edge of the chair.

"If I tell you who it is, he'll hurt me and my family. My boss is...horrible. He thinks of no one but himself, and places demands, needs and wants on all of us in different ways. He's always using me for his dirty work. And I know he was planning this for quite some time." She ground her fingers against themselves, creating an awkward rubbing sound.

"He, huh? A male then?" She peered over my shoulder, carefully, and nodded. My head was still whirring with more thoughts than I had ever had in my life. She looked down at her watch. "You in a hurry?" I squinted my eyes in her direction.

"No, I was told to keep you entertained until 8:30." I wrinkled my face, and pointed in Vayne's direction. "Well, our last meeting left me rather upset. I told the boss getting to you that way wasn't working." She shrugged.

"So, he's going to hurt me in another way?" Her face slipped again, this time to a darker, even drearier place. "Lizzie, tell me what he's going to do." She fiercely shook her head.

"Don't." She held up her hands. "Look," she leaned in so we were closer. "I already said too much. I'm sorry I had no choice. Just get out. *Please*?" This seemed so backwards. For weeks I'd feared even being around her devious ways, and somehow I'd not ever even noticed that she was putting on an act. *Why would you notice?* The time you spent with her years before had been just that—all an act.

"I just want to be extremely clear here- we're talking about the drugs, right?" She nodded, and I back to her. "So, if I step out of that side of the business, this will stop? Your boss will leave me alone?" She cleared her throat quietly.

"If I'm understanding it all, then yes." She motioned to use quotation marks with her fingers. "'There's only room for

189

one boss in Indiana,' seems to be on repeat whenever he speaks." She glanced at her watch again.

"Time?"

"It's 8:20. Almost time to head back." She fidgeted in her chair, and Vayne stood up to stretch his legs, slipping his phone back into his pocket. I fell back in the chair, needing to collect the swirling thoughts again. All this time I was plotting against the wrong person. And now, I don't even know who that person was. I exhaled deeply.

"Come on, Lizzie. It's time to head around to pick up and go. All these suits are making me nervous." Vayne's eyes never stopped moving around the beautiful extravagance that was this Estate. Exactly why someone now wanted what Donovan had. *Donovan*. What am I going to do with him? Tell him? Keep it to myself? Another week and the first models would be done of my product line, then I'd be paid. I rubbed my temples with my thumbs.

"You coming with us, Gabe?" She asked, flatly. I shook my head.

"No, I'll be back there in a few." I couldn't even turn to look at them. They, and whoever else was a part of this, all knew the history, the plans, and the details. How have I missed all of the signs? All of the warnings?

My head began to replay the conversations between Lizzie and I. Parts of what she said left swirling around leaving my questions unanswered, and with little direction. *Oh my God.* Over, and over again, Janie and I are forced into these games of fuckery!

"Damnit!!" I yelled, slamming my fists on to the arms of the chair. And then it fell over me..."*Your wife isn't safe.*" Images of Janie flashed through my mind, and suddenly I felt tense, and completely on edge. I felt a huge disconnect from her, and stood almost in a full sprint back into the house. *Was what she said a warning*? Jesus, I needed to get to Janie.

My feet only hit the floor a handful of times all the way through the house, and out on to the balcony. Looking over the edge to the pool, it was hard to find anyone in the mass of people. I could see Mylah in the bar across the way, and watched for a few moments to wait for Janie to pop out from somewhere. *Shit, Gabe!* Where is she? I pulled out my phone, and noticed it was 8:40. I started running down the sidewalk towards the bar.

"You seen Janie?" I asked, gasping, completely out of breath.

"No, not for about an hour. She said she was taking a break. You text her?" I shook my head and pulled out my phone. I was barely breathing, having the worst sinking feelings I'd had in years.

Answer Me.

"Give me a double bourbon, please." I could barely push the words out. Mylah stared at me like I was unhinged and dangerous. I didn't feel that way completely yet... but I was definitely getting there. *FUCK.* I rocked my head back, and downed the entire glass in one gulp. She wasn't answering. I stood up, looking past the bar into the gardens, and thought I saw a figure move. *Janie?* Shit.

22
Janie.

Only ten minutes in, and I was already questioning why I had come out here with Sean. The gardens were dark and too quiet. Too quiet for anything he and I had to talk about these days. We'd turned and circled so many different statues, I wasn't even positive what corner of the gardens we were in. We approached another statue, this one was a large Goddess Tara replica with benches surrounding. I noticed there was something on one of the benches, but didn't think much of it.

"Well, Janie." He cleared his throat, his voice dark and heavy. "I've brought you out here tonight for your help. Your help, and your…" he closed the gap between us, barely touching my shoulder with his clammy hand. "Your *expertise*. See," turning again, he seated himself on a nearby bench. "My business, *my* company has some competition right now, and we need that competition to go away. My boss is a ruthless sonofabitch, and he's forcing me to do this right now." He chuckled, and I felt my breath stop. *I think your heart did, too.*

"What? I don't know what you're talking about Sean." I turned to leave the garden, but his words stopped me in my tracks.

"If you leave, they'll *kill* Gabe." There was no feeling in his voice. No care for his friends, just nothing. I couldn't make my feet take another step with a threat like that. Slowly turning back to face him, my face distorted with confusion. My hands started to shake, and every synapse in my body began to shoot off the most insanely nervous feelings.

"What??" was all I could muster in a whispered panic. He nodded, standing up next to the bench where he sat. Reaching his hand to me, he motioned for me to sit with him. Cautiously, I inched towards him.

"I'm sorry to scare you, Janie." I sat on the far side of the bench, and Sean took seat on the other end. "I'm surprised you don't have more questions, honestly." I couldn't gage the situation, or his mood. The terror of the unknown was over taking me, and I just wanted to go home. He obviously wanted to play twenty questions, so I did my best to oblige.

"*Your* company?" I ran my tongue along my teeth. "You work for James Industries," I said flatly. He nodded sideways, and his expression turned contrite.

"Well, sort of. Not for much longer though, but that secret needs to stay between us." Swallowing hard, I took the bait.

"Not much longer? Who is making you do this?"

"Making me?" He laughed loudly, holding his belly and rocking back on the bench. "No one is *making* me, Janes! It's just part of my job." My head was spinning. He was talking in circles on purpose, giving only the parts he'd need to give me. He cleared his throat again, putting his hands on his thighs to

194

stand up. "There's another part of this job that I've got to take care of tonight."

Watching him slink around, he ended up near the bench with the box on it. He pulled out a blanket, and a bottle of something else, which he opened and promptly gulped down. With the darkness setting in and no other lights around, the moonlight was all there was to light the way. *A blanket? What the fuck? Is this for real?* Suddenly, there was a loud cheer from back at the Estate, and I turned my head in that direction, taking my eyes off of him.

His hand rested firmly on my shoulder and took me by surprise. I gasped at the sudden contact, instinctively attempting to pull away from the connection. Looking up at him, he was not the same man he was years before. *This is not your friend!* His eyes were empty and broken. With this realization, panic settled in the pit of my stomach. I recognized the look on his face, as I'd seen it in so many others before they'd taken my solace, yet again.

"Sean," I spoke softly. "Whatever you're thinking, you don't have to do it." He swallowed, and nodded.

"I know." He sat next to me on the bench now, his hands still forcefully holding me in place. His arm now laid across my shoulders. "I don't want to force you..." Our faces were so close together, I could feel the end of each beer stained breath on my cheek. One tear fell from my eye, and I broke our stare to look into my lap. My heart was breaking into thousands of pieces. *Just let it happen. If you don't... the consequences...* "But, I will fuck you tonight, if only to hurt your husband." He smiled deviously. I swallowed hard. He stood and quickly laid the blanket out across the bench, letting his pants slide to the ground.

Defeated. *There is no fight when your husband's life is threatened.* I fell to my knees on the ground, turning myself completely away from him. Pulling my skirt up around my waist,

I gagged when I heard him suck breath through gritted teeth. I'll never understand how people can be so turned on by forcing someone to do something against their will... More tears fell.

"If I do this, they won't hurt him?" His hand latched on to my hip, pulling me into his now stiff shaft.

"Correct. However, he still needs to get *out* of the drug business." He sank into me slowly, and I sighed, feeling the unwanted entry. I rested my forehead on my forearms so my head wouldn't hit the cement of the bench. I couldn't help but think how I was going to even approach the topic with Gabe. *Will you tell him about this?* The thought instantly made me tense, making every thrust hurt more than the last.

"Loosen up, Janes," he sputtered out, changing his position to try and entice my body to react. "I'm not trying to hurt you." His thumbs pushed into my hips, holding me tighter against his thrusts. His grasp was changing. He was pulling me closer, and preparing to finish the deal. In this moment, I felt so confused. So used, so broken. Only a few years before, at least the two of us had felt something for each other. At least back then friendship was valued. *I never would have thought he'd end up no better than Michael...*

Thinking back to the night he had come to Donovan's in the middle of our tryst. *He was so hungry for you.* His eyes burned with pleasure and need. Back in those days, his overly scented cologne hugs were the most annoying thing about him. *And now...* I lifted my head to look around the garden darkness, again stopping on the beautiful Goddess statue. The darkness made it hard to decipher which color Goddess she was. I was hoping it was black or blue, considering.

Where had I gone wrong? People constantly taking and taking from me over the years. It never seemed to matter how my life was going, either. For no specific reason, but their own selfish personal gains. Where in my history had I made these types of behaviors okay? I felt him pulling out of me, and in my deep thought, hadn't even noticed he had finished.

"Ahh," he sighed. "You really do get better with age." Nauseated by the comment, I couldn't will myself to move.

Sinking back on to the bench, I let my knees sink into the cool ground, and pulled my skirt back down around me. Sean stood a few feet away, fixing his clothing, and checking his phone. He walked towards me, and I turned away from him, hiding my face again in my arms.

"I need you to remember a few things, okay?" I did my best to be strong, and hold in any sobs for a different time. I slowly looked up, watching him out of the corner of my eye. "*This* is a secret." He pointed between the two of us. "Your job now is to get your husband to back out of this business. Okay?" The silence grew in the heavy air, and his foot impatiently tapped on the ground. I could see his phone light turning on and off in his hands, like he was checking the time every ten seconds. "If he doesn't get out of this business, I'll be forced to completely take him out." He stood, and I could feel his hand extended to me. "Come on, Janie. Stand up." He wasn't asking.

"Yeah, all right." I stood without his aide. "I understand. I guess." The smile the crept across his face shown a glimpse of the flashy colors I'd never seen in him before. Full of rage, desperation, anger and hate. *But towards you and Gabe? How did that happen?* One thought led to another, led to another... and suddenly, something clicked. "All for *your* company, huh?"

His smile fell a little, and he took a step back, speechless. I know I didn't have all the details, but I knew enough to see he was behind this. It had to be him. The cause of Gabe's lack of focus. The crazy vibe, and local run-ins. *But now what? Does Gabe know?*

"Exactly. It's all about business, and being on top." He dropped his phone back into his pocket, and turned to leave the garden. "I'm heading back to the party now, care to walk with

197

me back?" Almost laughing, I shook my head. "All right, well, until next time, then." *Next time? Oh, come on.*

I remained standing, frozen in place, until I could no longer see his shadowy outline. Taking seat on the bench again, I tried to steady my thoughts. *It's obviously Sean's company... a Location?* What was I going to tell Gabe about this? How could I approach the subject? He loved this job for so many reasons, and being the 'Midwest kingpin' was never one of them. I wiped my eyes again, and reached into my pocket for my phone. 5 missed texts, and even more missed calls. *Ohh, Gabe... I'm so sorry.* My heart sank even more.

Sorry! Out for a walk. Be back to the bar in five!

I headed back out of the garden in the direction I thought the party was. I crossed over a small hill, and around a tight bend. The lights of the party were starting to come into view as I came around the koi pond. I could see the bar, and a familiar figure coming towards me quickly. *I hope you have your story figured out, Janes.* Gabe's big body was barreling at me, and engulfed me in his arms before I could speak.

~

"Janie." I inhaled her in as deeply as I could, and almost couldn't let her go. I had no idea how I was going to tell her about what I'd learned, and I really just wanted to get her home. Her face looked tired and worried as her thumbs trailed across my cheek.

"I've got to get back to the bar and help Mylah. Are you done with the work part of this party?" Her words fell into my ears, but making the thoughts process to speak was a whole other story. A story that wasn't happening easily.

"Yeah, I'm done with the work part." I clasped my fingers with hers, and we slowly made our way back to the bar. It was almost 9, and some of the guests had gone. The music played loudly over our silence. "You want to head home?" I didn't even know if I could leave, but it seemed like the best option. I needed to clear my head.

"Sure, let me just wrap things up with the bar, okay?" We stopped next to the bar, and she put her phone on to the counter. "Go check on Don, then come back to get me." I squeezed her fingers one last time, and helped boost her back over the bar.

"There you are! I was beginning to worry." Mylah jokingly said as she shook up another Blue Lagoon.

"Yeah, I ah..." She was tripping over her own words, and she blushed a little. *What the hell?* "Sorry about that." She glanced up at me nervously, and smiled.

"I'll be back in a bit. I'm going to go find Donovan, and say some goodbyes." Without much extra thought, I headed up the path to the balcony where I had caught a glimpse of him moments before. There were cups and cans scattered everywhere, and lining every walkway. Looking to my left, the pool was now empty, and a few couples remained in the hot tub.

"Gabe!" Donovan was stumbling out of the kitchen sliding door.

"Hey Don, I need to take off and get Janie home."

"Oh, man! What?!" His drunkenness was astounding. He wreaked of his special punch. "You look upset, man. Are you okay, man?"

"Yes, Don. I'm fine. We're just really tired, and need to go home. It's been an extremely long day." He nodded, and raised his hand.

"Well, shit! All right then! I really do appreciate your help, G. And Janes, too." He set his drink down on the table, and extended his hand for a shake. He was oblivious to all of the crazy things that had happened tonight. I shook his hand firmly.

"See you Monday," I said, grabbing his forearm with my free hand. "Ease up there, tiger. You're about three shades to the wind!" I patted his shoulder, and headed back down to the bar to collect Janie. As I approached, I watched her cleaning up. She still looked distant. I leaned on the bar.

"Excuse me? Could I get a..." I asked, jokingly. Janie turned and smiled.

"Get outta here, ya crazy!!" Mylah yelled from across the bar, dramatically winking at me. "You taking off now, Janes?" She nodded in her direction, and said something that I missed. Janie leaned way over to collect her bags from under the counter, giving me a nice view through her white skirt. *No panties. MMmm...*

"Will you help me over?" She was wearing the bags, and had put her other things on the bar. Reaching for her, I picked her up under her arms, and over the bar she came.

"Come on, time to go home." She leaned into me, and we walked arm and arm to the cars. I followed her home being unable to form any legitimate thoughts about what had happened tonight. I knew I needed to fill her in, and there didn't seem to be a better way to go about it. Checking the radio clock, it was just past 10.

23

"Janes," I set her bags on the kitchen floor, and she turned to me yawning. "Want to join me on the deck?" She nodded.

"Of course, I'll be out after I use the bathroom." I locked the house up, and headed over to the bar. I was thankful to be away from the Estate, and the drama and conspiracies that seem to be looming over us there. Home always made me feel calmer, and more in focus.

Grabbing two glasses I filled them both with ice. Bourbon in one, vodka with lemons in the other. My mind drifted to the kids, and I wondered how their past few days at camp had gone. Soon they'd be heading to the lake with Sam and Paul. I was thankful for this, too, knowing they'd be safely tucked away from everyone causing these problems.

Reaching under the bar, I opened the tin of smoke. Opening the pack, I pulled out a joint and lighter, and slid them into my shirt pocket. Heading out to the deck, I took a seat at the bar. I couldn't decide how to tell her, or when to tell her. *Maybe a little relaxation, first?* She stepped out of the sliding door moments later, wearing only a robe.

"Here I am," she muttered jokingly, heading straight for the hot tub controls. She cranked the timer on, and turned on the tub's music and light system. "Hope you don't mind if I take a dip. After tonight," she paused and sighed. *Maybe she knows something?* "I could really use this." I nodded and watched in awe as she opened her robe, and let it fall on to the deck.

I was all but gawking at her. Completely naked, she glimmered from the hot tub's lights. Her toes touched the water, and I watched her sink in, inch by inch. My eyes stopped just above her knee to see a scrape with a small blood droplet running from it. *A fresh wound?* She winced a little lowering the wound into the water, but finally the pain must have eased. She relaxed into the hot tub seat, her breasts floating in the water, gently rocking in the waves.

I walked around the tub, setting her drink down behind her. Sitting down, I dipped my legs into the hot, steaming water. Watching her breasts was waking me up in all of the right places. I sipped on my bourbon, and took her in. There was a heavy silence in the air, until her hand landed on my knee.

"You coming in here with me?" Her fingers trailed gently up my thigh. I could feel her need, and hesitation. "Please?" *Don't make her beg, Gabe.*

"Of course," I drank the rest of my bourbon, and slipped my shirt off carefully. Pulling the joint out of my pocket, I held it up to her. She nodded, and gulped her vodka. It lit quickly and I sank into the tub next to her, passing it to her. "Did you have fun today?" I could barely push the words out.

"It was all right." Her eyes darted around, and she inhaled again. "You know," she turned herself to face me, holding herself up with an arm on the side of the tub. She stared into the water for a few moments. "Never mind." She shook her head and smiled, passing the joint back to me.

She leaned into my side, and finished her drink while I finished the smoke. Lost in the music, and taking in the beautiful night sky, I pushed my leg into hers, distracting her just enough. She wrapped her leg around mine, and her fingers began to wander around my abdomen. Pressing my lips to her forehead, I gently grasped her neck, trailing my fingers in between her breasts.

Her mouth turned up to mine and our lips found each other, first gently- and then overcome with hunger. She was on top of me after one blink. Letting my fingers explore, they dove into her soft folds that were already primed and ready for the taking. She moaned, and it vibrated deep inside of me. My cock throbbed and my hands rose to her shoulders, pulling her into me. Our bodies crashed together and I was lost in the moment.

202

"Gabe," she said moaning, reaching for my shorts. I lifted myself enough so she could pull them down, and they made it to my thighs. She handled me roughly, pulling and twisting in every direction. I gritted my teeth together, and pressed my face into the breasts bouncing before me. Sucking her nipple as it passed my lips, I ran my teeth along its pert length. She screamed out in pleasure.

"Do you want me, Janie?" I pressed out the corrupted words between intensely tightened lips. She tightened her grasp on my shaft, and leaned into my face. I could smell her lemony sweetness, and could hear her ragged breathing. She slid on to my shaft, causing waves to lap up over the edge of the tub.

"Yesss," she hissed, looking more deviant than ever. She smiled a little, and I felt her walls tighten around me. I could only let my head fall back against the head rest. She rocked against me, taking every bit of me she could. Her tongue probed in between my lips, and I willingly let her in. Clasping my hands around the back of her head, I dipped my tongue deeply inside her. My fingers found her nipples and my hands engulfed her breasts, that were overflowing out of my hands. Breaking our kiss I pulled her towards me, sucking her breasts in to my mouth. She moaned loudly, thrashing harder on my shaft.

"Give it to me, baby," I whispered in her ear. Slamming down on me again, clenching tightly, she was shattered. Her walls quavered, and my cock pounded. Her fingernails pressed into my shoulders, stinging enough to make my balls tingle. I felt her wave of fluid rush all over me, and couldn't hold myself back any longer. Reaching behind her, I grabbed my balls and gave them a hard pull.

"OOoohh!" She screamed as I hardened even more to come inside of her. The intense waves of pleasure fell over us both, and we both stayed connected, riding out all of the roller coaster of feelings. Her head fit perfectly on my shoulder, and she nuzzled into my neck. Wrapping my arms around her tightly, I pulled her body into mine. Lifting her head, her mouth found mine again. Distracting me with her kiss, she slid off of my shaft, and moved next to me in the tub, leaning her head back against the rest.

"Do you want to stay out here for a bit?" She moaned, and nodded. "Want more to drink? Smoke?" She nodded, and shrugged. I couldn't hide my laugh. She was completely sated. Peaceful and blissed out. I headed into the house to refill our drinks. *She won't be peaceful for too much longer with your news...* Right. Unavoidable. I headed back outside with a fresh refill of all our needs.

"Here you go," I handed her drink down to her, and carefully sat back down. "I need to talk to you about a few things that happened tonight."

"Okay, guess it's good that I'm comfortable?" I swallowed hard, chuckling slightly at her. Truthfully, I didn't think she'd be very comfortable after hearing this. "I found out tonight that someone is black mailing me, and they want me out of this business." I cautiously watched her face, but there was no change. She only took a long, slow drink. I mimicked her motion, taking a drink of my own.
"Whoever has been setting me up has been using someone from my past to get to me." Here we go.

She sat up a bit, sensing the shakiness of my voice. She put her hand on my shoulder. She looked upset.

"Go on," she encouraged quietly.

"Lizzie's boss. For the past few weeks, her boss has been forcing her on me." She sat back in her chair, stunned. "There were only a few specific instances, but I-" she raised her hand.

"Forcing *her* on *you*?" She swallowed again. "Like you *fucked* her?" I shook my head rubbing my temples momentarily.

"Yes, and no." Tears filled her eyes, and she did her best to hear me out. "The last time she was in my office, days before the party, we had sex." I could barely look at her face. "It wasn't enjoyable on my end. In fact, the last encounter was recorded." She wrinkled her face, and looked more disgusted than ever. "No, no. Not for pleasure. I recorded it because at first I had thought that it was just Lizzie trying to get at me. But after tonight-"

"Why is tonight any different? I don't understand." She was starting to spiral before my eyes. "How are they blackmailing you to have sex with her?"

"Tonight she pulled me away because her boss needed her to, and she had her orders, but instead she filled me in on their plans." *Poor Janie.* Now she just looked confused. "She wouldn't tell me who her boss *was*, but that they were going to move to take over the top dealer spot in the Midwest again. Somehow Donovan has stepped on some toes along the way." I glanced at her face to try and gauge what her thoughts were.

Tears were silently pouring from her eyes. I could tell she was hanging on to her composure with every thin string she had left.

"Lizzie. She's the one from the bar, right?" I nodded. "The one from the Phoenix, way back when?" I nodded again. "And *whoever* was using her to get to you? To get to me?" She pointed into her chest with her finger. I nodded again. Sobs rained from her swollen eyes now, and she quickly reached for me, burying her head in my neck.

I expected her to be upset, but this isn't exactly how I had figured it would go. She sat back, still sobbing, but visibly trying to calm herself. She held her pointer in the air, waiting for the first moment she could speak.

"Please don't hate me." It slipped from my lips before I could stop it. She paused for a second, holding her breath. She shook her head no, and looked at me adoringly through tears. The emotion flowing out of her was palpable, and so confusing.

I watched her intently, taking another sip of my bourbon. She took long, slow, steady breaths, doing what she could to settle.

She picked up her glass, and took a small sip of the vodka, wincing as it hit the back of her throat. I could feel my heart beating out of my chest. I had no idea what she was thinking, or about to say. I felt like I should brace myself for anything considering what I had just told her. She set her drink back down, and wiped the tears from her eyes.

"I'm sorry." She began, sniffling a little in between breaths. "Gabe, I know who is black mailing you." Just uttering the words caused more tears to fall, and I lost my breath. *What? How would she know this?*

"Who?" I said cockily, almost not believing what she was saying. She sat in front of me now unable to speak. Her mouth hung open, and her faced looked terribly pained. Her forehead wrinkled, and her eyes grew sad, and even darker.

Her face con torted as if she couldn't find the words to tell me who it was. Tears filled her eyes, and rolled loudly down her cheeks. Sobs escaped her lips, and then it all started to fall in to place. She calmed back down, steadying herself for more revelations.

"What time did Lizzie find you tonight?" I squinted at her, she was avoiding the answer. "Please, tell me what I need to know, so I know if I'm telling you the right truth."

"I think it was about eight? Give or take a little. She kept checking her watch. She had one of the Location workers with her, too." She nodded, and looked down to the water. "His name is Vayne. We sat on the front porch of the Estate, and Vayne was on the phone."

"Just before eight," her body visibly shook. "Sean came to the bar, and asked me to go for a walk." She gasped, and held in another sob. "We walked through the gardens, and he filled me in on things. He, too, kept checking his watch." Her eyes locked with mine, sealing the nail closed on my worst thoughts.

"Did he fucking hurt you?!" Leaning towards her, I very gently put my hand on her knees. "Janie?" I asked, my voice barely audible.

"He wants his company back on top in the area. He wants you out of the business, or," she stopped breathing, and her pale face looked hazily into my own. "Or he'll *kill* you. And me."

"WHAT?!" I was yelling, too loud, and she cried again. Wrapping her in my arms was all I could do. I could feel her entire body shaking, and her fingertips were cold. Freezing cold. "Janie," I pulled her into my view. "Did he *touch* you??" I didn't know her eyes could've looked any heavier than they already did.

"Yes." She whispered, laying her head back down, ashamed. So many thoughts were coursing through my head that it was becoming a dangerous place. I couldn't swallow all of the information I had just gotten, and how perfectly it all made sense. I threw myself away from her in the hot tub, as the rage I was feeling was pulsing through my body, and I didn't want to direct any of it at her. I felt hot, and crazy.

A hurricane of thoughts poured through my head. Sean had taken advantage of her years before, due to his own immature crush. That had only caused problems. I closed my eyes to collect my thoughts, and the flashes began. Flashes of driving with him in the James Industries van. Remembering how location four was attacked immediately after our delivery, and we were unscathed. Thinking of how he would show up, and disappear at all the right and wrong times. *Perfectly planned*. I leaned out of the hot tub, laying my head on the cool deck wood.

The water shifted in the tub, and I quickly turned to check on Janie. She was now sitting on the cushioned chair, curled back up in her robe. The fluffiness of the robe made her look even smaller, and more fragile. I climbed out and wrapped my towel around myself.

"He said if I didn't, he would do it *forcefully*." She swallowed, emphasizing the 'force'. "I couldn't even handle the thought... I think you need to make some decisions, and fast. Our kids will be home in a few weeks, and I don't want them to know anything about this."

"Sean?!" I asked perplexed, and feeling more lost than ever. She nodded. "After all these years, this is how it turns out." I felt broken and violated all over again. I wasn't even in this business for that reason. Working at James Industries designing new products and life-saving boats, was my dream job. This was all just extra. *Shouldn't he know that?* My head spun.

His company? *What does that even mean?* My poor wife. Now taking the torture because someone's got it out for me, and they know she's an easy target. Looking at her, I could see her strength and resilience was shaking. I wondered what she had endured, and if she would need time to mentally recover.

"I need to think this through. This is...a *lot*." I winced. "It affects *everything*." She nodded, still coiled around herself. I headed slowly over to where she sat trembling. Sitting next to her, I pulled her into my side. "I'm so, so sorry Janie." Stroking her forehead seemed appropriate. Her silence told me what her words could not yet do. "How about we head to bed? Look," I turned her face up towards mine. "He's not going to hurt me, Janie. We've dealt with so much worse than him." Her eyes closed, and she pulled her robe closed tightly around her.

"Sleep. Sleep sounds good. We can figure this out in the morning." I nodded, and stood quickly. Reaching my hand to her, I pulled her to standing, and into a steadying embrace. Walking through the bedroom, leaving all of the lights off, she turned the music on softly. There weren't many words said tonight, but I knew I'd come out on top of this. No one was going to hurt my wife again. She laid in the crook of my arm, and we both drifted off.

24

I awoke sweating profusely, lost in my dream, not even sure of my own surroundings. Looking quickly next to me, Janie was sound asleep, still curled in a semi-fetal position. Rubbing my eyes, I sat up and checked the clock. *Only 2:24? Ugh, come on.* I carefully crawled over and around Janie, and headed out to the kitchen to get a drink of water. I refilled the glass again after the first drink, and glanced out the window towards my mother's house. Her living room television was on. We both had bouts of insomnia, but for me, this surely wasn't that.

Grabbing my cell, I landed on the couch and was thankful for its plentiful fluff. I had a few missed calls. One from Donovan, and another from Greg. I could really use his advice about some of this, but I was hesitant to bring him into it at all. Heather had pulled away so much over the years, claiming the drama that follows us was just too hard to handle. Janie would be devastated if their relationship took any further assault.

I couldn't let this go. I feel like my choices are limited, and Sean's not given many options. He wants me out of the business, but what about Donovan? Donovan was signing off on my latest design this week, and the personal payment for the design patent would be coming. I took another long swig of the cool water. I needed to talk to Don before I made any big decisions. *How long do you have?* I had no idea, and I'd hoped that Janie would be able to discuss the events a bit more.

The sheer rage that overcame me when I thought of what he did to her. I was disgusted knowing that Sean knew all of her weak spots, and everything her past held. He played her, and used her for his own disgusting purposes. *How is this even supposed to be dealt with*? One of her oldest friends, now turned into a demanding, comfort stealing prick. *He's no better than the person he use to help protect her from. Guess he learned from the best.*

I opened up my email, and quickly shot one off to Donovan that we needed to talk, first thing on Monday. I felt like fresh air would be the best decision, and cool me back down. Sitting on the porch, to my surprise, my phone suddenly rang. It was Donovan.

"That was fast." I said flatly, yawning into the phone.

"I figured you were awake, and so am I." I heard him inhale. "I can't seem to get relaxed, so, what's going on?"

"You've hired a rat, Don."

"Oh, stop. Who's pissed you off now?" I couldn't handle his joking nature right now. This wasn't a joke.

"I'm being blackmailed, and I'm almost positive Janie was forced into sex tonight at your party." My temples were starting to hurt from gritting my teeth together so hard.

"How in the hell do you know this? Who is it?" I still didn't hear what I was hoping for. The backing, and concern I needed to hear so desperately.

"I know because I was told by Lizzie, who was so upset by our last feeling-less meeting that she couldn't do it again." I paused long enough to let it all sink in. I heard him swallow. "And then just a few hours ago, Janie told me how she was accosted by Sean in the garden. His demands? For me to be out of the business. If I don't, he'll kill me. And then her." Silence took over the line.

"Is this for real? I mean, I..." he stopped, tripping over every attempt to clarify. "What do I need to do? Is- How's? I-" he was speechless, and sounded emotional. "Is Janie okay?"

"She's still asleep, thankfully. I honestly don't really know how she's handling it yet. She was pretty quiet after she told me. Don, you need to get rid of Sean immediately. Change the codes, bump his location."

"But his bosses won't go for that!" I could hear how losing an account affected his psyche, and I knew he'd react this way. He still wasn't catching on to what was so obviously right in front of all of our faces.

"Don, he *is* the boss! It's *his* company. *His* location. *He* wants to be the Midwest kingpin! *He* wants me dead. Think about it, man. Up until now, he had the perfect plan. The perfect cover." Silence fell like a cloud over the conversation. It was then I knew he was putting it all together, just as I had.

"Jesus, Gabriel. I don't know what to say, except that I'm sorry. Can we talk about this some later on this afternoon, or this evening? I will absolutely protect the two of you the best I can. Are the kids safe? I will send security to them if you'd like." The thought had crossed my mind, but honestly I think the children would have me killed if they had to have security detail following their every move.

"Sure, I'll come over tomorrow, and we can discuss it in detail."

"Gabe," he interrupted, almost panicked. "I don't want to lose you from my company. Somehow, some way, we can fix this." He sounded very genuine, but at this point, it was only about our safety. *Mainly hers.*

"All right, I'll text you later. Night, Don." Hanging up, I did feel a bit of relief knowing that this wasn't an even larger conspiracy drawing my boss in, too. Maybe there was hope that we could get Sean before he got us. I muted my phone, headed back towards the couch, and turned on the television. *Law & Order SVU* played on the screen and I blankly stared into the image. I couldn't stop thinking about Janie, and what had truly happened in that garden. I wanted to rip him apart. I wanted to hit him once for every single touch and finger he laid on her. Who cares what he's done to me, I thought pausing to check the clock. *4:46.* What he's done to me doesn't matter. But he will surely pay for every hair out of place on my wife's head.

~

Waking to the sounds of birds chirping, and the smell of a fresh breeze wasn't what I had expected. Opening my eyes slowly, I realized I had never made it to bed again. I sat up, hoping the headache I had acquired during the night had gone. I could hear Janie out on the deck talking to someone. Hopping to my feet, I knew we'd still need to finish talking about what had transpired between her and Sean. I just didn't want to break her by doing it.

Peeking around the corner, she was sitting at the table, smiling and chatting away. I tried listening a little bit to see who was on the other end.

"Really? They had that for lunch?" She giggled, and I checked the clock. How long did you sleep, man? It was already after two in the afternoon. *Shit.* I turned back to see her real smile. The beautiful definition of what she was. A carefree, overly trusting, passionate, empathetic, highly intelligent, workaholic woman, who was now in the middle of another horrible situation. I smiled through my gritted teeth because I knew who she was talking to, and I was thrilled with the timing. "Aw, all right honey. I love you, too. Of course, I'll tell him. Okay, talk to you soon!" She looked towards the door and caught me gazing at her.

"Oh, quit staring," she muttered sardonically. I didn't get a full smile, but she did smirk in my general direction.

"I can't quit. I wondered who that was... Lilah?" I raised an eyebrow, and she nodded, smiling widely. "Oh, good. How're they doing? This is the last week at camp, right?" I turned my back to her to pull a banana off the counter.

"Yes, this is the last week. Lil's excited to head to the lake. I think she's about had enough of camp. Galen is still having a blast at camp, and he would like to live there." She stopped to giggle, making me smile, too. "He's loving the bog, and all the bugs and mud. Shocking, I know." She whizzed around me in the kitchen, organizing and cleaning. Reaching out, I grabbed her wrist, slowing her down.

"Hey. We need to finish talking about yesterday, and last night." Her head sank instantly. Using my pointer gently underneath her chin, I nudged her head back up so she was looking at me. "None of that, Janie. This isn't your fault. We need to sit down, and talk through this." She shook her head no, and tears sprung to her eyes. "Breathe, baby. Your therapist would remind you not to bottle it up, and that we've been through tough stuff before."

"This feels different. I'm scared." *Oh no.*

"How is this different than Michael? Or the abduction?" She shrugged, and headed out on to the side patio. She silently sat down in the chair, trying to control her breathing. She gazed into the wooded distance, and finally down to her toes.

"For a few reasons. One, I'm having a hard time okaying in my head that he didn't force me. Parts of me wish I would've fought him..." She looked at me, with an indescribably heartbreaking face. "What can I say now? I willingly had sex with Sean, while he threatened my husband's life." A few tears silently fell, and her hands covered her face.

"Janie," I began slowly, carefully plotting my words. She had just confirmed that he had forced her to fuck him. My blood was boiling, and my heart broke into a thousand pieces. Which is exactly what he wanted to happen. "He did force you, baby." I sat next to her, sliding the other chair closer to her. "Has he done this to you at any other time?" She shook her head.

"No, this was a one-time thing. So far." Clearing her throat, she added, "He did threaten a 'next time,' but that was open ended." She sat back in her chair nibbling on her fingernail.

"Was there anything else he said, specifically?" I was doing my best to remember all of this.

"Yeah, what happened between him and I is a secret. He didn't want me to tell you, and said that it needed to be secret." Lost in my own thoughts again, I found myself chewing on my bottom lip. "How about you? What info did you learn from Lizzie?" The long, slow sigh escaped my lips before I could stop it.

"A few minutes after we'd sat down in the front, away from everyone, she told me that you weren't safe." Her head snapped up instantly, forehead frowned, and she looked even more upset than before. "I know how it sounds. But she backtracked after she said it, and she was sort of threatening me with that, too. I talked to Donovan late last night about it all, and he's going to terminate Sean tomorrow." She sat up suddenly on the edge of her seat, almost jumping out of her skin.

"But that shows Sean that I told you! That you know! No! Please don't do it that way!" *Shit.* I put my hands on her legs, over her own hands, calming her down. I nodded, she was right.

"You're right. You're so right. Calm down, baby." I leaned in more wrapping my arms around her shoulders. She was quick to return the embrace. "This is why we needed to talk it through." Pulling back a bit, she smiled idly through the tears. "All right, so he'll continue to work there for now. We'll just switch up his job descriptions until we can get rid of him."

"You can't work on that side of the business...." Her eyes were distant and worried.

"I know. This week I'll be in the warehouse finishing up the project plans for my new design." I patted her lap. "So don't worry, for now, I'll be okay."

"How are we going to make this go away?" I didn't feel like there was an easy answer. After Janie had reminded me that Sean can't be fired, and cannot know that we know... everything changed, yet again.

215

"Honestly, I don't know. I need to think this through, and talk with Donovan before I make any decisions. But as for you," touching her cheek with my hand, forcing her to look me in the eye. "You're staying away from the Estate. I'd really like to tell you to stay home, and away from society too, but I know you'd divorce me if I did." She smiled a little, forgetting to hold her seriousness in place for a moment.

"I feel the same way about you, Mr. Lazarus. If someone hurts you..." she shook her head.

"I know, Janes. I've been where you are, and they *did* hurt you." She searched my eyes with her own, and I knew she finally understood my point. "Now that I know who it is, that's going to really help. If you hadn't told me..." I shuddered at the thought.

"But, where do we go from here? Are you going to keep working there?"

"Until this gets figured out, we just take one day at a time." It seemed like the most logical thing to say. "Sense would tell me this could be the best door for me to exit smoothly from that side of James Industries. Money could keep me there forever."

"But I'd prefer you safe over any amount of money." I smiled at her sentiment.

"I understand Janie, and I feel the same way. Just give me another few days to work through some things, and iron out some of the details. I'm meeting with Don in the morning to figure out what we need to do, and that reminds me." I fished into my pocket for my cell. Opening it, I dialed him quickly. It rang a few times before he answered.

"Gabe, everything okay?" He was a little on edge since our last conversation.

"As well as it can be during this chaos." I chuckled. "Yes, things are okay for now. Did you get any sleep?"

"Yes, thankfully. I feel a bit more like a human now. Except that convo we had a few hours ago- that was real, right?"

"Unfortunately, yes. And that's why I'm calling now. Please do not make a move to fire him now. I'll explain more later, but doing so will put Janie in immediate danger. I know this is all confusing, but we'll talk more tomorrow. You'll understand then."

"You're right about the confusing. I'd never thought someone that was a friend to both of us on completely different platforms, would work us both over at the same time. I'm still wrapping my head around it, and I'm having all of the records from location five pulled for review."

"Thank You, Don. I appreciate your care on this. I know you have a lunch meeting tomorrow, so I'll be there after breakfast."

"All right, sounds good. Talk to you tomorrow." Hanging up with him, I looked over at Janie. She smiled, telling me I'd done the right thing.

"I'm going to head inside," she stood in front of me. "I've got a load of emails to send out, and some new events to get planned." She opened the screen door, and took one step in. "And I'm doing it all in my PJs." She winked at me, and headed in the house.

I stayed outside for another hour or so, mulling over options and thoughts about Sean. I had a few ideas, but they were almost beyond my scope of reality. Nothing I was opposed to trying, as long as I knew I had the full support of everyone else involved. Tapping my fingers on the tops of my thighs, the picture images of Sean and my wife together from years before flashed through my mind. *No way. Never again.*

25

I was ready for work by eight. I needed to get this out of the way, and finally establish a legit plan. I buttoned my sleeves, fastened my belt, and watched her do her morning stretches. There was a heavy feeling, almost visible, floating through our air today. I could see her pulling away from me, just like years before. Janie was such a strong soul, ready to battle anything, until it ended. *That's when she always falls apart.*

"Hey love," smiling, I patted her rear. She stopped stretching long enough to slide into a full body embrace. *Okay, see?* She's still in there, hanging on as tight as she can. "I'm going to go to the Estate for a little bit today, talk to Don, and see about getting things signed off on my product line."

"Will he be there?" She looked suddenly nervous, and I shrugged.

"I'm really not sure, but I don't want you to worry. He's not going to know that we know." She nodded slightly. "Not yet anyway."

"I understand. I'm just worried. I've got a busy day today, so that will keep my mind busy, and occupied."

"What's on your agenda for today?" She began rolling up her yoga mat, and reorganizing her sunny corner.

"Just a business meeting day. Everyone should be here in about an hour to go over a few new clients for the cleaning side, and a few more planned events to go over. BIG events." She motioned how big it was with her hands and arms, making sure to widen her eyes, too.

"As long as they're not too big..." I winked, and she giggled. "I'll be home this afternoon." I pulled her close to me inhaling her exquisite scent. "Please call me if you need me, okay?" I could feel her nodding under my chin, where her warm skin was pressed so perfectly.

"I will," she kissed my cheek, and pulled at the collar of my shirt. "Hurry back." Tugging on the collar, she kissed my cheek again and turned towards the bathroom. Such mixed emotions this day held so far, and it had just begun. Grabbing my keys off of the counter I headed out to the car. Feeling a touch of rage, I floored it leaving the driveway, spinning the tires out on the highway. *Did that help?*

I headed straight into Don's office, where he welcomed me with a smile, and a motion to take a seat. I opted for the couch, and waited for his phone call to end.

"Yes, that will do it for today! No, for now just keep that between us. Correct. Yes, I'll keep you posted." He turned towards me, and smiled. "Thanks, Cal." As he hung up the phone, he collapsed into his oversized desk chair. So many times we'd sat in this office working, partying, or doing completely mind-blowing things...and now we're riddled with fixing blackmail and threats on my life. "Jesus." I nodded in agreement.

"I don't even know where to begin. You know the basics." Glancing up at him, we made eye contact, and he nodded. "Sean told Janie in the garden that if she told me he did this to her, and said what he said, he'd kill me, and hurt her more." His hands came to his forehead, and he sighed aloud.

"Where does he get off, Gabe? I mean, why pull Janie into this?" I'd always known that Don had favored my wife over me, but times like this just proved it. In some ways, I was thankful for it, and in others, I wanted to rip his fucking head off.

"It was his best way to get at me. And he's right. Don," I sat on the edge of the couch. "I can't put her in danger, and if I'm around Sean, I'm going to kill him. If he finds out that I know he raped my wife, he'll hurt *her*." My hands wrung together in my lap. "I've thought about this constantly for the past two days. I've barely slept. There's no give on either side. I can't find an angle to take him down with."

"How about his ex-wife? Their kid?" I shook my head.

"He doesn't care about his kid, and he's moved on past Delaney now. I just don't think that would affect him much." Donovan nodded again.

"I've got him working solely with Lonnie in the warehouse. I've told Lonnie to keep him in eye sight at all times, and take breaks at the same time." I chuckled. "Told him to chalk it up to new security procedures, for now."

"Hopefully that'll hold him for a few days. At least until I can come up with something." Looking back at Donovan again, his face was covered with revenge. His fingers tapped in a rhythmic pattern on the top of his desk. I could hear his foot tapping underneath the desk, and the corner of his lips turned even farther to the dark side. "What now, Don?"

221

"Can I be frank?" I nodded, my lips pulling into a faint smirk. "I don't like threats, especially when they're against my *family*. Business aside, I don't like it when people fuck with my *family*." He squared his hands on his desk, marking the point of his conversation. "That said, someone who threatens my business had better have his footing. Because the second he missteps, I'm going to take him out." His balled his fists on the desk, and smiled.

"Where do I fall into this?"

"You really don't. I mean," he paused, and flipped through his rolodex. He stopped abruptly on one of the cards, and pulled out his cell. Typing quickly, he set the cell back down on his desk. "I've changed my mind, Gabriel. I don't want to tell you anything further." The words fell out of his mouth slowly, with twisted feelings and connotations falling all around us.

"What?" I stood, and moved towards his desk. "Donovan. Come on. This is serious. My *life*." He nodded, and turned his chair around to his side bar, mixing himself a morning Bloody Mary.

"That's exactly why we're going to be done with this conversation. In fact, let me get you your work schedule for this week. I don't want you in the office much." My forehead wrinkled, and I felt abandoned. Being left out of the plan wasn't something I enjoyed, and my mind was spinning. *Is there a plan?*

"Don. Come on. We need to know what's going on! This is our safety." He held his hand up to my protest, to calm me back down. "I'm sorry, I-" I ran my hand through my hair.

"Gabe! Please, relax. Trust me. Trust that I will take care of you, Janie, and my business." He stepped around the desk, and over to me. He extended his hand to shake. "Come on, Gabe. I promised you on day one I'd never let anything, or anyone hurt you. Let me keep my promise." His eyes squinted into mine. I took his hand, and he squeezed it extra hard, as if delivering a silent message.

"Okay. Okay Don." I sighed, unable to hold off the shakes any longer. My hands turned clammy and cold, and my body shook from nerves.

"Now, you're on house arrest until you hear from me. I'll have jobs for you mid-week, until then," he turned, and slammed a pile of folders down on the desk. "Touch base with these customers? Fill out the new sales plans for them, if you feel like it. Mainly, just relax. Have some friends over." He patted my back, pushing me to his office door. "Oh, and I'll have one of the guys bring over your paperwork from the completed product design, too. And Gabe?" I turned back to face him. "Make sure that Janie understands she's safe, and I've got this under control."

Walking away I nodded in his direction, raising my hand in the air to wave. I checked my watch, and it was only 10:31. Climbing back into the 370z, I headed towards home. Janie would be deep into her meeting by now, and I'd do my best to sneak in with little interruption. There's no way we needed to be discussing this in front of her employees.

Pulling into the driveway, I'd noticed that our usually empty security shed was now full of a person. I stopped by the check in window, and he opened it slowly.

"What's your- Oh, hello Mr. Lazarus." He reached through the window, and into mine, extending his hand. "I'm Shane Hunter, your new day security guard. You'll have a new night guard, too, but I'm not sure who's taking that role." I took his hand in a firm shake, knowing better than to question whatever Don was up to.

"It's great to meet you, and we appreciate your service. When are the change-over hours? I'd just like to let my mother and wife know when to expect cars around the station." I pointed to his vehicle sitting on the edge spot near the road.

"Oh, I didn't even think! My apologies, Mr. Lazarus. Our shifts run from eight to eight." He smiled, obviously nervous from the questioning.

"Ok, thank you. You're familiar with our alarm system and codes?"

"Yes, Mr. James filled me in on everything I would need to know. He gave strict instructions, and I assure you I will follow them to a T."

"Please let me know if you need anything out here." Smiling, he raised his hand and opened the gates to the house. Slowly pulling down the driveway, there were a few cars parked at the house. I had wondered if Janie was aware of our new security guard yet. Personally, I was hoping she hadn't yet noticed.

Parking near the house, I saw Janie and her employees sitting on the deck. Getting out of the car, I was struck with just how beautiful it was outside. The sun hung perfectly, just off center from being in the top of the sky. There was a steady breeze that was cool for the end of June. The clouds passed just enough to give little bits of shade here and there. Before I knew it, I stood leaning on the car, tilting my face towards the sun. The warmth felt amazing, and took my mind off of the pressing issues at hand.

"Gaaabriellll!" I heard squealing from across the yard. Lowering my head again, I saw Bradley waving as if on parade. "Get over here, stud!" Janie shook her head at their antics. Slowly, I aimed myself in that direction.

"Hey Brad," I extended my hand to him, which he took and pulled me into a full body hug. I instinctively put my hand on his chest, trying to hold him back a little. *Impossible.*

"Oh no you don't! I get my one summer hug!" He laughed loudly, and stepped back, leaning against the deck rail.

"How've you been? Business good? Boss treating you well?" The girls giggled, as Mylah refilled everyone's lemonade.

"You know, your wife is one amazing woman! This job has been the best thing to happen to me in quite some time." He sipped his lemonade, pinkies up. His personality was the best, and I loved the sassy punch he packed. "I absolutely love my coworkers, and my clients!" Turning his head to the side, with an ornery smile, he added, "Some of them I love a little extra, if you know what I mean!!" His elbow nudged my side gently.

"Good, I'm really glad to hear it. I'm really proud of Janie, and all of you, for your hard work." Making sure to make eye contact with all of them, recognizing their effort and ability. *That's right, praise the good ones.* I finally found Janie, back by the sliding door, smiling at my simple effort. She closed the door, and walked over to me. She wrapped one arm around my side, eyeballing me.

"You're home pretty early today!" She poked my ribs.

"Yeah, I've got some "at home" work to work on this week," I said, pointing to the pile of files on my hood. "Speaking of, I'd better get to it. It was great to see everyone!" I leaned in to Janie's side, grabbing a handful of her ass, and kissing her forehead. Her eyes closed peacefully, and I was almost positive I felt her lean into my hand.

I carefully picked up the files, and headed into my office. Closing the door, a sat back in my chair, letting my head fall on the headrest. Staring at the ceiling fan, collecting thoughts, and attempting to process any of them was only giving me a headache. Instead of working, I opted to rest my eyes for a little while in the silence.

26

"Gabe? Gaaaabe?" I could hear her faintly calling my name. Pulling my eyes open, their focus was rough, and blurry. Blinking rapidly, I'd realized I must've fallen asleep and had no idea what time it was. "Honey? Where *are* you? Your mom is here." Rubbing my eyes, I stood too quickly, grabbing the desk loudly for support. The door swung open. "Here he is!"

"Sorry, I ah," I yawned. "I guess I fell asleep. Did I miss anything?" I asked jokingly.

"Oh Gabriel, always the comedian!" My mom greeted me with a hug, and a shoulder punch. "Listen, I don't mean to bother you, but I wanted to let you know that I'm going on a spontaneous vacation!" She was beaming, and looked so happy.

"Mom, that's great! Where are you going?"

"Well, I guess we're going to Las Vegas to see the Cirque du Soliel show!" I could always tell when she was excited. Even in my childhood, the happier she was the more she talked with her hands.

"Who is going with you?" She grabbed my forearm almost in disbelief.

"My whole bridge group!" I was taken back a bit, as this seemed like a big trip all of the sudden.

"Oh, that's wonderful! I'm so thrilled for you!" I hugged her again, this time a little tighter. *Ahh, less to worry about this week. Here's hoping Donovan gets this shit under control...* "I'll be sure to take in your mail, don't worry about that."

"Jean, how long will you be there?" Janie looked peaceful enough, and tired after her meeting.

"I'll get back on Saturday morning." They smiled at each other, and turned back to me.

"When are you leaving?" I wasn't sure if she would need help with her bags, packing, or anything else.

"Now! I was on my way out, and stopped long enough to tell you!" She laughed, as if she'd made a joke. Turning, she headed out towards the kitchen door.

"You're a riot, Ma." I followed closely behind her, Janie interlocking my fingers with hers as we went. "I hope you have a great week. Send me a text or two so I don't worry about you." She hugged me again, pulling Janie in, too.

"Bye Jean, safe travels!" Janie patted her back, and took a seat at the bar. I opened the kitchen door and stepped out on the patio, watching her get into the limousine. She waved once more, and slammed the door closed. The tinted window rolled down, and her face popped back out.

"I feel famous in this thing, Gabe!" I waved as the car pulled out of the driveway, and glanced at the guard tower. *Shit!* I didn't get a chance to tell Janie what was going on. Sighing, I stepped back in to the house. She was smiling that telltale going-to-kick-your-ass-for-information smile. She tapped the seat next to hers at the bar.

"Care to update me on things?" I smiled at her and took the seat.

"Yes, Donovan is handling it." She raised both eyebrows, and pulled her head back.

"What does that mean?" Her head shook in disbelief, obviously not satisfied with the answer.

"He thought it better that I didn't know the details, but has me working from home this week, or until I hear otherwise." I shrugged, looking her dead in the eye. "At first I wasn't satisfied with that, either. But then I pulled in the driveway to find our new day guard, Shane." I turned to her, "did you notice that?" She shook her head.

"No, I hadn't really looked that direction all day. So, we have a guard? That's it?" I shook my head.

"Not the way Don was talking. He's really upset about this...especially that Sean's hurt you." She lowered her head, looking now at the bar. "And me, a little, I think." I shook my own dark thoughts. *You've got to trust someone, man.* "We've been given strict work instructions to have some friends over, and try to relax. According to Shane, there's a night guard, too." Slowly she raised her head, matching my gaze.

"Okay," she sighed heavily. She took another breath in, blowing it out through pursed lips, closing her eyes. "I'm putting my trust in him. I really hope he doesn't let us down."

"I know," I draped my arm around her. "So, how about we have some friends over Wednesday afternoon? I need to call Greg, and I could see if they'd want to cook out." She didn't immediately turn down the idea.

"Do you really think that's a good idea in the middle of another chaotic crisis?" I could see her point, but I didn't think this was the same. At all.

"I think we're fine. We know the threats this time, right?" She nodded. "Then let's give it a shot. I'll talk to Greg, update him and stuff. If he's not comfortable with it, he'll never mention it to Heather. I know that's what you're worried about." Her eyes quickly darted to mine, and she nodded.

"Okay, yes, that sounds good." Her voice was a little peppier, and she looked over my shoulder to the guard station.

"Guess it's good we got that out of our systems a while ago..." she directed me with her eyes to the front corner station, where we had spent a wonderful hour of our time the other night.

"I'd like to head in, I think. I'm in a movie mood." She pushed her knees into mine. "What are you going to do?"

"I'm thinking I'll contact a few of James Industries clients, and get a little of the real work Don gave me done. Do you mind?" I cocked my body to check her facial reaction, as those were telling me more than her words today.

"Not at all. I'll be on the couch if you need me." She stood, bending over to kiss my forehead on her way back into the house. I stayed on the porch a few seconds longer, just admiring the outdoors. I was pretty confident that for the time being, Janie would leave things go to Donovan. I just wasn't sure how *long*. Standing to stretch, I headed back through the house to the office. Janie was comfortably reclined, watching *Little Children*. She always loved those love triangles.

Flipping on the computer, I dove into work and planning as many new sales plans that I could muster. The sheer amount of profit James Industries would have from these clients and businesses alone were astounding. This was the business I was fighting to stay in, no other part meant anything to me. By the time I emerged, it was dark outside, and Janie was half awake on the couch. I sat next to her, propping my feet up on the coffee table. Before I knew it, I too was succumbing to the music of *Jurassic Park*, and it was lulling me to sleep.

~

We awoke the next morning to a pile of crumpled blankets, and our twisted legs between the couch cushions. The sun had reached the point of the morning where it burst through our front windows, off of the coffee table top, and into our eyes. We both squinted, and pulled ourselves from the blaring, screaming sunlight. Her hair was completely mussed, which made her look that much more edible.

"Morning baby," I leaned over for a kiss. One quick one was all I got, and I was surprised. Normally morning breath was not something she tolerated. "MMmm…" I moaned.

"Morning, yourself!" She stood, pushing me away from her, and headed over to the coffee pot. Pressing a few buttons, she had the new pot brewing in mere moments. "What's our agenda today? Anything specific?" I shook my head.

"I need to call Greg, and maybe we could put a call in to the kids?" The way her face completely lit up with their mention was just another reason why I loved her so much.

"Yes! I'll do it right now! Normally they call back in the evening before or after dinner." She headed towards her cell, and dialed the camp. Distracted by something outside, I noticed a different car parked by the guard station. Pushing the button on my cell, the clock came to view. *10:06. Maybe it's a different day guard?*

Walking to the window, I opened the blinds a bit more to assess our surroundings. Nothing seemed out of place, or unordinary about the station. I shrugged it off, and turned to find Janie smiling at the bar, pouring two cups of coffee.

"I left a message. She'll have them call us back later."

"Thanks, love. I've missed talking to them." I took the cup from her, and walked out to the side patio. She stayed in the kitchen, cleaning up some dishes from days before.

"I'm going go to your mom's for a bit, and lay out by her pool. You're welcome to join me." I leaned to the side so I could see her through the screen.

"I just may do that. I think I may work outside a bit first. Get a little yard work done." Looking around again, I nodded at my decision. *Don did tell you to relax.* Yard work is sort of relaxing. She nodded and disappeared into the house. I took my coffee, and headed out to the shed. Walking up to the shed, you could still see the burn marks from the half-assed attempt to blow it up years before.

There were memories all around us of everything that had happened over the years. As hard as it was to face the truth, the scars were everywhere. On her arms. Her back. Her chest. Left there from Michael. Then Simon and Cain. And now Sean. Memories from the house. The tree line. This shed. It all seemed so significant to me, all connected. My mind wandered to life without Sean, with the last of the drama and torture bringing people. *What would life even be like without all of this happening?* A blackbird flew overhead, lower than usual. *Would Janie be the same if all of that didn't happen?*

Opening the shed doors, I hopped on the riding mower, backing it out carefully. Filling the trailer with the garden tools, I drove to the back of the house to work on the flower bed. Seconds later, Janie emerged from the door, heading back to Mom's house. *Wow. That is amazing.* She walked with a purpose in a steady beat across the yard. Leaning on my shovel, I couldn't help just stop and watch. Her skin was shimmering, and the navy bikini was a little snug. She wore a translucent cover up, revealing how the top made her boobs all but fall out of their loose-fabric top. I closed my eyes, trying to forever burn the image into my head.

I opened my eyes again to find her staring at me, waving from Mom's porch. She disappeared into the side path gate, and I continued on pretending like there was nothing else happening in the world. Unexpectedly, my phone rang. Dusting the dirt from my hands, I carefully pulled it out of my pocket. *What the fuck?!* Sean's number showed on caller ID. *You have to take this, Gabe. He thinks it's just a normal day in paradise, remember?* I didn't know what to say, but I knew I had to answer.

231

"Hello?" There was an idle pause, but I couldn't tell if it was from the cell connection, or him.

"Hey Gabe! I missed you this weekend. Did you guys have fun at the party?" Looking again to the sky to calm my breathing. I guess we really are going to carry on this charade.

"Oh yeah, it sure was an exhausting day. We were both glad to get home." *Stupid mother fucker.* "Did you enjoy *yourself* at the party?" I couldn't believe I even asked, and I knew any answer would make me want to hurt him more.

"Oh man, the best time! Met lots of new people, and had some hot reconnections." *Hot reconnections? Jesus Christ!* My blood began to boil. I could hear it thumping in my ears.

"Oh? Anyone I know of?"

"Oh I'm sure you know them, you knew almost everyone there!" He chuckled. "I don't mean to bother you, I just hadn't heard if we were doing our normal deliveries this week, or not." *Don't trip.*

"Actually, I'm working on the new product line coming out for James Industries. My design was approved a few months ago, so this week Don's got me wrapping up a few loose ends." *Nice literal description!*

"Oh, well, that's cool. I guess I'm stuck in here with Lonnie then. Let me know if you hear otherwise?"

"Of course, you'll be the first text. I need to get back to it, did you need anything else?" *Like, oh I don't know, sucking my wife into a garden where you can take advantage of her and threaten her?* I waited patiently, but hoped for nothing.

"Nah, not really, I should get back to work, too. Need to make a few phone calls. You and Janie having any parties coming up?" All I could do was shake my head. "I could really go for some wild and crazy about now." I laughed, trying to keep my composure. I was glad he couldn't see the anger ripping across my face while we spoke.

"Sorry man, nothing anytime soon. I'll let you know though! I'll talk to you later, okay?" I heard him chuckle a little, almost feeling the creepy smile spread across his face.

"Sounds good, adios!" I'd never hit the red "off" button so quickly in my life, sliding the phone back in my pocket. Back to leveling the dirt. My mind was racing again. As I dug, I remembered more and more things I'd tried to forget.

As far back as the Phoenix, I could remember Sean being nothing but a follower. A weak man desperate to fit in with whoever would accept him. I could remember the days he'd follow Michael in to the store, and he'd stand a few feet behind him, silent. No matter what insanity that demon spouted, Sean just stood there and took it. *Michael had powers that no one knew about.* I can understand that, but... The images of the pictures from the kidnapping were growing more vivid in my head again. Seeing my wife in the throes of passion with two men.... Two men I'd grown to know, and appreciate. *Temporarily.*

Somehow, over the years, I had okayed what had happened between Janie and Donovan. Donovan was no threat to me, and wanted... No, still wants, only the best for both of us. I can tell he cares for Janie, but I'm not threatened by him. I don't think I've ever been okay with what happened between her and Sean. And I think she knows that. *Gabe, I don't think she's okay with what happened between them either.* And now she's feeling left up a creek with no paddle, yet again.

I finished packing up the trailer with garden tools, and sat back on to the riding mower to head back to the shed. Still lost in my thoughts, I went back to the night in the hot tub, where I had made the worst decision ever. Letting him watch Janie and I that night must've really fueled his fire. I shook my head. The signs were all there, even from Janie. *That's true...she did all but beg you to not include him...* But yet I did it anyway. *What a stupid motherfucker I am.*

In all of these situations, I'd let her down. There was no way I was going to let it happen again. Sighing aloud, I made note to keep this phone call to myself. She'd only worry herself even more. His call was nothing more than a check-up, to see what Janie had said, and if Lizzie had gotten her point across. I unloaded the trailer and tools, and parked the mower in the shed. I headed back into the house to grab a quick shower.

My phone was ringing the minute I stepped out, and I'd hoped with everything I had it wasn't that fuck-face. Wiping the condensation off of my phone from the shower steam, Greg's number was visible.

"Hey, Greg!" I answered jubilantly. "I've been meaning to give you a call all day long!"

"Hey Gabe! Guess smart minds still think alike, huh?" He laughed. "How're things going? Heather's really been missing Janie, and I know, sort of weird to say aloud, but I've sort of missed you, too!"

"That's great! Actually, we were wondering if you two would like to do dinner, say, Wednesday evening?" I heard commotion in the background.

"Let me check real quick," he turned away from the phone, and asked loudly, "How about Wednesday? Dinner at Gabe & Janie's?" More commotion, and then he was back. "Sounds great, man! Just us, like the old days?"

"Absolutely. Special requests?"

"Well, I have requests, but nothing legal." He chuckled, and I heard Heather's tell him to shut up in the background.

"Rest assured I've got you covered, brother." I laughed. "Text me when you're on your way...whatever time is fine. We're working from home this week."

"Perfect! We'll see you on Wednesday! Bye G!" His cheerfulness was contagious, and I couldn't help feel a little better knowing that real friends were still out there, and didn't want anything from us but laughter and fun. I couldn't wait to tell Janie.

27

We sat at the bar for dinner, still waiting for the phone to ring. It was in between us both, so we could race to answer, I was sure. It had been such a long month without them. I couldn't help silently wonder if he had done this on purpose, too. Timed everything perfectly so the kids would be away if anything did transpire. *So, should you thank him for that?* I shook my head, and took a bite of my tenderloin.

"MMMmmm..." I moaned. "This is soo good baby. You really out did yourself on this one." In the past few years, she'd really taught herself so many new tricks in the kitchen. This was a prime example.

"I thought it was really good too," she said, taking another bite. Picking up my phone, I checked my email. No news was good news, I kept reminding myself. The phone rang, and before I had any time to react, Janie was already all over it.

"Hello?!" she was almost frantic, I couldn't hold in my snicker. "Hey Honey! How are you??" I loved listening to her on the phone. Her voice inflections with excitement or emotion, and her faces made throughout the conversation were some of the best I'd ever seen. "Oh, that does sound like fun! Yes, you'll be at the lake by the weekend." Her eyebrows bent a little, which instinctively made me worry about whatever was being said. "I know baby. Camp is a tiring, but a really fun place. All right, here's your dad." She smiled, passing the phone to me.

"Hey Lilah! How are you princess? Tired?"

"Oh Dad, I'm so tired. It's been so hot, I can't even get comfortable at night. I did go canoeing though! It was so much fun!!" Listening to her tell me about this week, and learning how to canoe made my smile beam. *Oh, to be a fly on the wall at camp...*

"We'll definitely have to go canoeing, and you can show me your new skills." Her giggle gave me goosebumps.

"You guys are coming to the lake, too, right?" Her laughter ceased immediately, and I could tell she missed us.

"Oh honey, I cannot wait to get to the lake! Your mom and I both need some down time." I glanced at Janie out of the corner of my eye, and she was nodding in complete agreement.

"Good! Ok, Galen really wants to talk to you. He's missed you a LOT, Dad." Aww, my man. *The dude!*

"Ok, put him on. We love you, Lil." I could hear the voices get loud, and soft again. I could hear her ushering him to the phone, and telling him to be quick so others could use the phone too. I let out an audible laugh.

"What's so funny, Dad?" Oh, his voice had changed. Somehow, in one month, my boy's voice was different. *Deeper?*

"Hey Galen! How are you, man?"

"Oh Dad. Camp is the BEST place ever! I found frogs and toads and bugs and we saw a snake! I wish you were here though." Very frank, and to the point. That was our Galen.

"I'm so glad you're having fun, bud! I wish I was there too, but you know, we'll all be at the lake together in less than a week!"

"YEAH! With Grandma and Grandpa, too! And snacks!" *Oh man.* This kid, I swear. "What are you and mom doing?"

"Right now we're eating dinner. We've been working lots, and missing you guys, too."

"Oh, my counselor says I need to go eat now. I love you dad!"

"I love you too, Galen!" I heard the line go dead, and I turned to Janie. "Guess he hasn't figured out phone goodbyes yet?" We chuckled, and I put the phone back on the bar.

"I really miss them," she said, quietly. Her fingers found mine on the bar, and they intermingled for a few moments. With her other hand, she sipped her wine. Talking to the kids had warmed her heart, and dampened her spirit. This week was really turning into a challenge.

"Want to watch a movie with me?" I squeezed her fingers a little. "I'm thinking we should take advantage of our alone time, and watch a movie that not made by Disney." I joked, and she laughed.

"Sure, that sounds wonderful." She took her plate to the sink, carefully fitting it in the dishwasher just so. "I'll meet you over there in a minute. I'm going to go put my pajamas on." She vanished into the bedroom giving me long enough to shoot off a quick text to Donovan. I quickly cleaned off the bar, grabbed a couple bottles of water, and went to sit on the couch. I could still hear her in the bathroom. Opening my phone, I typed as fast as I could.

All clients contacted. Any updates? Contact was made. Friends over Wednesday night. Tell me something.

Closing my phone, I checked through the pay-per-view movies. There wasn't much on, but for Hot Tub Time Machine. Displeased with the selection, I thought it best to wait for her. Impatiently, I kept pushing the button on my cell to check for a missed reply. Moments later she appeared in an oversized t-shirt and boxer shorts.

"What are we watching?" she fell into the couch next to me, sighing once her head hit the pillow.

"There isn't much, really. Do you want to look?" I handed the remote in her direction, to which she declined. "How about Hot Tub Time Machine?" She shrugged, and I clicked to accept the charges. She cozied into my side, and we watched the movie. After an hour or so, the tension fell out of the moment, and I felt her body finally relax next to me.

~

Janie.

I woke up in the living room, curled up in a blanket that usually lays on the top of the couch. The sun was shining through the bottoms of the curtains, almost shouting into my eyes. I rose slowly as to not wake Gabe. He looked so peaceful, and with all of the stress, sleep seemed like a better idea. Tiptoeing to the coffee pot, I quickly brewed a pot, and poured myself a cup. *You'll need more than coffee to pull yourself out of this internal hell...*

That was the truth, and after getting myself some, I quietly exited out the back door letting the sun warm my skin. I noticed the mail truck at the end of the driveway, so I decided to grab the mail on my morning adventure. It looked like it was going to shape into a beautiful day. The sun was already hanging nicely in the sky. I was glad we had decided to stay home today.

Approaching the guard station, I was a bit taken back by the size of the guard. He was taller than some of our trees, solid, and with an angry face, was quite scary. Thankfully, his beaming smile caught my eye, showing me just how dangerous he really was.

"Good morning, Mrs. Lazarus. It's nice to meet you." He first extended his hand to me, and then my mail. I took his hand in a firm shake, and put the mail under my arm.

"Hi, please call me Janie. You must be Shane?" He nodded. "Thank you for holding my mail for me." I used my hand to cover my forehead from the sun. *You should've brought your sunglasses.*

"It's no problem, mam. Is there anything I can get for you?" I shook my head.

"Not really. But, we are having friends over tomorrow night, so please be sure to see that they get inside the gates safely." He nodded and smiled. "Otherwise, I need to get back to the house. It was nice to meet you!" I waved and pulled the pile of mail into my hands. On the top of the pile was a letter. From the Indiana Department of Corrections State Penitentiary.

I pushed my feet to keep walking, at least up to the deck. It had been so long since everything had happened with Michael, and over the years, I would like to think he would just let go. *He hasn't done that yet, Janes!* For the most part, his letters were friendly and informative. Sometimes they would have repeated apologies, and other times he would be back to placing the blame. Blaming me for inciting his temper. Blaming me for making him put his hands on me. *And in you.* And now, all these years later, the random notes always brought everything back.

Luckily, life was already giving me shit, so I was ready to read whatever he had to say. I'd secretly wished that there was some way to make this all okay, get some sort of real closure, and move on. Truth is, that was never going to happen, and I knew it. I finally got back to the deck, and sat on the chair. Taking the envelope carefully into my hands, I read the back of the envelope. "Mrs. Janie Lazarus. South Anthony Extended. Fort Wayne, IN." My hands began to shake, and I slipped my finger inside to pull out the note paper.

Dearest Janie,

I hope this letter finds you well. For once, maybe life is leaving you alone. I hope your kids are doing well, and that Gabe is successful. I've been thinking a lot about everything, and I know more than ever that I've done some serious wrongs. Some I'll never be able to apologize for, and some that I know permanently changed you. I wish my brother hadn't done what he'd done, and I wish somehow I could fix that, too.

All in the details. Reading even the most minor sentence about what happened brought the flashes and recollections of each moment that I still held on to right back. *One paragraph to go. You've got this.* I looked towards the sky, took a deep breath, staring into the bright blue.

I don't know if there's room for me in a world like this. I don't know if my temper will ever be better? Do you, Janie? Do you think I can be rehabilitated? Sometimes I wonder what you think of me...you've never written back in all my letters over the years. Sometimes I wonder if I should stop writing you, but then something compels me to do it again. When I get out, I'm scared I'll screw up again. I wish I could talk

to you one last time, but your lawyer made your
thoughts on that perfectly clear. I'll respect it Janie. I
can't say if this will be my last letter....sometimes I can't
help but write. I know it's hard to believe, but I am sorry.

Admiration,
Michael

I took a few slow steady breaths, and closed my eyes hoping the tears would suck back inside. They didn't, and came falling down my cheeks. Why hadn't I written Michael back? Searching my heart, I found the box marked Michael. I opened it slowly, trying to pull the memories of the good times that we did have. I smirked remembering the mornings before school, but then I was reminded why I had to go over there each day in the first place. *If he couldn't see you before class, he'd suspect you were screwing another classmate.* Shaking my head I tried again, remembering one of the school events he attended with me. After my award ceremony, he'd become enraged because some men were googling at me, and ended up taking it out on me afterwards. *Stop!*

It wasn't possible to look inside that box, and now I knew that. My chest hurt. I couldn't tell if it was because I had stepped into the past, or because I couldn't find a reason not to write him back. But maybe writing a letter would help burn the box? Staring into the distance, I was startled by a noise in the house. Gabe must be awake.

"Good morning," I put my arms around him from behind while he poured himself a cup of coffee. "Did you sleep well?"

"I sure did," he sipped at the steamy brew. "You were pretty tangled up in the blanket." I shrugged.

"I met the guard this morning, and collected some mail."

"Oh yeah? Anything good in there for me?" He smiled his flashy, take-of-your-pants smile, testing out the waters. It wasn't that I wasn't in the mood for him, because truthfully I was craving him. My brain was just so heavy from all of the extra thoughts, sex just wasn't at the forefront.

"Just a magazine or two." I jokingly stuck my tongue out in his direction. "I got another letter, too." Watching his reaction, he face grew pained, and he shook his head.

"This one just as bad as the last?" He hated the letters, regardless of what was written in them. He didn't believe a "sad word" that Michael wrote, but he did believe the nasty, negative ones that were sent.

"Nah, this one's apologetic." I swallowed hard in the silence. "Maybe I'll write him back." His head snapped over to me quickly, before I could explain.

"What a waste of time, baby. I thought you were past that." I wrinkled my forehead at him.

"I know it's hard to understand. Jesus Gabe, I don't even get it." I picked up my glass, and pressed it into the refrigerator door to get some water. The cool felt good going down my throat. "It's nothing I'll be seriously revisiting, if that makes you feel better. But what could a letter hurt?" He looked into my face, searching for something. "If I don't try this, I'll be searching for closure the rest of my life." My phone rang on the counter. It was Donovan.

"Hello?" I turned away from Gabe, and walked into Lilah's room. "Yes, that's the schedule I'm working from." He couldn't know anything about this. If he did, he would try and stop me.

28

The day had passed quickly after our morning chat. Janie had trailed off into the garden, and I had stayed inside to work out a few client issues on the new sales plans. Walking through the house, I smelled the fresh cut Hyacinth and Lily of the Valley in the kitchen. It smelled so perfect, crisp, and relaxing. Looking through the kitchen window, I could see Janie sitting next to the grill, deeply engrossed in whatever she was working on. I filled my water glass, and took a few long drinks.

Stepping out on to the deck, I was met by her beautiful smile. She closed her notebook, and motioned for me to come over to the grill.

"Come 'mere!" She was excited. "Look at this." She opened the grill, and the sultry, rich smelling steam poured out.

Oh my…. You're eating well tonight! My mouth began to water almost instantly.

"Oh baby! What *is* that?" I'd not been this excited about dinner in a long time.

"This is a new one! A bacon and balsamic roast. I wanted to give it a try, and then make some pulled BBQ with it for our dinner tomorrow." I leaned over the grill, and inhaled another huge breath of tasty. My stomach growled.

"I think you've outdone yourself!! I cannot wait to try this!" She raised an eyebrow, and snagged her giant fork, pulling off a small piece. She blew on it for a few seconds before offering it up to my mouth. Her lips in the perfect 'o' shape. *Sexy as ever, don't you think?* Hungrily, I accepted. I couldn't help but lick my lips a little bit, too. "Oh man! Janes!" I yelled loudly. "Melt in your mouth, perfect." She smiled proudly displaying her excitement.

"Thanks, I was sort of worried it wouldn't turn out. There were so many different spices!" Pushing into my side, she curled herself into my arm. "Anyway, there are baked potatoes in the oven, too. I'm pretty hungry, so we could eat now if you'd like."

"Sure, sounds like a plan. Can we eat at the bar?" She nodded, turning back to the grill to take the meat off. I headed inside, turning on the sound system, and setting the table. Tracy Chapman blared over the speakers, filling the house and the outdoors with a heavy, steady beat. I could hear Janie singing along, filling a container with her shredded masterpiece. Searching through the wine cabinet, I found a 2007 bottle of El Pecado that I thought would pair well with everything else. She came inside, and set the third of the roast she'd not shredded in between our plates. I grabbed the potatoes out of the oven, and met her at the bar to sit.

"Thank you, baby." I kissed her forehead. "A wonderful dinner." She grinned, obviously having other thoughts.

"You're welcome. I'm glad you like it." The mouthwatering meat melted in my mouth, invoking the most illicitly intimate thoughts. It didn't help that she seemed to be slowly pulling the fork back out from between her tight lips. "Do you have plans this evening?" *Oh God, finally. Please, please want it like I want you.* I couldn't help shift in my chair.

"Well, no plans that I can think of at this moment." I shrugged. "Why, what do you have in mind, Mrs. Lazarus?"

"I was sort of thinking about sitting by the fire, maybe having a drink." She stood, and put her dishes into the dishwasher. "Want to start *my* fire?" She smirked, cocking her head to the side.

"God yes." Her hands gently caressed my neck as she headed into the bedroom.

"I'll meet you out there, just going to put on some different clothes, and grab some stuff." Turning back to finish my delectable dinner, my thoughts raced of Janie sprawled out across the counter top. Next to the hot tub. Laid out over the outdoor lounger. I couldn't deny my need for her. The stressors we'd faced again on a daily basis had my nerves fried. I needed relief in the worst way.

Clearing off the plates, I heard our bedroom patio door close. Out of the corner of my eye, I caught a glimpse of her long white robe falling around the lounger. I closed my eyes, momentarily picturing Janie's nakedness before me, knowing I couldn't push her or I may end up pushing off a few in the shower. Grabbing the lighter out of the junk drawer, I stopped by the bar to grab a few glasses and bottles, and proceeded to the deck.

She met my smile for a moment, and sunk back into her notebook. Only the end of June, and already she'd drawn such a deep golden tan. I built the fire in my favorite pyramid tee-pee style, and put flame to it only minutes later. The flames quickly rose, giving a glowing ambiance to the entire deck area.

"Hey love," I motioned to her, holding up the bottle of vodka. "Do you want any of this?" She nodded, and again, fell back into whatever she was doing. Probably work. *Damnit! Sometimes she's positively worse than you!* I poured her a glass, dropping a few ice cubes and lemons. As I stirred the glass, my phone rang. Quickly glancing to see who it was, Donovan's name shone brightly.

"Hey Don." I walked her glass over, setting it on the table next to her.

"Gabriel! Sorry I didn't text back, I was working out a few issues on my end." I sighed to myself, happy to know that nothing major had happened as of yet. "Your product line was approved, and you should be receiving the payoff amount for the idea very soon." Leaning my head back, I couldn't help but smile. Working so hard on such a long project had really paid off.

"Oh, that's great news!" Using one hand, I poured myself some bourbon, and dropped in some ice. Taking a quick drink, the burn crawled down my neck and into my belly.

"As for the other, I'll need you to stay in touch towards the end of the week, and be sure to follow my direction. Okay?" I wanted to ask what the plans were. I wished I could know what was going to happen, and keep my wife out of the mix.

"I'm fully trusting you on this, Don. I'll make sure to have my cell on me at all times. We are having some friends over tomorrow night, so, maybe you could make sure-" His laughter cut me off.

"Gabe, come on. I got your text. Of course not." I could hear Mylah's laughter in the background.

"What's going on over there?" He laughed again.

"Ah, our good friend Mylah has gotten into some of the Forget-Me-Nots again. She's such a riot. I need to go deal with that, actually. So, just know I'll be in touch, and everything is going to be all right." I nodded, trying to make myself believe what he was saying.

"Okay, talk later." The line went dead, and my mind replayed his words over and over. *Everything's going to be all right. But is it?* Turning back to Janie, she was closing her notebook, sticking a toe into the hot tub water.

"How's Don?" I set my phone down on the bar, and took another long swig of bourbon.

"According to him, 'everything is going to be fine.'" I smiled, and she bent her brows at me. "I know, but, he also said I should get my payment for the rights to the product line soon! That means that I-" *What now?* My phone rang again, but this time was no one I wanted to deal with. I frowned in Janie's direction, and held up a finger. This may be the only link to him I'll have in the next few days.

"Sean." It loathingly slipped through my gritted teeth. "What can I do for you?"

"Hey man! How're things?" I tipped my head to the side, cracking my neck repeatedly.

"Things are good. Enjoying the week with my wife."

"Oh, well, I don't mean to keep you. I just wondered if you knew when the next delivery for Location 5 would be." My mind raced with questions and observations and I knew I needed to keep myself in check. Perfect timing for the bourbon to kick in.

"Oh, sorry man. Since I've not been at work this week, I'm not sure of what Don's plans were. I'm just stoked I just sold the rights to my first product line!" I knew he wouldn't care about that, and I knew what he really wanted. *No way, don't give in.*

"Well," he grunted. "I've heard some things around the shop about some of the locations, and things happening with the delivery business." *Keep reachin', buddy!* "I just want to make sure I'm going to have a job next week, you know?

Delaney would kill me if support stopped." *Oh, two can play at this one.*

"Delaney? You two are speaking again? You're seeing Dominic again? That's great man! I'm really glad to hear that." *He's so full of shit.*

"Oh, well, I hadn't seen Dom for a little bit, but I'm going to be seeing him really soon. So, you don't know anything about work then?" I had to bite my cheeks to keep the smile from speaking through my voice.

"No man, sorry. I could call in, and see what I can find out, if you want."

"Oh, sure, that'd be great. I'm sure Donovan will tell you what's up before any of the rest of us."

"All right, next time I talk to him, I'll ask. I need to get going now though, I was in the middle of something." He chuckled.

"Understand that, I'd want to get back to it, too. I'll talk to you later then." He hung up, and the line went dead.

"Wow." She cautiously smiled. "You good?" I nodded.

"He was desperate for information." I swallowed the last few ounces of bourbon in my glass, and gave it a refill. "Do you need some more?" I pointed at her glass, and she shook her head. "Well, I need some more." I took off my shirt, hanging it on the bar. I slid into the hot tub with ease, turning on the back jets. I leaned into the head rest, taking another long drink.

"What did he want to know?" She dropped her long white robe down her shoulders, and tossed it on to the lounger. My eye trailed up her legs slowly, stopping to check out the intricate pattern of black lace covering her groin. Following the curve of her hip and up her rib cage, the black lace appeared again, covering her rounded, supple peaks. The lace looked to be in the shape of flowers and skulls, holding in her flesh well. "Wellll?" she joked, stepping slowly into the tub before me.

For the first time, in what seemed like forever, my cock throbbed and began growing for her. The water lapped up on to her thighs, and quickly covered her belly. She sat back in the higher seated chair, allowing her breasts to bounce freely at the water line. As she leaned back, her hair fell over her right shoulder, and her breasts fell out to the sides of her bikini top. *Swallow your hunger...*

"He ahh," I fell over myself. "He wanted to know when the next delivery was to his business. To his location." I could hear my words slurring. *How much bourbon did you have?!* "He tried to say he needed to know if he had a job because he was going to see his kid." I shook my head, and she frowned.

"I'm sure we'd be some of the first to hear if he'd shown up to see Dom. Delaney would be so thrilled. She hates Sean, but she knows he needs his dad." She took the last long sip of her vodka, and dripped the cold condensation on to her bare chest. She giggled, and my cock all but jumped out of my shorts.

Closing the distance between us, I set my glass down, and floated to the seat nearest hers. Putting me directly by her thighs, I carefully set my hand down on her. Her cheeks instantly flushed, and her fingers locked my hand to her. As the saddest music came across the radio speakers, Janie seemed to come to life hearing Sarah McLachlan play through the air.

She sat up abruptly in her seat, sloshing water into both of us. Her eyes searched mine for any stops, "don'ts" or "cants," and there was nothing stopping her on my end. She smiled, and our mouths crashed into each other. Her tongue was eager, needy, and probed straight into me. Her hands fisted my hair, pulling my head back so she could access my mouth with ease.

Pulling her on to my lap, she reached around and unclasped her top, revealing the most suck-able nipples I'd ever had the pleasure of seeing. Lifting my knees raised her breasts directly into my mouth. Pulling her nipple to me, it hardened on my tongue. Gently rubbing my teeth around its short length, she clawed into the back of my head.

My hands coursed down her sides, squeezing into her hips. My fingers found their way into her sweet spot, which was already dripping and ready for me. Sliding a digit in, she thrashed on my hand. Her body speaking what her mouth could not yet say. Her juices flowed all over me, while she bit my chest and neck, sucking and licking along the way.

Sliding another finger in, I really drove into her. She moaned and screamed my name. With the sound of her pleasure, I became unglued.

"Gaaaabe!" she screamed again. Quickly flipping her around, I stood in front of her still wrist deep in her hole, and let my shorts fall into the water. My hard shaft bounced up and down, but was quickly rescued by her tight grip. She con torted herself so her own pleasure would not be interrupted, and sucked me into her mouth. Her tongue was still just as needy, now sliding around every inch of me. Every time she sucked, I could feel the intense throbs that followed.

She broke the suction long enough to make fast eye contact, and lifted my cock higher, taking my balls straight into her mouth. My knees started to shake, and I could feel the rumbling. Reaching down to her, I stroked her face, and put my hand around her neck, gently tugging her back up to my mouth. She tasted of salty skin, and I wanted to do nothing but bury myself into her. Turning her away from me, I pulled the bottoms down as fast as I could. Our mouths met one last time, pushing into each other in our twisted position.

"Hard," she moaned into my ears as we broke the kiss. She leaned over the side of the hot tub, exposing herself and opening up to me completely. *So fucking beautiful.* Palming my cock, I lined up with her deep, tight hole. Lunging inside, her walls opened up to me without hesitation. She screamed into the night, and I braced my legs with hers to give it to her just as she ordered.

I thrust into her as hard as I could, ramming her into the side of the hot tub over and over. She held tightly to the side, pushing back into me every time I withdrew. I felt her walls begin to quake, and the warmth poured from her all over me. Our bodies spoke silently, and I picked up the pace, pumping into her feverishly. Her hands stopped me suddenly, and she pushed hard on my thighs.

"Wait," she lifted off my shaft. "I want to turn around." She piled up a few towels, and opened herself back up to me, this time leaning on the pile facing me. Grabbing my hips with her feet, she pulled me back towards her. I slipped right back where I was before, but this time she diddled her clit with her fingers. Her walls locked down on me harder than before, and my balls pulled into me, preparing for their final explosion.

"My God Janie," I pushed out between breaths. "So. Fucking. Amazing." She smiled, and circled my shaft, still pumping deeply inside of her, with her hand. Her folds were so slick, there was little friction to slow my speed. Her fingers left her clit, and trailed around to her back side. My mouth fell open watching her finger her bum. Slipping her pointer inside, everything clenched tightly, and sweat poured from my brow.

She moaned loudly, coming again and again. My cock was so full of blood, I thought it might explode. The throbbing hot feelings coursed on and on, leaving me longing for the relief of coming. She screamed out as my last throb shot deeply into her, sending her into another round of orgasms. Pulling her closely to me, our nerves were misfiring and parts so sensitive, I couldn't help sink into her again.

Smiling, she pulled back enough so our eyes could meet. She was slowing her breathing, but could tell I what I wanted.

"Again?" she asked, coyly as ever. I nodded, letting her fall on to my hard shaft. "Slowly, okay?" I nodded again, barely breathing from the extreme feelings running up and down my shaft. My insatiable wife, now riding me so slowly. So deeply. Taking every inch of me inside. Her fingers found their way back to her clit, and she circled it slowly.

"You feel so good. I never want to leave." I felt her start to quiver and shake again. Once those hot juices touched the tip of my dick, I blew into her again. Our bodies sat intertwined, unable to move more than a finger. With every pulse into her, she throbbed and I twitched again.

"Stop that shit," she jokingly said, sliding off of me. "So sensitive..." Readjusting herself, she cuddled into my side restarting the jets in the hot tub. I draped my arm around her, and we both leaned back on the head rests, staring at the stars. "I love you, Gabe," she whispered.

"And I you, my love. Forever." I kissed her forehead, and closed my eyes. My mind was still full of thoughts and wonder, but now I understood why Donovan didn't tell me the details. The end of the week was approaching, and would be here before I knew it. *Just relax, and be patient. Everything is going to be all right, remember?* I did remember. I just wasn't sure I believed it.

29

"You know what they say about hump day?" she jokingly nudged, while washing some cherry tomatoes for the appetizers. Sauntering over to her, I spun her with one hand.

"I'm taking that as an open invitation," our lips met and the kiss was full, passionate, and strong. "MMmm..." I moaned. Her hands gently ran down my chest, and she turned back to her vegetables, smiling all the way.

In a few hours, Greg and Heather would be over for a visit. Janie had decided to drag me along to the store this morning, so I hadn't gotten a chance to get any work done like I had hoped. *Really you just wanted to check your email...* Gazing out the side windows, down the drive to the main street, I couldn't help think of what was coming.

I hadn't backed out of James Industries like I was ordered to do. I hadn't been entirely forthcoming with the information Sean was seeking. My mind trailed off to Don's call, and then Sean's. What would he do if Don cut off his deliveries? Running my hands through my hair, I tried to clear my head. I was to enjoy this night with friends, bosses orders.

"Can I help you with anything else, baby?" I asked my stunning wife. She turned for a moment, and used her head to point to the side counter that housed a pile of unopened groceries.

"That needs to all go into that," she turned again, this time aiming her head across the kitchen near the stove. "Crock pot, right over there."

"All right, any measuring?" I was handy in the kitchen, but I was definitely no Janie.

"Nope, just open it, chop it if it's too big," she stopped to giggle. "Mix it up, and cook it on high." There it was again. I got lost in that big, bright smile. It, that smile, reminded me of every memory, thought, action, person, and major event that it was tied to. That was the thing I'd vowed to protect. *At any cost.*

"You've got it. Hopefully my chopping skills are up to par!"

A few hours later, the food was made and looked great. I changed into proper outdoor attire, and headed out on to the deck. My breath left me when I saw her. A simple black sarong wrapped around her, perfectly hugging her body. *Holy shit, man... control yourself!* You're gonna have guests! Smiling at her, I joined her at the bar.

"Pre-guest drink?" She nodded, and I mixed a few on the rocks. She turned on the sound system, and opened the table umbrellas. She leaned over the table to turn on the lights, and stopped suddenly, looking down at the table. Wrinkling her nose, and stopping momentarily as if deciding something. She reached down and picked up her phone.

"Hello?" Her voice was flat. "Yeah, I remember, and I think I could." Her body language changed, and she partially turned away from me. "Yes, I understand. When? Okay." I saw her sigh and she turned back to me, smiling idly. *What the hell?* "Yeah, okay. Just tell her to plan for a morning swim. All righty, talk later!" She thumbed the phone ending the call.

"Everything okay?" I asked.

"Sure is," she picked her drink up, and sat back down at the bar. We both heard the rumble of the car turning down our drive, and knew it was Greg's old Mustang. "Hey, the guys are here!" Suddenly animated again, I hoped she would fill me in later on whatever that call was about.

Greg and Heather walked up to the side deck, and quickly tossed their things down at the table. Bags of clothes, towels, booze and fireworks scattered the everywhere.

"Hey man!" I extended my hand. "It's been too long!"

"It has! Glad we were able to meet up!" He turned, picking up a bottle and handing it to me. "Here's an old one for you." Opening the bag, I pulled out an old Four Roses bourbon.

"Oh, no shit! This is great! Let's crack it open." For the next few hours we ate Janie's delicious food, and talked all about our kids. While our lines of work were completely different, our home lives were remarkably similar. I wasn't sure what time it was when the drinks started flowing, but they were fast, and furious.

Darkness fell over the backyard, and the glowing lights around the patio kept everything perfectly visible. Laughter rolled through the night, as we all ended up around the hot tub.

"I loved working with you at the Phoenix! I never knew what I was going to get with you... Turned out, I liked the excitement you brought."

"For a while..." Janie added, shaking her head. "You have no idea how bad I feel knowing it was my fault everyone got involved with everything." I winced. Going there wasn't normally a good thing when she was drunk. Just be ready.

"Janes, that wasn't your fault! I don't blame you," Heather took Janie's hand. " Except you did have some pretty questionable judgment with guys for a bit." She giggled. "I just didn't want to deal with it, especially with the kids. I know I've been a shitty friend lately." She sat up quickly raising her glass, sloshing water everywhere. "But no more of that!" She laughed.

"The headaches finally stopped a few months after the fight." Greg spoke up. "I was extremely disappointed in my fighting skills, and that I couldn't ram that fat fuckers face into a tree." He took a long drink of the purple punch. "Since then, I've practiced a lot." He looked over both shoulders, and back to us, smiling widely. "You know, just in case the shit hits the fan while we're here!" I couldn't hold in the hysterical laughter. It made my sides hurt, but looking at Janie, she was barely laughing. She looked stuck. I nudged her knee with my toes.

"Hey you, what's up?" She smiled, and scratched the back of her neck. "Tell us, Janes."

"It's probably the last thing that any of you want to hear about though..." her eyes darted from person to person. "I just wondered if I could run something past you guys. Read you something I wrote?" I wrinkled my brow, confused about the secrecy of the moment.

"Well, I don't mind." I glanced at Heather and Greg. "Either of you?" Heather shrugged.

"I guess not. What'd you write?" She smiled at Janie, who let out a demented chuckle.

"That's the part you won't like. I feel like I need to explain." She held up a finger, took a long, slow drink of her vodka, and sighed. "I wrote something to Michael." She paused, as if waiting for a reaction. I think we were all stunned into silence.

"Okay... why?" Heather said what we all thought. Janie sunk into the seat in the hot tub.

"I know it's hard to wrap your head around, and it's not like four pages front and back or anything. It's just," she paused, looking directly at me. "He's written for years, and I've never responded. He asks questions in letters I honestly want to answer, or at least give my opinion on. While he's still in there though, safely away from me."

"But he's a demon. Janie, I don't think I like it." She smiled at Heather, and nodded.

"I understand. I don't have to read it aloud, I just thought it would help. I hope it gives me the closure I need to not be reminded of him with every bad memory." She adjusted in the seat against the jet. "Maybe I could learn to not get stuck on old memories, and just let them go. I don't know." Right then, I think I understood why.

She needs closure, just as he is seeking. Rubbing my fingers together, I thought of all the times over the years she'd received letters, and fallen apart. Not because the letter had been too negative, or too normal. Just because she'd get lost in all the memories, all at once, like it had happened again just yesterday.

"If you want to read it, I'll listen." I wanted her to know I understood, and was right here if she needed me.

"Yeah, Janes, if it'll help you, I'll listen, too." Greg nodded in her direction, and smiled. She turned back to Heather, looking for her approval as well.

"Of course I'll listen, Janie." She nervously smiled, pulling herself out of the water, and wrapping up in a towel.

"Thank you. I'll be right back." She disappeared into the house, and I turned back to Greg and Heather, who were both nervously looking at each other.

"Hey, I don't think it's going to be as bad as you're thinking. I think this has been coming for a few years." They seemed to relax with that statement, and both took another drink.

"So, did you ever get that product line designed?" I pumped my fist in the air.

"Yes! In fact, I sold the rights this week. This turned into a highly lucrative deal for us." I couldn't hide my pride for this project. *It had just made us millions.*

"That is great news! You always were the more creative one between the three of us," he joked. "Where will it be available? Overseas only?"

"Actually, we've got over a hundred stores ready to carry the line through the Southern states, and yes, overseas as well." Janie appeared again the deck, with a printed paper in her hand. "I'm really excited about my future with James

Industries, and falling solely into design." Truth was, I was ready to be done with the cartel.

"Well, mazel tov!" He raised his glass in the air, and everyone toasted. Silence fell over the deck, and the tub's bubbling and jets were all that could be heard. Janie sat back on the side of the tub, dipping her legs into the water. She held the paper higher, making sure water didn't splash and distort the words.

She looked around at us all, checking our faces. "I'll be quick, I promise." She looked back to her paper, holding it out in front of her, and began to read.

"Dear Michael,

It's hard to believe that this much time has passed since we were teenagers. Sometimes I feel like all of this was happening last week, and sometimes you haunt my dreams, still to this day. You were someone I trusted, and counted on. You shaped me into the untrusting, paranoid, worried person I am today. To this day, I pay more attention to what's in the shadows than I do what's in front of me. You taught me to never take someone at face value, and how to immediately understand their motives. You taught me people are horrible, and those with joker smiles, such as yourself, are demons. You taught me that safety isn't something I'm automatically granted.

You asked me specific questions in your letter, and the only reason I feel safe writing you back is because you're still in jail. Behind bars. I think your tendencies will always be there, because it's how you were raised. A spoon-fed, mama's boy who was never taught how to handle his emotions or feelings. It's not my place to say if I think you can be rehabilitated, but seriously, don't you already know my answer? I'd fear

259

for any woman in your path that you choose to sink into again. Your mentally abusive ways were no match to that of your physical demands. I worry that in another decade you'll be free, and seek me out to carry out your promises of "forever." I worry that all my life, I'll be partially turned around, wondering if you're watching me. "

She paused for a moment, glancing up over the top of the paper at me. I smiled a little, letting her know she was doing fine. I had always known, but hearing her words say these things was incredibly heavy. My heart broke hearing she was still afraid of him. I was there for most of it, and I don't know how she survived him. *And you see the things she didn't write about, like the night terrors, nightmares, and her intense paranoia...*

"Go on, baby, you're doing just fine." Her eyes were filled with tears, but she managed to give a small smile, and her eyes fell back into her letter. Heather looked upset, pained even. Greg was smiling, like me, hoping she could finish reading it aloud.

"I've spent years working on myself, to fix the fears you've instilled, and rebuild myself for my family. I'm come to this point by the grace of something, and fate. Fate brought me Gabriel, and gave me a chance. I'd like to think you are owed that same chance in life, but far away from me. There's no way I ever want to be your neighbor. There's no way I could ever be. I hope you find whatever you're looking for, and stop trying to find it in the past. In me. Your letters take me back to every horrible memory you created, and I would appreciate it if the letters stopped.

I'm sure you can remember why, I do, every time I look at the scars. You've known me almost all my life...but still to this day, you've never truly known me.

I wish you the best your life can bring, and I hope that for once, you can respect my wishes. Someday, I hope you have a daughter, and I hope that she finds someone like you. Because I don't think you'll ever really get it, until that time comes.

Goodbye, Michael.

"If ever words were spoken
Painful and untrue
I said I loved but I lied
In my life
All I wanted was the keeping
Of someone like you
As it turns out Deeper within me
Love was twisted and pointed at you..." –
Pantera

Janie"

She cautiously lowered the paper, laying it on the lounger behind her. She wiped a tear from her cheek, and smiled at us all. The heaviness was back, and silence filled the air. *Wow.*

"That was really good, Janes. Right on point." Heather smiled, and scooted around the hot tub, putting her arm around Janie. "You know, I remember a lot of the past, too. The times you would come into work in tears, with wounds and bruises..." she shook her head, trying to expel the horrible memories. I couldn't help think of just how many people Michael had touched in some way.

"I'm sorry," her voice was small, and meek.

"No Janie," Heather was quick to correct her. "It wasn't your fault, and I'm happy I was there, that I could be for you."

"Yeah, don't apologize, Janes." Greg sat up, facing Janie. "I remember when Gabe came home, and first told us about you. Before you two were 'you two,' he worried about you constantly. His worry made us worry, and when he asked if we'd help protect you, I jumped at the chance." I remember the moment he was talking about, and he did jump up and down.

"Hell yeah you did!" I laughed. "Any chance to fight an asshole you're usually in on," I joked, and Greg laughed hard.

"Anyway, I think it's a good letter. First and last, then?" Janie nodded. "And the lyrics at the end?"

"I hope so, not something I want to dwell on constantly. Or, any more than I have to." She sighed, and the stress was almost visibly lifting from her. "That's an old Pantera song. I fucking hate Pantera." Wrapping in her towel, she stood again glancing in my direction. "I appreciate you listening. Soundboards are nice to have. I'll be right back." She picked up the paper, and headed back into the house.

"I give her so many kudos," Heather said, taking a drink of her wine. "She's been through so much. She deserves a little peace and quiet." *Oh, God. How true is that?* I nodded in complete agreement, and suddenly wondered about the situation with Sean. *If I just knew when...*

"I do everything I can to make her feel safe..." I couldn't even finish the sentence. How could I even say that? I didn't protect her from Cain, Simon, or Sean, and we're in the middle of a cloud of bullshit now, too. *You do try, Gabe, but you can't stop the world from spinning...*

"Gabe," Greg began. "You're torturing yourself. I can see it. Stop, man. These paths are set up years before by fate. These things that keep happening are unstoppable. But look at how strong they've made you both. And how close it has brought you together." He was right, as twisted as it sounded.

"I know. It just seems so never ending sometimes. I'd hate to think how wonderful life would be without all of these stressors and incidents over the years." They chuckled.

"I think some people are predestined for life's worst situations." Janie rejoined the group, sitting next to me and dipping her legs in the water.

"What are people predestined for?" She smiled, curiously.

"I just think some people are predestined for hell in life, the worst, you know? I think those people are the strongest people on the planet." Janie's face flushed, understanding the point, reaching for her drink.

"I didn't mean to turn our evening heavy, but I can't tell you how much just reading that aloud made me feel... It's been so much fun getting some time with you guys again. We'd love it if you visited us at the lake next weekend, with the kids! Lilah and Galen would love to see them!" She rested her hand on my thigh, and her smile seemed a little bit brighter. She looked lighter.

"That sounds like a plan, Janes!" He turned to me. "Man, I haven't seen the parents in years!" We filled our glasses, and talked a few hours away. In the still of the night, we said our goodbyes until the next weekend at the lake. Walking arm and arm with Janie back up the driveway in the starlight was romantic, and we were both incredibly drunk.

30

Locking up the house, we both fell into bed. The chill from the air conditioner made her cold. She had draped her arms over my waist for warmth. I had drunk myself almost to the point of room spin, so I threw a foot down to the floor. She laughed into my side.

"Little too much, honey?" she asked, raising her head so she could see me. Her hair was extremely messy, and hanging in her eyes. Her eyes bore into mine, heating up every extremity and appendage I had. Green and brown, blazing with need. I slid my fingers into her hair, making my intentions much known. She leaned in, and kiss me gently on the lips.

She seemed to be moving in slow motion, relishing every touch and every kiss. She barely took her eyes off of mine, except to close them. She sat up slowly, untying the top of her bikini letting it fall to her abdomen. She laid back on her side, her breasts falling over with her. *Delicious*. Forcing myself through the spins, I propped myself up to a more upright position. That's a little better.

Sticking with her slow, steady pace, my hands sought out her bottoms, and pulled the strings. The small piece of fabric fell away in the sheets, and I was left with exactly what I was seeking. She laid back on the bed, eyes bright with desire, and opened herself to me. I couldn't resist dipping my fingers into her. *Oh god... so soft, so hot...* I watched her squirm and twist around on the bed. *So fucking wet...* Squeezing her nipple between my fingers, her hips jutted towards me.

I couldn't wait. I pulled her on top of me, and she sank on to my rock hard shaft. I held her still, taking me entirely in and felt her walls shake and shatter.

"Please, oh, please, move!" she begged between breaths. Obliging the best I could, I linked fingers with her, helping her rise into the air for leverage. It was then she took over, riding me quickly, breasts bouncing everywhere. Catching them to suck on became a new game.

Suddenly, she twisted around, and was facing away from me. *Jesus Gabe, what a view...* Watching myself sink into her never got old. It was home. Janie had always brought this calming comfort that let my head go to all sorts of places. Her walls began to quiver, and she soaked me with her essence. Her body shook, and I held her tightly to me. Her orgasms rolled on and on. Pumping into her, I was deep, and she felt every eruption.

Before I knew it, her mouth covered mine. Her tongue probing deeply, fisting my hair, moaning into my mouth. I could feel her throbbing and twitching on my shaft. Her hand cupped my cheek, and she nuzzled into my neck. I wrapped my arms around her tightly, and pulled her into me once more.

"Easy Mister," she warned, still quaking from moments before. Steadying herself on the bed, she pulled herself off of me. Grabbing a towel and wrapping it around her waist, she was quick to avoid creating any wet spots. She laid back down next to me, cuddling into my side, and covering us both with a sheet. "I needed that, thanks," she yawned.

I couldn't move, just exhausted and spent from sex. Instead I laid there, watching the most beautiful woman in the world fall asleep. Her hair was still a disaster, but I loved the way it fell around her face. Her skin was so soft no matter where I touched. Carefully, as to not disturb her, I ran my fingers over her shoulder and down her side. She only leaned into me more. I let the sleep win, and drifted off hanging on to her.

~

I could hear Janie in the house, mulling around like normal. Eventually she made her way into the bedroom, sitting on the bed next to me. She gently tapped my shoulder.

"You awake?" she whispered. I tried to stifle a giggle, but I couldn't.

"Of course I'm awake. Who could live through that violent shaking?" Hiding my face under a pillow, she patted my legs.

"Well, come on and get up! Don's been trying to reach you, he needs you to come into work for a little bit today." She patted me again. I felt my throat dry…maybe this was it? *Or maybe he's just filling you in on things?* Either way, I couldn't wait to find out. Tossing the pillow off of my face, I aimed straight for her. The pillow made her hair poof behind her. "You ass!" she yelled, smacking my rear as hard as she could before leaving the bedroom.

I headed into the bathroom and jumped into the shower quickly. Climbing out, I could hear Janie talking to someone in the living room. On the phone, maybe? I'd hoped so, as I'd left the bedroom door wide open. I stuck my head out and listened for a moment, determining how sneaky I needed to be.

"I know, I know. I've gone over it tons of times. No, that's okay. I'm comfortable enough with it." She laughed a little, in between sentences. *She must be on the phone.* I headed the closet, settling on my nicer business casual outfits. Giving myself the once over in the mirror before heading out, I noticed Janie's phone flashing on the counter. Checking around, I nudged the button, turning her screen on. A text from Mylah shown on the screen. "I'll be by in an hour or so." *Well, nothing off about that.*

"You look good today," she patted my shoulder, and reached up on her tip toe to kiss my cheek. "I really like the new work polo's. You look hot." Her hands fell down my back, and rested on my ass. "Know how long you'll be yet today?" I shook my head.

"Nope, I haven't even checked in. Probably should, but I figure I'll just head over." I leaned in to her, pulling her in to my lips for a quick, chaste kiss. "I'll let you know once I find out what's going on, okay?" She smiled, and nodded. "What are you going to do with yourself while I'm gone?"

"Oh, not much. Mylah's coming over in a bit. I thought about swimming at your mom's, since she's on that RV camping trip with her friends." She shrugged. "Our possibilities are limitless!" She sounded happy, and didn't seem as distracted or as unfocused like I was. I suppose that's a good thing though.

"All right, baby," one last kiss. "I'll talk to you in a little while." I swatted her ass as I walked by her and out to the car. I slowed on the way out of the driveway to nod, and wave at the security guard. My drive in to work was mindless, and frantic at the same time. I couldn't wait to hear what Donovan had planned for the day, or how we'd be dealing with Sean.

I parked quickly, all but running into the offices. Donovan was hanging up the phone when I walked in, and greeted me with a smile.

"Hey Gabe! How're you doing? Have a nice night last night?" I nodded, and forgot for a moment I had told him that Heather and Greg were coming over.

"Yeah, we had a good time. It had been a while since we had seen them. So," I sighed, still out of breath from running down the hall. "Today. Janie said you needed me?"

"Yep, I sent you a few texts this morning, but I figured you were sleeping, so I messaged her to wake your ass up!" He closed a few books on his desk, and stood from his chair. "I need your help with some deliveries and such today. Meet me in the big delivery truck in ten?" I nodded, feeling more confused than ever.

On my walk to the truck bay, my tornadic mind swirled freely. Where were we going? Sean had made it a point to say if I delivered, something bad would happen. To me? *To Janie?* What kind of delivery did this apply to? What kind of delivery were we making? I was getting a headache, fast. I climbed into the passenger seat, now in no mood to drive anywhere. Donovan hopped in a few moments later.

"Don," I couldn't take it any longer. "What's the deal man? About Sean? I need to know." He turned his lips into a frown, turned and looked out the windshield for a moment, and then back to me.

"It's being handled. That's what you need to know right now. I have two of my best employees on it right this minute, actually." *Right this minute?* Ok, that sounds promising...

"I'm just so eager for it all to end." Sighing, I caught Donovan awkwardly chuckling towards the window of the truck. Getting off on the highway ramp headed towards Indianapolis, he glanced at me out of the corner of his eye.

"Gabe, Jesus! Trust me. It will be over soon." His voice was serious, yet sarcastic. I never knew what to believe and what to ignore.

"I'm trying. So, if we're not meeting to discuss that, then what in the hell are we doing today?" He smiled at me.

"I thought you'd never ask. We're just moving a load of playground equipment for the local after school programs down to a different district." He flashed me all of his teeth. *Playground equipment?* Well, I doubt that will be an issue...

I couldn't believe my stress level. I pulled out my phone to text Janie, and let her know what was happening with my day. Don cranked the radio up, poorly singing the Rolling Stones that was playing on the radio, and I did my best to relax and enjoy the road trip.

~

Janie.

I waved at him as he left the driveway, and I could tell that he thought they were going to take care of Sean today. I'd managed to keep the plan a complete secret from him, although I don't know how. This was the loosest plan I'd ever been a part of. There were so many parts that could go wrong, and most likely would.

Before Mylah arrived for our pool day, I verified all of the security tapes were clean, and that they were all recording. I was careful not to tip off our security, knowing that anything extra may blow this out of the water. I needed to make the contact now, but I was extremely nervous. My hands shook as I held my cell phone, and opened up the text message to Sean.

Do you know where Gabe went? Is he at work yet? Just need to talk to him. Thx.

I hit send, and tried to continue with my day. I grabbed a basket and four towels, some tanning lotion, and my cell charger. I heard the sound of squeaking breaks, and I looked up to see Mylah's car stopped at the guard station. He waved her through, and she waved out the window at me. I waved back, but my nerves wouldn't let me smile. The familiar ringtone came through my cell, and I opened it to find Sean's reply. *Pearl Jam.* So many memories of band practice days gone past...

I'll check for him and let you know.

Mylah parked her car next to mine, leaving the windows down. She pulled a big cooler out of the backseat, smiling widely.

"I brought some goodies, and leftovers from the big party. There's even a tad bit of Don's punch left." I shook my head. Only Mylah could remain this level headed. "Don't worry, Janes. We've got this under control." I smiled, hiding all the doubts I was having.

"Let's head back to the pool, and we can get ourselves settled." I took a step to pick up my towel basket, and got an extremely sharp pain in my abdomen. "Fuck!" I yelled, bending over in pain. The familiar pull of my PCOS syndrome showed its ugly head. It had been quite a while since I'd had any issues. *Must be the stress...*

"Janie!" Mylah ran to my side. "What's happening?!" I shook my head, and steadied myself on her arm.

"Really bad cramp, or something. I'll be fine. Perfectly normal for all of this excitement." I stood slowly, testing out my muscles. They had relaxed a little, and now there wasn't as much hurt around my middle. I took a deep breath, and rested my hand on my stomach. "Must just be the stress."

"Let me know if you're not feeling well, or if I can get you anything, ok? Let's just go enjoy a little bit of pool time." She punched my shoulder gently. "Just us girls." I picked up my pile of stuff, and we headed back to Jean's pool area.

Walking up into the back yard, Jean had a solid shrub line with one path in, and one path out of her backyard. The pool was L shaped, and we took our seats at the far corner, where the sun was the brightest. *And also because you're on camera here… give it a wave and a wink.* I nonchalantly looked up, and made sure the green light was on. *Excellent.* From my chair, I had a blurry shot of our driveway, and the grassy area between our houses. I swallowed hard knowing that soon, if this all went according to plan, I'd be rectifying the problem.

We laid our towels out across our chairs, got ourselves comfortable and ready for the long day in the sun. For now, I left my cover up on, not wanting a sunburn on top of everything else. Mylah put the giant cooler between us, opened it up, revealing the premade Bloody Mary's for breakfast.

"How about we get some vegetables in for breakfast?" I nodded, my mouth was actually watering. "I've even got extra hot sauce." She winked, pouring my glass with extra ice, too. The ice cold drink felt great to hold on to in the warm morning sun, sweating cool water that dripped on to my skin. I drank it in only a few sips. She plugged her phone in to the outlet, and turned on her iPod. She finally laid back, and took a drink of her own Bloody Mary. "Ahh," she smacked her lips with pleasure. "That's really fucking good." My phone buzzed, and I unburied it from my towel basket. I had a few missed texts. *Shit.* Gabe, too. I had to deal with Sean's first.

He's not here, and neither is Don. Where the fuck are they?

Hello? Weren't you supposed to keep him off of runs? I just Heard he's out on runs with Don.

One more chance.

Shit. I turned to Mylah, and made a face. If he was angry, would any of this stay on track? "He's really pissed off, Mylah."

272

"Well, just answer him. Stick to it, for now." I nodded, and typed as fast as I could. I needed to get these texts in to ensure that our asses were covered.

I'm sorry, I'm not sure where he is. He left for work early this morning. Hasn't texted me yet today.

"Now we wait." My hands shook so I took a long drink of the punch, hoping that would help calm my nerves. Mylah was almost done with hers. Suddenly, her phone rang. She answered very cheerfully.

"Hey. Yep, all is well. We're just laying by the pool, drinking some Bloodys." It must've been Donovan. "Janie? Oh, she's good. Cool as a cucumber!" She laughed, "Oh, I'm sure. Of course I will. Cool. See ya." She hung up, and shaded her face with her hand. "Gabe and Don are almost in Indy. Did he tell you what they're doing?" I shook my head, wondering if not knowing would be better.

"No, I still haven't talked to Gabe since he left this morning." I tried to hide the worry in my voice.

"Oh, well, they're perfectly safe. They're transporting some new playground equipment for an after school program in another district." I smiled, a bit taken aback by their task.

"That's really cool, actually." She nodded, and I finished off the last sips of my drink. My cell phone buzzed, but it wasn't Sean. Or Gabe. Just Bradley reporting on his last few clients. I checked the time, and it was almost 11am. *Why isn't Sean responding?*

Mylah baked herself in the morning sun, with Zeppelin blaring. My head felt heavy with so many details floating around. I found myself scanning the yard like someone was going to pop out of nowhere. *Stop it, Janie.* Everything is going to be all right. Out of the silence, *'Whole Lotta Love'* came blaring through my cell. I answered quickly, afraid to miss an important text.

"Hey Gabe," I tried to not overthink the massive secret I had been hiding. "How's your day?"

"Hey love, we're almost to Indy. That's where we're delivering today. I wasn't sure if Mylah filled you in yet, or not." There were lots of road sounds in the background, and Donovan swearing at all the other drivers.

"Oh, we're good. Mylah and I are back at your mom's pool. We just finished our breakfast Bloody Marys, and now we've moved on to baking in the sun." I giggled.

"Sounds fun, I wish I was there instead. Hopefully I will be later this afternoon. Don's talking about a get together this weekend if we're up to it before we head to the lake." I was starting to worry. I wasn't sure what Don had ended up telling him, and what he hadn't. I didn't want to risk saying the wrong thing, or give too much away.

"Sure, we can give it some thought."

"All right, I'll let you go. I just wanted to check in, and hear your voice. I miss you something crazy today. I can't get you off of my mind." I knew why he missed me more. His senses were on high, just as mine were.

"Let me know when you're on your way home, okay? I'll try to be done baking by then." He chuckled, and I knew I was in the clear.

"Sounds good, I love you." The line went dead, and I sighed and sunk into my chair. This entire situation was giving me too many intense feelings. But, for the first time in forever I felt strong, and powerful. I felt like I could control how this was going to play out, and I'd never felt that way before. As if on cue, I looked up to see the car pull in to the driveway, and stop at the guard station. Sean had arrived. Just as we had planned.

Silently reaching next to me, I grabbed Mylah's hand, alerting her of our company. We both watched across the distance, and the guard did exactly as he was told allowing him in to the drive. He drove quickly to my house, and parked behind Mylah's car. Stopping so quickly, he stirred up a cloud of dust from the gravel. We watched him storm into the house, and heard him screaming my name. She squeezed my hand. I could hear doors opening, and slamming closed. Loose picture frames shattered against the hard tile floor. He was angry as ever, and I knew it was time.

31
Janie.

"I'm going to go in Jean's guest house now. If anything goes wrong, just say the word." She nodded, picking up the flask she kept at her side, and took a long drink. I quickly headed in to the guest house living room, and cracked the window to the pool so I could hear what was happening. Sean was storming across the yard, closing his distance to the pool.

I watched Mylah sit up, acknowledging he was coming towards her. She gave him a small wave, and I saw her adjust something underneath the cooler lid. It looked like a black handle... I had debated for weeks, and had finally decided just a day before. I turned around and reached underneath the kitchen counter. The handle of the Sig 9mm fit perfectly into my hand.

I proceeded to the living room, checking underneath the couch cushion where I had left the other Walther automatic. Sliding my hand under, it was exactly where I had put it. I went back over to the side window to see what was transpiring. My heart was beating out of my chest, and I was worried for us both. Sean was walking into the pool area via the only real entrance there was.

"Hey Sean!" Mylah said nicely. "How've you been?" She was being so jovial.

"Where the fuck is Janie? I need to talk to her." His fists were balled, and rage sprayed from his pores. Witnessing that anger brought it all back. *No one is ever as they seem...*

"She'll be back in a minute. What's got you all hot, man?" He was silent for a few moments, and finally started to pace back and forth.

"Just need to talk to her. Can't seem to get a straight answer from anyone else." His eyes searched the pool grounds, and now he'd turned to the pool house.

"Oh, I'm sure she'll talk to you when she's back. I think she had a phone call." He nodded, trying to hold on to the little patience he had left. "Can I give you some advice?" He looked at her blankly. "Maybe tone it down a little? She's not in the best mood, and you know how that can be..."

"Oh yeah?" he shrugged it off, but pointed his finger sternly at the pool house. "Is she in the pool house?" He started to walk towards the sliding door, and I was instantly in action. I punched in the code as fast as I could for the inside and outside cameras to begin recording at Jean's. The beep let me know it had worked. I hit record on my cell phone's voice recorder, and pretended I was on the phone to the kids just in case the videos were not enough. I could see him walking up to the door, and reaching for the handle.

Come on, Janie. You've got this. Now's the time you stand up for yourself, and your family. No more getting walked over, or on. No more being forced into anything. You do what you have to do to protect yourself. To reclaim yourself, and your life. I swallowed hard.

"Oh! That sounds so wonderful!" I said into the voice recorder. I could hear him yelling from the minute the door opened.

"Janie?! Are you in here?!" he left the door open, and headed in the house, almost walking by me in the kitchen. I leaned on the counter, holding a finger up to him to wait a minute.

"Aww, that's great news! All right buddy, I'll let you go for now. Uncle Sean is here, so I'm going to go chat with him. Okay, I love you, too. Always." I pretended to turn off the phone, really just dimming the screen. "Hey, Sean. What's up? You didn't text me back, did you?"

"No, I didn't. We have a problem, Janes." He took a few intimidating steps towards me, and I put the kitchen island between us.

"Why do we have a problem? Gabe's not been working on that side of the business." This was a fact, and now I knew it.

"That's a lie. He's out on a run with Donovan right now. I thought we had a deal?" He rested his hands on the counter top, mulling over his next move. I was just satisfied he'd left such great prints on the counter top without much hassle.

"That's not a lie at all. You've obviously been misinformed, again. They're delivering playground equipment for a school." Even if he didn't listen, I wanted to say it out loud. I shifted on my feet, getting ready for whatever was next. "So, what're you here for?" I pushed.

"You really think I believe that? I told you that you'd pay if he didn't get out! First you, then him, then maybe your kids. Your friends." Had he really just brought my children into this? *Wrong. Dead fucking wrong.* I swallowed my rage and disguised it as terror, so he would think he was getting somewhere. "Get over here, and give me what I want."

"I don't want anything to do with you," I stepped away from him making myself closer to the living room, than to the gun under the kitchen counter. "You need to find a new method, Sean. I'm not in the mood for this!"

278

"You were never in the mood for this, Janie. Not with me, anyways." He reached for my arm, and I pulled away, knocking myself purposefully on to the couch. "That's it, stay right there. I'd like to bend you over the back of that couch." The bile rose in my throat. "I can't imagine how Gabe's going to feel knowing I'm violating you on his own property. In his mother's own house."

"I can't believe this is what you've turned in to! You use to be my friend! Now you just like to use me to get whatever else it is you want! Whether its sex, or stimulation...you're disgusting!" Taking another step towards me, I spit at him and I held up my hand. I began to yell. "Don't come near me, asshole!! I'm done with all the fuckwads like you in my life! I don't owe anyone shit, and I'm tired of this! You're a spineless pussy of a man who hides behind false promises, and can't take care of his own family!! You think I give three shits about your business or your life? You're very, *very* wrong. Consider that your final warning." He rolled his eyes, his hands lowering to his button on his jeans, fumbling to undo it.

"Oh Janie, trouble for you is, I know your secrets. We both know what's going to happen here, so just make it easier on yourself and take off your suit. If I have to do it for you, it's not going to be done smoothly." *Hear that, kid? He thinks he knows what's going to happen here. Do you think he knows what's going to happen here?* I smiled at my own thoughts. His pants fell a few inches once he undid his zipper, and a few more inches when he pulled out his straw-thin penis.

"Don't take another fucking step towards me, Sean!" I screamed. He took one step, and in one suave motion, I pulled the gun from under the couch cushion, and aimed it at his chest. *Safety off.*

"Whoa, Janie..." he froze, speechless and unable to move. His hands began to shake, then his arms. We stood silently for a few seconds, staring at each other. The power that

279

came from holding a loaded gun on someone who had forced you into doing things you didn't want to do was insanely righteous. *This feels good, feels right... just like taking down Michael.* There was no more talking, he had crossed every line I had ever had. My anger raged, and my hand clung tightly to the gun with little thought. *What good was he?*

My mind spun out of control, and in front of me was Michael. Heavy breathing, with fists of rage. I saw myself holding the gun on him, and ending the hell I faced once and for all. Squinting my eyes, shaking the visions away, I steadied the gun assuring it was aimed square at his chest. Opening my eyes again I saw Simon, and my body started to ache, remembering all of the hurt and pain. *Janie, calm down...* I felt the tears spring to my eyes, and I knew there wasn't anything I could do to stop myself. Cain's words rang out in my ears, *"This is all your fault."* So many years of fear have now boiled down to this.

"You shouldn't have pushed me..." I managed to speak in a dark, shady whisper. He shifted, slowly pulling his pants up. "You shouldn't have used Gabe, or Lizzie. Forcing people to do things isn't very human. But neither are you." We stood at an impasse, only feet apart. Reading his face, he was planning out his best method to take me down. I could see it coming, and there's no way I was giving up this gun.

"Maybe there's another way we can work this out. What do you say, Janie?" I wasn't sure there was anything left to say. Memories from years before flooded back. Sean never acted against Michael, never stood in my defense. I'm still unclear on his exact role in the kidnapping, but after all of this, I'm sure he had a hand. My heart sped up, and my pulse raced. Tears streamed down both cheeks. My tears peaked his worry. "Janie... you wouldn't." *It's now or never... it's time for you to reclaim everything that's been taken from you. Everything.*

"I warned you, Sean! I *fucking* warned you!" I whispered, knowing the cameras didn't have very good sound recording. My finger tightened and pulled the trigger. I held my eyes wide open. The gun fired, and rang into my ears. Without much thought, I squeezed the pistol once more, and another shot rang out.

The silence that overcame the room was intense. Sean grabbed at his chest, wide eyed. He stumbled back a few feet, holding himself up on the counter. I couldn't take my eyes off of him, as he started to collapse to the floor, I was distracted by Mylah at the doorway.

"Janie!" She yelled, and as if I was in a trance, snapped out of it. Looking back to Sean, he reached out for help. I dropped the gun on the floor, and ran out of the guest house. The adrenaline was pushing through my veins, and tears were pouring down my cheeks. I finally caught up to her as we ran across the yard. Only small glances were exchanged, like a silent acknowledgement of the events. As planned, she reached the guard station first and began banging on the door.

"Hey Shane!! Call 911!! Sean just tried to attack Janie!" He looked dumbstruck, and fumbled with his phone calling for help. I reached the station, out of breath, sweating, and pale.

"Please get the police, and an ambulance. He tried to rape me, and I defended myself. He's in the back pool house."

"Are you okay, Mrs. Lazarus? Ms. Bush?" He spoke the address to the dispatch while looking us both over. I knew things were going to start to happen quickly, and I was confident that Mylah and I had this all covered. The stress made it easy to cover all the bases, and I let the waterworks begin. "Okay, I'll tell them." He turned back to us, repeating what the dispatch had asked. "They're only minutes away. Should I alert Mr. Lazarus and Mr. James?" I shook my head.

"No, I don't want to worry them yet. The police will contact them, too." He shook his head in agreement. I sat down on the grass, feeling a little overwhelmed with all of this. Mylah took a seat next to me.

"We've got this Janie. You did great," she whispered, wrapping her arm around my side, kissing my hair. "Now we let the videos tell the story." She was right, but emotions were getting the better of me. I had just shot a man, twice, and I felt little emotion about it.

The police cars pulled into the driveway, and past where we sat. The ambulance followed them through the grass, and back to the pool house. Two cars parked by where we sat, and two male officers came over to us.

"Mam, could you come with me?" One officer said to Mylah. She nodded, stood slowly and walked with him. The other took a seat next to me, noticing the tremors my body was having.

"Mrs. Lazarus? I'm Detective Charles Witt. I need to take your statement, and find out what happened here today. Is that okay?" He handled me with porcelain gloves. I nodded, auspiciously, still crying. "Start at the beginning, slowly." I nodded again, sniffling up tears.

"We were just out by the pool, just sitting there enjoying the morning sun." I replayed the entire scenario in my head as I spoke it. "We heard commotion across the yard, but couldn't really see because of Jean's trees and shrubs around the pool." He frantically jotted down everything I was saying, and looked up at the tree line around Jeans'.

"Are you referring to those tree lines back where the other officers are?" I nodded. "Okay, what happened next?"

"I heard some noises, so I went into the pool guest house to call up to the guard station. I was taken off guard when I heard Sean's voice, and Mylah started to argue. I went back to the window, and saw Sean barreling towards the pool house. I tried to hit the alarm button to lock all the doors, but I was too slow, and they didn't lock." I took a slow, deep breath, calming myself again.

"He entered the pool house?"

"Yes, he came into the kitchen where I was, and tried to grab me around the bar. He was angry about something that had happened at work. He works with my husband at James Industries, and was angry that his job was coming to an end."

"Why would he bother you then?" I shrugged. "Continue please, if you can."

"He started to fumble with his pants, and told me to take mine off, or he would do it for me." My eyes filled with tears again, as with every other time I'd become the fetish and desire of the most unstable men in America. *Don't fumble, Janie.* I let the tears fall, and it was easy considering everything from my past.

"Just a moment, Mrs. Lazarus." He radioed for another officer to bring a bottle of water to me, and to Mylah. "Sorry about that, just wanted to get you a cold drink. It's intense out here today." He nodded, and held his pen to his small tablet of paper.

"He dropped his pants, exposing himself to me. He took a few steps towards me, and I pulled the gun out on him. I warned him, and told him to leave... But he wouldn't go." I sobbed, now thinking of what I had done. I thought of Delaney, and all the years we had been friends. I thought of Dom, and how I just took away his chance to ever get to know his dad. *Stop it. What about what he was going to do to you? Again?*

"And you shot him?" I nodded, covering my face in my hands. He nodded, and patted my back. "I'm sorry you had to go through this, Mrs. Lazarus. I need you to stay put here, while we finish taking Ms. Bush's statement, and gather evidence."

"Can I move under the tree please? For some shade?" I asked, he smiled and nodded and went to confer with group of officers back by the pool house. Sitting back against the tree, I couldn't stop playing it all through my head. Detail by detail. Over and over. I noticed that the ambulance hadn't left yet, which was a little disgruntling. *Did you make the shot? Did you miss?*

The police scurried around for over an hour, keeping myself and Mylah apart. Of course this was policy, but being alone wasn't helping me out at all. Finally my phone rang, and it was Gabe. I hadn't been instructed not to answer, so I did.

"Hello?" I said nervously.

"Janie?! What's going on?! We just heard the police are there? Are you okay?!" He sounded shattered, and in pieces.

"Everything is fine, Gabe. I'm just a bit shaken up. Mylah is okay, too." There was a long pause, and a heavy sigh.

"What happened?"

"Sean was pissed off. I mean really, really angry. He showed up to take it out on me. Just like he promised. I just wasn't going to take it again."

"I'm so sorry I wasn't there. I'm about an hour away. We're heading straight to you guys. I love you, baby."

"I love you, too." I hung up, and noticed Mylah was strolling back across the lawn, escorted by an officer to sit with me.

"Go ahead and sit here, Ms. Bush. We'll be back with you both shortly. They're just finishing up with the crime scene." I nodded, and looked at Mylah. She waited until the officer was out of ear shot, and leaned in to whisper to me.

"Don and Gabe will be here soon. Gabe just called." I said flatly.

"I heard them talking... we're in the clear. We are the victims here." I fell back in the grass, hoping I'd made all of the right decisions. Hoping that I'd just given my family the peace we've sought for almost a decade. Leaning up on my elbows, I heard the ambulance start, and begin driving back down the driveway, past where we sat in the grass. No lights. No sirens. No rush. It was then I knew I my mission was successful.

Laying down I looked up at the clouds. They were huge, puffy like cotton-balls, and perfectly white. There wasn't much of anything that was perfectly white in my life anymore. *You're just as strong as ever, Janes.* I smiled a little, picking out an alligator flying by in the big clouds. After everything over the years, it took me to end the drama. Me to stand up and take control of my life. Never again will I be forced into anything. *Ever.*

32

"Janie!" I screamed from the street, being held back by
the police officers. "Please, this is my house, and that is my
wife!" After checking my credentials, and verifying I lived there,
he let me pass. Janie looked pale, and emotionless. I engulfed
her in my arms, and turned back to Donovan, bending my brow
at him. "I love you, Janie." I didn't let go, and neither did she.

I knew what had happened here, especially after seeing
the police surrounding the pool house. I couldn't believe he'd
put her up to handling this. *Amazing...*

"Are you and Janie okay?" I heard Don ask Mylah.

"Yeah, we're good. Everything went just as it
should've." I couldn't believe what I was hearing.

"And what if it hadn't!?" I asked abruptly.

"Then we would've stepped in to plan two." Janie spoke
up, looking up at me with tear stained, truth telling swollen

eyes. She took a step back from me, still hanging on to my arms for support. "I'm done being taken advantage of, Gabe. And there was no way I was going to let him hurt you. I was just reclaiming and protecting everything that's ours." Her eyes searched mine, and I pulled her back to me. "The ambulance left about an hour ago, and the police are just cleaning up, and documenting evidence."

"Yes, the officer over by the entrance said they'd be over in a few moments to update us on what's happening. This will be over soon." My eyes met Don's again, and we exchanged some unspoken words. We'd bonded years before, over other bad decisions, and our understanding of each other was deep.

"Janie," he began. "You are the strongest among us. I wouldn't have trusted anyone else with this. I'm forever in your debt. Gabriel, your wife is amazing, and just saved us all." I nodded, and noticed the police were taking down the tape, and some were getting in their cars and leaving. Two detectives approached our group.

"Mrs. Lazarus," one said, and then extended their hands to myself and Donovan. "I'm Detective Huff. We've spent the last few hours collecting and reviewing the evidence. We'll be submitting the videos, as well as both of your statements to the prosecutor to determine the outcome. As for Mr. Westing, he expired due to his injuries after the attempted assault of Mrs. Lazarus." He opened his notepad to a separate page, "Yes, they did call the tow company, so his car should be removed from your driveway in the next hour or so. Does anyone have any questions for us?"

"Can we go back into our house? What about my mother's?" The detectives turned and looked back towards the pool house.

"You're free to go into your own house, but please stay out of the back area until we are completely done with our investigation. We should know more for you on that by this evening." He handed me a business card. "If you need anything before then, please call me." Janie stood emotionless, looking lost after the afternoons events. He turned to Janie, and extended his hand to her. Without hesitation, she took his hand, and her eyes filled with tears.

"Mrs. Lazarus, I commend you on your bravely, and self-preservation. I'm told this is not your first experience with someone like Mr. Westing, and for that, I'm truly sorry. You looked incredibly terrified in the videos, and I think you did the right thing. It was obvious what he was ready to take from you, and your quick thinking may have saved both yours, and Ms. Bush's lives." Janie sobbed, and I did my best to support her shaking body. "Will you be staying here, or staying somewhere else for a few days?"

"We will be going to stay at her parent's lake house for a few weeks. We were planning on leaving next week, but I think we'll leave much sooner."

"I think that's a great idea. We have your phone numbers in case further testimony is needed, but I feel that the evidence is clear." He extended his hand to me, and I shook it firmly. "Thank you, Mr. Lazarus. Mrs. Lazarus." He turned on his heel, and headed to his car awaiting him at the mouth of our driveway.

We all stood in silence, still taking in what had just happened. "I don't even feel like this is real." Donovan let slip from his lips. "I think we should all take some time and let things calm down and cool off. Why don't you guys head up to the lake, and plan on staying for a few weeks? I'll have things cleaned up here, and Jean will never see the dismay." I nodded.

"I think that's a good idea. You guys can still join us up there next week if you'd like." Mylah nodded, and Don smiled. "Is there anything else that needs to be discussed about what happened today?" Each pair of eyes met the next, but no words were exchanged. *Are you having a hard time understanding why no one filled you in?*

"How long was this planned?" I had to know.

"A week or two, right after he accosted her in the gardens after the party." My mouth fell open. "Well, after you filled me in, I mean." I understood, but I didn't like any of it. Looking at my wife, I could tell that this had affected her in some deep way. With Janie, it could be a while before anyone really knew how.

"Now that this has been worked out, I'm assuming you'll stay on board with the company?" I hadn't thought of it much, other than I needed to be done with the cartel. *Now is as good a time as any to throw that out there...*

"Yes, I'll stay in James Industries. I'm done with the cartel though, and I hope you can understand that." He smiled, and slid his hands into his pockets. Janie looked up from the ground, finally, giving me a genuine smile. She mouthed the words "thank you" to me, and my heart melted. *Why didn't you do this sooner?*

"Oh, Gabriel, many of our locations will miss you, but you'll be the best I've got on my business side. I'll spend the next few days wiping your name off of everything involving the cartel. I've not done the greatest things for either of you since I've known you, but I swear to God I'll make up for it all to you both."

"It's not all your fault, Donovan. We've all played our parts. This connects the four of us together forever, and I'm okay with that. I know the people standing around me now would do absolutely anything for me, and I hope they now know that I'm capable of providing the same kind of protection." She wiped her eyes, and let out a huge sigh. "I'm going in now to pack for the lake. I need to see my people, and from what I've heard, they're all at the lake waiting for us."

Donovan extended his arms to her, and she willingly accepted the hug.

"Janie, you're such an amazing woman. On so many levels, you've saved me. You're the best friend I've ever had, and I love you for it all." He looked back to me, and lifted a hand, but I knew he meant no harm.

"*Real* friends. There when you need them most, regardless of the situation." She turned to Mylah, and hugged her tightly. "Thanks for helping me with this. I'd never of been able to pull it off alone." *What? She'd never of been able to pull it off alone?*

"Listen boss, I'd do it again in a heartbeat. I can't wait to see your parents and Lilah and Lil G at the lake. I've missed them. I'll handle Caty, Kiara and Bradley this week, okay?" They locked eyes, but did not speak. Instead, their arms locked tighter around each other, solidifying their strange, but forever connected friendship and business relationship.

"Thank you," I heard her whisper as they broke their hug, sniffling noses and wiping eyes. Janie turned to walk away from us, "I'll see you both soon." *Something is still off with her...* I turned back to Don and Mylah.

"Well buddy, we're going to head home. We all have some quiet adjusting to do, and I've got some things to fix at work. Please let me know if you hear from the department about today, and know that my lawyer is your lawyer, and don't you dare hesitate to call him." He patted my shoulder, and I walked him to the end of the driveway. "Oh, and security," he pointed at Shane and Craig who were both standing in the guard station. "They are here for the rest of your lives. No question. I've never met two people more prone to dealing with the worst people and situations in the entire fucking world, Gabe." One loud chuckle slipped through my lips, and it felt oddly great. I laughed again, this time louder, and the stress, agony, pain, and confusion from the day fell away.

"See you later, Gabe." Mylah leaned in for a quick hug. "Take care of our girl, please." I nodded, and opened the truck door for her. Once safely inside, I closed her door, and waved. Donovan joined me in front of the truck, and we both stared at each other. There was so much to say, yet so little needed to be said.

"My brother," he tipped his eyes to the ground. "I owe you an apology for not including you in on Janie's plan. She knew it wouldn't work if you knew any part of it, and she's scary when she's serious." He shrugged, and I nodded. "She loves you so much Gabe, it's almost disgusting." This I knew today more than ever.

"I know." I patted his back as he climbed into the truck. Before I knew it, the truck was out of sight. Walking back up the driveway, I couldn't help notice the crime scene tape still up around the pool house. It dawned on me I hadn't seen the videos, so I turned around back to the guard station. I knocked, and Craig smiled from inside, unlocking and opening the door for me to step inside. "Hey, I need to check the tapes from the pool house today. Can you cue them up?"

"Of course, Mr. Lazarus." I watched him typing away, pulling the codes from the recorded videos on the hard drive. "Here it is, just hit start, and it will play through all of it."

"Thank you," I took the seat.

"Hey, uh, do you mind if I step out and have a smoke? I don't really want to see it again." I shook my head, and he stepped out of the station. My heart started to beat a little faster as the video played on. It showed Janie and Mylah walking back to the pool carrying all of their things. I could see them laying in their chairs in the sun, and on the same camera, could see Sean's car pulling into the driveway and parking. His fists were clearly clenched, and he was visibly angry. *Jesus, what would he have done to her if she hadn't fired?*

291

The video shows Mylah in her chair, and Sean approaching, but where is Janie? The outdoor cameras stopped picking up Sean, but I could still see Mylah. She laid on her chair, listening to her music. Her sunglasses hiding where her eyes were looking. Suddenly, the cameras changed, and the inside cameras were tripped on. There stands Janie, behind the island counter, moving from side to side, step-for-step opposite of what Sean was doing. *Look at her face.* She was calm, and straight faced.

The cameras shifted just as a scuffle happened, and Janie ended up on the couch. I could see his pants hanging down, unbuckled and cock out. *Disgusting!* The violent, angry look on his face told me all I needed to know. After he stumbled to the ground, I watched her spit on him, running away from the pool house. I didn't need to see more. I closed my eyes for a moment, rubbing my temples a bit.

"All done, Mr. Lazarus?"

"Oh, yes, I'm sorry. Let me get out of your way. Thanks, again." I headed back up the driveway towards our house. I was desperate to see her. I needed to tell her how much I loved her, and how proud I was of her.

Walking in the house, the luggage was sprawled out everywhere. The music was blaring, and its tone was very melodramatic. She came out of Galen's room, zipping up a smaller suitcase for him. She froze when she saw me. Her face still strained, she looked physically ill. I took a few steps over the suitcases, and threw my arms around her tighter than ever. Her arms eventually found their way around me.

"I'm so sorry I wasn't here, and I'm so thankful you're okay." She pressed her nose into my neck. "You were right though... I never, ever would've let you do this." She laughed a little, finally, and pulled away from me. The smirk remained on her face, and she shook her head at me. When she crossed her arms, I knew I would get an explanation.

"I won't lie. At first, I was doing it to save you, and take the threat away." She leaned to her other foot. "But then he was here, all raging and angry, and he was seriously going to rape me, again." She shook her head, now in disbelief. "My friend? My friend." She nodded. "I didn't have a choice. Being confronted with that again, brought everything else right to the surface. For those few minutes, I only wanted my life back. I just wanted to reclaim what's rightfully mine. *Ours*."

"You're so much braver and stronger than I'll ever be."

"No, no I think we're both incredibly strong. You've saved me plenty of times. It was definitely my turn to return the favor." This was the best woman in the world. She's been through hell multiple times, and every time manages to come out like a Phoenix, burning brighter and more beautiful than ever.

Our lips met passionately, and we stumbled over suitcases and lake toys to the couch. There was a certain peace that overtook our house knowing now that there was truly no one there to beat down our door. Probing into her mouth, she tasted like sweet cherries...

~

Janie.

The drive to the lake was a beautiful one. So many trees and open fields to take in while the Indiana air takes your breath away. Gabe decided to drive, and sing loudly to *'Secrets'* by One Republic, leaving me to my thoughts. Being away from the house is just what I need to get past today, and everything that's happened in the past decade. *Chin up, it's time to start anew... your secrets are safe.*

I've let others run my life, and steer my decisions. I've been walked over, on, and forced into doing things I didn't want to do. Forced into being with people I didn't want to be with. I've been manipulated, taken advantage of, and physically assaulted. I've been emotionally raped repeatedly. I've also been strong, stubborn, smart and successful. I've grown two beautiful babies, and a marriage that I know will last through the trenches. I've started my own business, and it's thriving, slow and sure. I've made the deepest of friendships in the most awkward of situations. I'm lucky enough to get a new start, again.

And regardless of what the future has in store for us, we'll handle it just like we've handled everything else. *Together.* I intertwined my fingers with Gabe's, as we drove into our personal lake paradise. I could see the kids jumping on the trampoline, and the water looked shimmery and warm behind them. My happiness was all around me.

And if anyone ever threatened that again, well, this time I won't give any warning at all...

The End.

*Follow Author Skye
Falcon to stay updated on
new releases!
www.facebook.com/skye
falcon*

Or follow the blog:
http://skyefalcon.in